The Marked Men Series

Asa

Rowdy

Nash

Rome

Jet

Rule

recovered

Cover design by:

Hang Le

www.byhangle.com

Editing by:

Elaine York, Allusion Graphics, LLC / Publishing & Book Formatting

www.allusiongraphics.com

Copyediting & Proofreading by:

Beth Salminen

www.bethanyedits.net

Interior Design & Formatting by:

Christine Borgford, Type A Formatting

www.typeAformatting.com

recovered

NEW YORK TIMES BESTSELLING AUTHOR
JAY CROWNOVER

Dedicated to first love.

Also dedicated to anyone and everyone who was affected by Hurricane Harvey. Port Aransas was hit so hard in the storm, which happened shortly after this book was finished.

introduction

I KNOW MOST of you are in my reader group or subscribers of my newsletter, so you've heard me talk about where the idea for Cable and Affton's story came from, but for anyone who was waiting until publication day for this book, I want to go ahead and catch you up.

Cable is based entirely on a real person. He is based on the boy who taught me all about love and loss. My first love. My first crush. My first taste of disaster and heartbreak. Pretty much everything about the way Cable acts and reacts to things is 100% taken directly from my actual experience dealing with my own broken boy. I throw that out there as a qualifier, because I want readers to understand this isn't a book dealing with addiction and depression from a researched and documented place. This book deals with those things from the point of view of someone who was watching a train wreck happen right in front of her and was helpless to stop the crash or the carnage.

I know there are no simple textbook symptoms for dealing with things like depression and anxiety, so I want to be clear that all the symptoms, outbursts, reactions, and emotions in this particular book are ones that I witnessed with my own two eyes and felt with my own young heart. I would never want to misrepresent the struggle associated with these issues, so this book is singular and unique to my own life experience.

I'm writing fiction here folks. I will freely admit to taking creative liberty with some of the medical help Cable seeks along the way. I wanted a connection between my characters that I felt was important to Cable's journey, so the representation of his relationship with his therapist is not the standard! I am aware. It was done on purpose to enhance the story, please don't send me angry emails. (I put this declaimer in after all Beth, my copyeditor's many-many notes about Dr. Howard's unethical conversations about Cable's mental health with characters who were not Cable. Lol. I know therapy is a safe space and this doesn't happen in the really-real world.)

I met my Cable when I was sixteen and had been living a pretty sheltered, quiet life as a small-town mountain girl. A mutual friend introduced us about a week after he was released from a court-ordered rehab program. The friend thought we'd be good for each other; he would get me to loosen up, and I was clean and uninterested in all the things that got him in trouble before. It was a terrible plan. We hated each other on sight. I was terrified of the way he lived his life like there were no consequences and no remorse. He hated that I wasn't impressed by him, that I didn't automatically think he was the coolest guy in the room. There was a lot of animosity between us for around a year, until he got in trouble again, did a stint in juvie, and was ordered back into a rehab program.

When he got out the second time, he realized he was going nowhere fast and contacted me out of the blue one night to ask if we could give being friends a shot. All of his friends used drugs, drank, partied, and lived just as wildly as he did. He told me he needed someone around who would keep him on the straight and narrow, someone who wasn't afraid of him. I was terrified of him, but I was even more afraid of what would happen to him if I turned my back on him. I was young enough at the time to believe that if I told him no and he overdosed or did something even more drastic like attempt to take his own life, it would be my fault. So, I agreed.

It was ugly for the first three months. We didn't like each other, and we weren't very good at being friends. There was so much temptation around all the time, and it was a struggle to try and help someone who wasn't exactly sure he wanted the help. Just when I was getting ready to bail, to tell him it was too hard I had my own life, my friends, my future to worry about something changed.

Maybe he realized I had one foot out the door and I was the only person still fighting for him.

Maybe it was the fact one of his friends died in a drunk driving accident.

Maybe it was the night he got into a fight with a skinhead over something stupid and ended-up with a sawed-off shotgun shoved in his face.

I don't know what flipped the switch, but he went from night to day. He ditched the friends who were always urging him to jump back off the cliff. He went from pushing against me to actively trying to pull me deeper into his life. He got his GED and blew through his first year of college like it was a piece of cake. He woke the fuck up. He realized there was a whole lot of life to live . . . all he had to do was start showing up for it.

Things changed with us as well. We went from always fighting to something else. I knew I was the center of his entire world and that his obsessive-compulsive tendencies had switched from drugs to me. It was never healthy. But when you're young and this guy with all the charisma and all the right words tells you he needs you, that he can't make it without you . . . man, it's impossible not to fall in love with that feeling and get swept up in all that emotion.

We were together on and off for a little over five years. We called it quits for good when he moved to New York and then Scotland after 9–11. He's still the most enigmatic, complex, and compelling man I've ever known. More than a couple of decades later, I still compare every man who enters my life romantically to him.

We weren't meant to be in so many ways. But when I think about that all-consuming, overriding need to be with someone when it comes to first love, I wouldn't give any of that time up for the world. I love that I get to write stories about that kind of love and passion.

So, that's it, that's where Cable came from, and Affton . . . well, let's just say she's the person I wish I could have been back then. She does everything right, whereas I did everything very wrong . . . that's about the only similarity between the two of us.

This is the place where I make it clear that my mother is nothing like Affton's mom. Affton actually has to deal with the loss of a family member to addiction in her life, so she's very empathetic and compassionate when it comes to dealing with this particular disease. My mom is great, one day I'll write her into a story, so I don't have to put a disclaimer that all the terrible moms I write about are nothing like her.

My mom is awesome. No doubt about it.

This love story has history and memories on every single page. I sure hope you enjoy my first love as much as I enjoyed sharing him with you.

(Yes, I'm going to email Ry—my Cable—and tell him I wrote a book loosely based on him. He already knows he's the physical inspiration for Rule. I doubt he'll be surprised.

prologue

AFFTON

I HATED CABLE James McCaffrey.

I loathed him.

I detested him.

I despised him.

My dad would tell me that it's dangerous to wish ill upon someone, that it's risky to borrow trouble by thinking bad things about a boy who had the means to buy and sell us both several times over. But I couldn't help it. I really, truly hated him, and every single day it seemed like he did something else to justify my complete and utter disdain. The boy was a year ahead of me in school. When I was in the sixth grade, my dad moved us to Loveless, Texas. I'd shown up skinny, shy, and uninterested in the world and my new school. My world had flipped upside down, and though my dad viewed the move as a fresh start, all I felt was failure and loss. I wasn't impressed by the tall, attractive blond boy who ruled the school. I wasn't impressed by anything. I felt nothing when he smiled at me in the hallways. I was numb when that smile turned to a sneer. I didn't want his attention or his scorn.

I'd never been fond of his antics and total disregard for the rules, mostly because, even then, he got away with murder, since his family practically owned the entirety of this small Texas town. As we got older, the behavior that already bugged me got even worse and more outrageous. Cable's indifference to authority and apathy toward common decency spiraled out of control. When I was a junior and he was a senior, I realized the reason he always rubbed me the wrong way.

He was a user.

He used his family's status and wealth to do whatever he wanted; he wallowed in entitlement. He didn't show up to class if he didn't want to. He drove a car that was nicer than all of the teachers' and parked it right out in front of the school—in employee parking—without any worry that it would be towed. He never adhered to the dress code even though the rest of us had no choice. I'd never seen anyone stop him from smoking as he walked across the campus, even though all tobacco products were strictly forbidden. There was no suspension or detention for the likes of Cable James McCaffrey. There was no worry the school would pull his parents in for a meeting about his behavior. The principal went out of her way to turn a blind eye to the boy's antics, and in return, she got sizable donations from the McCaffreys every year to improve and enhance the school.

He used girls . . . an endless string of them. It turned my stomach the way my female classmates couldn't wait to take their turn going through the revolving door that I was sure welcomed them into Cable's bedroom. He never stayed with any of them for more than a hot minute, and he acted like he couldn't remember their names as soon as he finished with them. The dismissive and rude behavior didn't stop them from rushing to do his homework when he asked, and it didn't keep them from clamoring for his limited attention when he walked down the hallway. He was the closest thing our small town had to royalty, and he knew it. We were the peasants who existed in his kingdom, nothing more, nothing less.

He used his friends . . . or the people who were foolish enough to think the bare minimum of attention and time Cable offered was friendship. He wasn't nice. Not to anyone. He was short-tempered and rude. He was always surrounded by people telling him how great he was, how interesting and fascinating his every action was in their eyes. He didn't make a move without a horde of admirers telling him he was the coolest and greatest thing to ever happen to Loveless High School. All they wanted was to be seen with him and score an invite to one of the legendary parties he threw every time his parents were out of town on business. The McCaffreys owned a sprawling ranch on the outside of town that was opulent and ostentatious. Both of his parents came from money and had made fortunes on their own along the way. Everyone in my school wanted the chance to get inside the mansion Cable called home to party, unsupervised, with unfettered access to his parents' high-end liquor cabinet, heated pool, and unchecked debauchery. Several bragged they had even seen the real Van Gogh his mother had, and I was positive the only reason they knew it was a Van Gogh was because they had Googled it for bragging rights.

But the main reason I never joined the Cable James McCaffrey fan club was that he was not only a user of people, but also used that which was scary and risky. He *used* in the literal sense. I don't know if his teachers saw it, if the girls who couldn't look away from him could tell, or if the boys who were so far up his ass they were looking at his brain stem recognized the signs . . . but I did.

It started sometime during my freshman year when Cable was a sophomore. He'd always been moody and quick to fly off the handle, but almost overnight his behavior became even more erratic. The mood swings got dangerous and unpredictable. He took a swing at his history teacher, and while anyone else would face immediate expulsion, Cable got the week off from school and was welcomed back with open arms as soon as his parents offered to buy the school a new scoreboard for the football field. His man-whorish behavior also started around that time. He was searching for something inside someone else over and over again. The harder it was to find, the angrier he became. Which in turn made him callous to the person who he deemed lacking whatever it was he was looking for. There was always a new girl crying over him in the hallways, and each time I walked past her, I was so thankful I'd been immune to him that first time he smiled at me. My broken emotions had nothing to do with Cable, and as long as I had a say in the matter, they never would.

The way he looked also started to change that year. Cable was tall for a teenager. If anything other than a good time and the frantic need to escape from himself motivated him, he would be perfect for our school's sucky basketball team. He was long and lean with shaggy, dark blond hair and the brownest eyes I'd ever seen. He was good looking in a rough and unkempt kind of way. But that year and the next, his rumpled appearance turned gaunt and ragged. He lost weight. His dark eyes started to take up his entire face as his cheeks hollowed out and his jawline sharpened. Instead of being intense, forceful, and furious, he became twitchy and paranoid. It didn't happen overnight, but the changes were significant and scary. The further away he drifted, the more I wondered why someone who loved him didn't try and catch him before he was too far gone. I recognized the trip Cable was on and knew the final destination wasn't anywhere I'd ever want to be again.

I mentioned my suspicions to a friend of mine when Cable appeared even worse at the start of his senior year. She looked at me like I was crazy and asked me *why* someone like Cable would need to use drugs to cope with the crap the rest of us had to deal with daily. He was privileged. He was beloved. In her mind, someone who had everything wouldn't risk any of it by succumbing to something as common as addiction.

I knew from firsthand experience that addiction didn't discriminate.

Addiction didn't care about the square footage of your house or the kind of car you drove. It didn't care about your pedigree or your GPA. Addiction was an equal opportunity life-ruiner, and I was positive that Cable was deep in the throes of it. I hated him, and I hated how he was carelessly tossing away his picture-perfect life. I shouldn't care . . . but I did.

I cared because I couldn't *not* care. I'd had a front row seat to the kind of destruction addiction wrought, and there was no way I could stand idly by and let it get its grubby, gross, insidious, infectious hands on someone else in my orbit. Even if that someone else was someone I wanted to dropkick and throat-punch on a regular basis. Anyone rational would point out that I had no reason to loathe Cable the way I did. He's never outright attacked me, embarrassed me, or victimized me. All he'd done was notice me when it was the last thing I wanted. It might not make sense to anyone, but it made perfect sense to me. I'd wanted to hide, but he had no trouble finding me. In my mind, that made him my enemy from day one.

I'd never said a word to Cable James McCaffrey. In all the years we'd been in school together, never, not once had there been an occasion where I needed to converse with him. I watched him from afar and judged him endlessly. I watched him because he was impossible to ignore and because I knew I was on his radar. I was always waiting for the day he would finally try his luck, test the waters, even though he knew I was a shark that could tell he was bleeding out from a mile away. Cable wasn't nice to the people who liked him; there was no way I wanted to find out how he treated the people who detested him. I had a couple of years left before graduation, and I wanted to get through them as quickly and quietly as possible. I did not doubt that Cable could shred the ease of my remaining high school days with minimal effort. So, I stayed out of his way until I felt I had no choice but to throw myself directly in his path. Someone had to say something to him before he slipped so far down the rabbit hole there would be no reaching him. Someone had to try and save him before it was too late.

It took a couple of days for me to work up the courage to approach him. I didn't want to do it while his entourage surrounded him. I didn't want to do it when he was in the center of his female fan club. I didn't want to do it where anyone could overhear what I had to say to him. It was like trying to get close to a celebrity or a member of a popular boy band. Frankly, it was ridiculous that I had to put so much thought into it, that I had to plan out my attack precisely and carefully, but I did, and finally, toward the end of the week, I saw an opportunity.

I was sitting in my AP English class, and I just happened to be gazing out the window that overlooked the front of the school. There was no missing Cable's long-legged lope as he slipped out the front doors, cigarette dangling from his lips as he headed toward his flashy sports car. It was early in the afternoon, we hadn't even had lunch yet, and he was leaving for the day. It annoyed me enough that I asked for a bathroom pass and hit the front doors running so I could catch him before he reached his car.

I caught him just as he was opening the driver's side door. I was winded, sweaty, and more than a little belligerent when I caught up with him. All the carefully constructed concern and gentle censure I'd been working up to vanished. I put a hand on the door and narrowed my eyes at him as he glared at me over the metal and glass that separated us. This close, I noticed he smelled like expensive cologne and marijuana. The cigarette in his mouth wasn't lit and bounced in irritation between his lips as he snapped, "Can I help you with something?"

His narrowed eyes were bloodshot and his dark eyebrows pulled into a V over his nose. There was a red flush staining his throat and the blade of his cheekbones. He was always ready to snap, but I'd never been close enough to see just how near to the edge he was. Everything about him was sharp, pointed, and dangerous.

I let go of the door and crossed my arms over my chest. I could hear my dad's voice in the back of my head telling me to walk away, to let sleeping dogs lie, and I could practically see my best friend, Jordan, shaking her head and telling me I had no business bugging Cable about his habits. There was no denying that this was a bad idea, but I couldn't stop the words that tumbled out of my mouth as we stood there in the world's most uncomfortable face-off. "My mom was a drug addict." I sucked in a sharp breath through my teeth. "She died a month before I moved here. She overdosed. My dad wanted to start over, to get me away from the loss and pain of losing her, but it never goes away. All of that hurt followed me here, and it will follow the people who love you if you don't do something about your problem."

His pinched eyebrows shot up so high on his forehead they almost touched his hairline. "What in the actual fuck? Who are you? Do I even know you?"

It shouldn't sting that he had no clue who I was, but it did. That was my fault. He looked at me and I looked away. I tried to keep my head down and blend in; all I wanted was to bide my time until I could put Loveless in my rearview. I guess I had done a good job. Our school wasn't massive, and Loveless was a relatively small town, so even though our paths never crossed and I never engaged, he should still know my name.

"Who I am doesn't matter. What does matter is that I know what's going to happen if you don't get help. You need to talk to someone about whatever it is that you're using and why. Get in some kind of program, Cable. If you don't get help, everything you have, everything you love, is going to go away. Addiction takes and takes and keeps on taking. It's the most greedy and selfish thing in the entire world." My voice broke a little, and he continued to stare at me like I'd lost my mind . . . which I might've. I couldn't believe I laid all my baggage concerning my mom open at his feet like that, scattered between us, messy and ugly.

"I haven't ever spoken to you. I don't know you, and you sure as shit know nothing about me. Who are you to stand here and accuse me of having a drug problem?" I expected fire and fury. What I got was low questions and quiet contemplation as he continued to stare at me with that unlit cigarette dangling from his lips.

"I'm someone who lost someone I loved to addiction." I blinked back the sudden rush of tears that burned in my eyes. "That's who I am."

He shook his head and reached up to pluck the cigarette out of his mouth. His sandy hair fell over his forehead, and his dark eyes seemed to get even darker as he did what he did best . . . dismissed me. "Sucks for you, but I'm fine. I have a good time fucking around. None of it is serious, and none of it is a problem. It's not a big deal, and it definitely isn't any of your business."

Whenever I told someone about my mom, I usually got the standard sympathetic look followed by awkward condolences. It was hard to hear she was gone, but it was even more difficult when they realized *why* she was no longer in my life. We got into a car accident when I was four where she had injured her back. What followed was years and years of addiction to painkillers, followed by an unstoppable addiction to heroin that resulted not only in the loss of our house, but also in her custody of me. Dad left her after her second failed trip to rehab when I was six and fought tooth and nail for full custody of me. He was too nice of a guy to pull me completely out of her life, which is why we stayed in Arizona after they split. After she died, he decided there was nothing for us in Tucson, so he packed us up and moved us to Loveless where his family had spent generations making families and building lives. But, like I told Cable, no place was far enough away from lingering ghosts of the damage from my mom's addiction.

I spent my entire childhood watching addiction steal my mother away from me, and all this boy could say to me was, 'sucks for you'? I wasn't sure how it was remotely possible, but I hated him even more at that moment than I did the moment before.

"You're not only hurting yourself, Cable. You're hurting the people who care about you. You should let them help you." I took a step back and waved him off. "Not that you care about whom you may or may not hurt. From what I can tell, you don't seem to care about much of anything or anyone."

He cocked his head to the side. "What's your name?"

I shrugged. "Does it matter?"

"You seem to have some pretty strong opinions about me for someone who won't even look me in the eye when we pass each other in the hall. You might want to worry a little bit more about you and less about strangers." He circled a finger in the air in front of me and sneered. "Get a haircut. Go buy some clothes that are from this century. Put on some damn makeup and maybe practice smiling in the mirror. Maybe you should work on yourself before trying to save the rest of the world."

It took every ounce of self-control I had not to wince. I knew I didn't spend enough time obsessing over the way I looked or the image I presented to the people who I spent my days actively avoiding. I was too busy doing everything I could to make it out of this town to worry if the wing of my eyeliner was on point or if my jeans were skinny enough. My hair was a few shades lighter than his and straight as an arrow. I kept it chopped in a messy bob so that I didn't have to do much other than wash and dry it. I wasn't interested in being a knockout, but that didn't mean I wanted this boy, or any boy, to give me fashion and makeup advice. I didn't want him to see me, and I'd never given him, or anyone, a reason to look.

I took a breath and let it out slowly. We stared at each other silently for a long minute until Cable broke the tension by sliding into his open car and dismissing me, the same way he did with everything he deemed unworthy of his time.

Before he had the door closed I told him, honesty and sincerity heavy in my tone, "I hate you, Cable James McCaffrey." I felt it like a weight in my chest.

Our eyes met through the window as he reached forward to grab the door handle. "Join the club."

He shut the door, cranked the engine, and peeled out in a shower of gravel. It was so very him and so very disappointing. I don't know why I expected him to admit he had a problem or what I hoped to accomplish by letting him know he was not alone in his struggle against something that was so much bigger than him. It felt futile and silly after it was all said and done. I'd wanted to help him, and I'd wanted to help my mother back then. My dad warned me about losing myself in lost causes, but I couldn't seem to help myself.

Later that night I sent an anonymous email to Cable's mother after asking my dad to find her work email address for me. She was indirectly my dad's boss, so he had a million questions in his eyes when he handed it over, but he didn't ask them. And I didn't offer any answers. We'd been through so much together he trusted me to steer clear of the things that left wounds that never healed. We'd both been burned, but I couldn't seem to stay away from the fire.

I warned Cable's mom that her son was on a perilous path, and if she wanted to save him, she better intervene on his behalf. It was reckless and crazy, but I couldn't let it go.

She never responded, but Cable wasn't in school the following few days, and rumors started to swirl that his parents were pulling him out of school and shipping him off to a prestigious boarding school in Europe.

I was breathing easier, patting myself on the back for making a difference, when something happened that made it clear I'd done too little, too late. That weekend the entire town of Loveless finally stopped pretending its golden boy wasn't tarnished. They had no choice other than to face the truth because it was a bloody, brutal mess right in front of them. By the end of that weekend, everyone decided they hated Cable James McCaffrey just as much as I did, and I regretted that those were the last words I said to him.

one

AFFTON

The day after high school graduation

"**Y**OUR FATHER WORKS for me, doesn't he, Affton?"

The woman lifted a perfectly groomed eyebrow at me and cocked her head to the side as if she was honestly waiting for me to answer. She knew for a fact that my dad, my uncle, and two of my cousins worked for her and her ex-husband at the brewery and bottling plant which had been in her family for years. I also had an aunt who worked at the McCaffrey grocery store, and my best friend was a waitress at one of the three restaurants they owned. Nearly everyone who lived in this town worked for—or knew someone who worked for—her and her ex-husband, so I thought the question was ridiculous and misleading. I was supposed to be celebrating my freedom and relishing my escape. I was meant to be soaking up the last hours I had with my friends and the last few days I had with my dad. I was not supposed to be pandering to Melanie McCaffrey.

"Yes, ma'am, he sure does." I forced a smile and fought the

urge to roll my eyes.

I had no idea why Cable's mother had tracked me down almost two full years after I sent her the email clueing her in to her son's hazardous habits, but here she was. She was standing across the counter from me, waiting for her non-fat latte while she picked me apart with her narrowed gaze. The coffee shop was one of the few businesses in Loveless the McCaffreys didn't own; however, that didn't stop my boss from comping her drink, and readily agreeing when she asked if it was okay for me to take five minutes to speak with her. No one bothered to ask if I was okay with it . . . I wasn't.

Sadly, I still had a couple of months left before I left for California. I'd been dreaming about Berkeley since I decided I wanted to go into psychology. It didn't take . . . well, a psychologist . . . to figure out that I wanted to work with broken people because I'd been raised by one. I was forever searching for answers that no one could give me. Why couldn't she love me more than her habit? Why wasn't I enough for her to want to fight it? How could she throw everything away? Wasn't I enough for her?

I followed the perfectly polished and severely elegant woman to one of the four tiny tables. Love & Lattes was about as far from Starbucks as a coffee shop could get. We didn't even play the requisite, mellow, college rock. It was all Willie, Waylon, and Johnny Cash. Not that I was complaining. My dad loved classic country, so I was one of the few high school students working here who could sing along to almost every single song. It annoyed the crap out of my coworkers, so obviously I did it during every single shift.

We sat in silence for a long moment. I had no clue what this woman wanted, but everything inside of me screamed it was nothing good. The *haves* did not lower themselves to mingle with the *have-nots* without reason. Cable didn't come out of the womb a user; he learned it somewhere, and I would put good money on that somewhere being at-home with this woman and her equally entitled ex-husband. Mr. McCaffrey was no longer in the picture if the rumor mill was to be believed. Cable had a hand in that as well. Apparently his parent's already strained relationship couldn't handle the pressure of trying to save their son.

Melanie tapped her manicured nails on the side of her cup and lowered her eyelashes so she was looking down at the table and not at me. "I know you're the one who sent me the email about my son before *the incident.*"

I blinked, and then blinked again a little faster. No one talked about *the incident.* Not unless they wanted to be run out of town and ostracized. No one brought up *the incident* when one of the McCaffreys was within earshot. The whole family had done their very best to erase *the incident* from the town's memory. *The incident* was nothing more than whispers in shadows and rumors bandied about after too many drinks. No one wanted to bring down the wrath of the McCaffreys, and no one wanted to acknowledge that maybe, just maybe, *the incident* would never have happened if someone, anyone, had reined in Cable or intervened on his behalf.

I fidgeted nervously across from the woman who could end my father's livelihood with a single phone call and wished I had listened to him all along and not borrowed trouble. "That was a long time ago. I thought I could help."

Cable's mom cleared her throat delicately and lifted her eyes back to mine. "You were the only person in this entire town who even noticed Cable needed help. Everyone else was too busy trying to please him or wanting to be exactly like him, so much so that they encouraged his behavior. His father wasn't around much to notice one way or the other. And I'm ashamed to say I was so consumed with worry that my former husband wasn't around, that I wasn't paying attention. I didn't do my most important job. I didn't protect my son." Her voice cracked slightly, and I watched as her lips tightened and her eyes started to shine. Talking about her lack of parenting skills was a sore spot. It had to be hard to have your failure tied to every single heartbeat and every minute that passed without the person who was supposed to be able to rely on you.

I wanted to be sympathetic. I wanted to be understanding and forgiving, but the place inside of me where all that lived was taken up by resentment and anger. I was too little, too young, to help my mom. But this woman had forever to get a grip on her son before he slipped away, and she hadn't even tried to reach for him until it was too late. He ran through her fingers like rushing water.

"How did you find out I sent the email?" And why did it matter now . . . two years later? The damage had already been done, and no matter how deep *the incident* was buried, there was no taking back the consequences of her son's actions that night. The hairs on the back of my neck stood up as alarm buzzed across my skin. "Did I do something wrong? Is that why you brought up my dad?" I was so close to getting out. So close to being someone better than this town let me become, but I would never leave my dad in a lurch. He was all I had.

"When I confronted Cable after I read your email, he mumbled something about 'that blonde bitch ratting him out.'" Eyes as dark as her son's softened a little. "I figured it was a classmate. Maybe one of his ex-girlfriends, but he wouldn't say anything more. He kept telling me he didn't have any idea who sent the email but he was very upset about it. He was going to a very exclusive, very expensive treatment center the day *the incident* occurred. I told him if he didn't go he was going to lose his inheritance, and I would legally bar him from the family trust he gains access to when he's twenty-one." She exhaled slowly. "I forced my only child to get help and it blew up in my face. I want to help him for real this time around, and the only other person who seemed interested in Cable's well-being was the person behind the email. I hired someone to trace the IP address it came from. Luckily, you haven't upgraded your computer in the last couple of years, and your father often brags about you. He couldn't wait to tell me all about what a hard worker you are. And Berkeley, that's impressive. I went to Stanford."

I wanted to laugh, but I bit it back. Our computer was old enough that it could be in a museum, and there was no chance it was getting updated until I could afford to get my dad a new one. "Yeah, impressive." The sarcasm was thick in my voice as I forgot for a hot second that I was speaking with my dad's boss and the woman who had the means to track me down like it was no big deal.

She made a little sound in her throat and tapped her fingers faster on the side of her cup. She was nervous and agitated. I was surprised she wasn't trying to hide it. I was the one who should be fidgeting and restless simply because I was sitting across from her. "Cable was released from prison three months ago; he's been living in a group home for recovering addicts as part of his parole. He gets to leave next week. He's refusing to come back to Loveless . . . for a lot of reasons. Obviously."

In the grand scheme of things, eighteen months in prison and three months in a sober-living facility was nothing more than a slap on the wrist. As usual, Cable James McCaffrey came out of a horrific situation mostly unscathed. Nothing stuck to the boy . . . nothing.

"Cable wasn't evading your questions or lying about not knowing who was responsible for the email, Mrs. McCaffrey. We didn't exactly run in the same circles, and our paths rarely crossed." I was in AP classes, studying my ass off to get as close to a perfect SAT score as I could. Cable was skipping class and scoring the kinds of things that landed him in prison. "I'm happy to hear Cable is getting some help, but we were never friends or even casual acquaintances, so I'm a little confused as to why you felt the need to track me down and update me on his whereabouts." It was information I didn't ask for and didn't need. It was information that would send the rest of my fellow graduates into a tizzy. Half the graduating class were still loyal members of the Cable fan club. The other half . . . well, the blinders had been ripped off, and they were pretty pissed they'd been worshiping a false idol for so many years. When a god falls, he leaves a pretty big dent in the ground where his worshipers walked.

I couldn't deny there was a tingle of relief working its way down my spine at the knowledge that he had no choice but to stay clean. For his mom's sake, since she seemed to really care, I hope it stuck. I wanted someone to beat addiction, even if that someone was Cable.

"You may not have been close friends, but it's clear you cared about him. You didn't want him to keep using drugs. You were looking out for him, and that's why I'm here. He needs people in his life who have his best interests at heart. He needs someone who won't automatically tell him what he wants to hear." She looked away, and I realized she knew as soon as she said the words, that person should be her or her ex-husband. She knew, but her hands were tied because Cable had shut her out. "He's not talking to me at the moment. He hasn't since he was sentenced."

I couldn't hold back a snort. "That's rude. The least he could do was thank you for paying for all those lawyers who got him three years instead of five." They were also the ones who made it possible for him to get out after serving only eighteen months. She made a strangled noise and picked up her coffee to take a sip. Our five minutes had bled into fifteen, and I purposely looked at the screen of my phone to indicate I needed to get back to work. "I need to get back. I'm not sure what kind of relationship you think I have with your son, but I assure you that I'm not the sympathetic ear or understanding shoulder you seem to be looking for. I know what addiction can do to a family. I couldn't stop it from ruining mine, but I thought maybe I could stop it from ruining yours." I shouldn't have bothered. Addiction always seemed to win. So far in my experience, it was undefeated.

I went to stand up when one of her manicured hands shot out and locked around my wrist. I stilled instantly and felt my eyebrows shoot up as high as they could go. Her fingers were shaking and her lips were trembling. She looked like she was about to cry, so I slowly lowered myself back into my seat. "I don't want you for me, Affton. I want you for Cable."

I felt my jaw drop and heard my breath suck in so loudly she couldn't have missed it. I was sure I misheard her, so I narrowed my eyes and snapped, "Excuse me?"

Her fingers tightened on my wrist and her perfectly painted lips pressed into a tight grimace. "Cable's father owns a house on the Gulf down in Port Aransas. It's a vacation property he rarely uses. Cable is going there for the summer, but his father and I only agreed that he could use the house if he stays clean and continues seeking treatment for his addiction. He's going to be called in for random drug screens for the next ninety days, and if any of his tests come back positive, he goes right back to jail."

I tugged my hand until she reluctantly let go. I rubbed the spot and continued to watch her through narrowed eyes. "All of that sounds reasonable, but again . . . I'm failing to see what any of this has to do with me." Letting Cable loose in a tourist town packed with sun chasers and party people didn't seem to be the brightest idea, but what did I know about the rich?

"The deal is that if Cable manages to stay clean for the entire summer, if he takes his sobriety seriously, then we'll return control of his accounts back over to him. Right now, he has no access to anything. No money. No cars. None of our connections. He is only given what we allow him to have. That's part of the reason he won't speak to me."

I snorted again and crossed my arms over my chest. "The last thing a recovering addict needs is unfettered access to money. That's part of the reason it was so easy for him to develop a habit in the first place. Your son is a drug dealer's proverbial wet dream."

She nodded seriously. "I know that now. I'm not risking my son's life again. If I can't be the one watching over him, then it needs to be someone else who cares about him. I don't want to push him. I'm worried he would use again just to prove a point if I hover over him too closely."

"What point would he be proving?" For having everything anyone could ever want, the McCaffreys were all kinds of jacked-up on the emotional front.

"That I'm a bad mother." This time there was no *almost* about it. She was crying. Big, fat crystal tears that looked like something you would see on a daytime soap opera. Real people didn't look pretty when they cried. "I didn't save him. I didn't stop him. I didn't protect him." She sniffed loudly and lifted a hand to wipe her damp cheeks. "I can't be there, but you can."

I laughed so sharp and short that it hurt my chest. I put a hand on my stomach and leaned back in my chair. "This is some kind of joke, right? There's a hidden camera somewhere or something." I looked frantically around the quiet coffee shop, but nothing seemed out of place. Reba was singing along to *Fancy* over the sound system, and my boss was watching my bizarre meeting from behind the counter with undisguised curiosity.

Cable's mom folded her hands together on the table and lifted her chin. This was no longer the grieving mother. This was the legacy who made millions while most of the town slept at night. She was battle ready and taking no prisoners. "I'm very serious, Affton. Cable's father and I are finally on the same page about our son's health. Relapse is not an option, so we want to hire you to be our son's sober companion for the duration of the summer. It will be your job to monitor his behavior and let us know if he's slipped up at all. You'll oversee his monthly allowance and be responsible for making sure he goes to meetings and keeps his appointments with his court-ordered counselor." Her shoulders stiffened, and her chin lifted a notch more. "Berkeley is impressive, but it is also incredibly expensive. I'm fully prepared to make you an offer you would be insane to refuse."

I let out another one of those painful laughs and ran a hand over my astonished face. I'd heard of sober companions before . . . on TV. No one in the real world could afford a glorified babysitter for a mostly capable adult. Plus, she was asking for the impossible.

The only way an addict got clean was if they wanted to. No amount of love, supervision, or pressure could make a junkie go straight. She was fighting a losing battle; it didn't matter how many soldiers she sent to war.

"Berkeley is expensive, but I got a scholarship. I understand what you're trying to do, I even understand why you're doing it. But you have to understand, the only person who can keep Cable clean is Cable." It wasn't going to be because he wanted his cushy life back either. It was going to have to be because he wanted *a life*, period.

She gave a jerky nod, and her lips tightened. "I know about the scholarship; your father told me. He's very proud of you. California is very expensive. The money will make your life so much easier,

Affton. You'll be able to study and have fun while experiencing new things, instead of working two or three jobs to make ends meet. The world is so much bigger than Loveless. Take the money, and you'll get the chance to experience it."

I shook my head reflexively. I didn't want to make any kind of deal with this woman, and I didn't want to try and save another addict and fail. "I'll make do with what I have, Mrs. McCaffrey."

She sighed and climbed to her feet. She smoothed a hand down the material of her skirt, and I watched as her fingers curled into a fist at her side. Her dark eyes narrowed, and I tilted my head back to gain a few millimeters of space. I got the sense that I was in the path of a predator and I was about to be eaten alive.

"Most teenagers see an opportunity for easy money, and they take it. I was hoping it would be that easy with you, but I suppose I should have known better. Every other teenager in this town ignored the signs my son was turning into a junkie because they were worried he wouldn't like them anymore." Her eyes rolled over my lopsided ponytail and my typical uniform of a plain tank top and jeans. "You clearly aren't concerned with the things typical teenage girls worry about."

Again, with the dig about my appearance. I was even more certain that Cable inherited his worst traits from this woman. Someone taught him how to go for the unprotected underbelly and exploit that weakness.

"I didn't want it to come down to this, but I'm afraid you have left me no choice." She met my gaze unflinchingly as I started to shake at her blatant threat. "You're off to college soon. You have your entire life ahead of you . . . but what about your dad? What does he have after you're gone, Affton? What's he going to do if he suddenly finds himself unemployed and all alone? You've got a way out, but we both know your dad is stuck here, his roots are buried deep, and if I want to make his life difficult, I can, with very little effort."

I balked and briefly considered grabbing the last of the latte she hadn't finished so I could throw it in her face. "You're unbelievable." I got to my feet and placed my hands flat on the table to prevent myself from reaching for her instead. My eyes narrowed to slits as we faced off. Fury was clear in every line of my body, and determination was evident in every curve of hers.

She shook her impeccably coiffed head in the negative. "No, I'm a desperate mother."

"Remember how well it worked out for you when you blackmailed your kid into rehab?" If she could throw *the incident* around, then so could I. "What makes you think this is going to be any different? What if he uses even though I'm there? What assurance do I have that you won't mess with my dad?" I put a hand to my throat as I tried to bite back bile and a flood of bad words. That was too much responsibility. It had nearly crushed me once; I didn't know if I could survive it again.

"It will be different this time because it has to be. There is too much at stake. If he uses, he goes back to prison for violating parole, and he gets cut off. If you do everything in your power to keep him clean, you'll get a sizable fee for the summer, and your father's position will be secure." She reached for her purse and pulled out a business card. I stared at it for a long time, refusing to take it from her. She put it on the table with a heavy sigh and took a step around me. Quietly, so that only I could hear her, she told me, "I'm willing to do whatever it takes to save my son. Whatever. It. Takes."

She swept out the door leaving me reeling. I had no doubt that she would dismantle my father's easy, predictable life to get her way.

Growling under my breath, I snatched up the card she left

and tucked it into my back pocket. I thought I hated Cable James McCaffrey . . . but I had no idea what hate was until his mother came calling. I wanted to strangle her. I wanted to run her over with my old, beat-up Volkswagen. I wanted to claw that desperate look off her face.

All I'd ever wanted was to be out of Loveless. Ever since I was old enough to understand that I was the only one that could make things happen for myself, my every move had been carefully weighed to get me out of Nowhere, Texas. I was proud of the choices I'd made, pleased with my progress. I'd earned my freedom through blood, sweat, and tears . . . suffered through years of being the girl no one knew because I was singularly focused on one thing, and that one thing was not my social life. All the sacrifice was for nothing if Melanie McCaffrey handed me a golden ticket and offered me a ride out on easy street. All the hours of working to be at the top of my class to guarantee a shot at my dream school meant nothing if I took her blank check. All the years, the hours of hard work my dad put in to support us and to make sure I had a good life were worthless if one determined, desperate woman could strip it all away without even blinking an eye.

That trouble I borrowed when I was silly enough to try and save Cable was the gift that just kept on giving, even when I was more than ready to give it all back.

two

CABLE

Port Aransas

I LIKED THE water.

I appreciated the way it could be calm and serene one minute, but as soon as something disrupted the surface, it could rage and churn with a scary kind of violence.

I also respected that you could never tell what was lurking beneath the surface. There was no telling how deep the water was until you waded in. One minute your feet were solidly on the sandy bottom, the next you were in over your head. Sinking, falling, flailing as you went under.

That was pretty much how I felt every single day of my life. Some days I could touch the bottom, but more often than not I was struggling to find my way to the surface, desperate for a breath of air.

I watched the water roll up over my toes, touching the torn hem of my jeans. My ass had been planted in the sand for a couple of hours now, and the tide was starting to come in. I was soaking wet, and my jeans were going to weigh a ton by the time I made my way back up to my dad's waterfront beach house. I couldn't find the energy to care about the tide or the hazy knowledge that I was going to be entirely uncomfortable when I finally got to my feet. My impending discomfort had little to do with wet denim and clammy underwear and everything to do with the reality that the solitude I'd been searching for was about to be snatched away from me. All I wanted was to be alone. I had spent the last year and a half of my life surrounded by criminals and correctional officers, and addicts and counselors. I'd been swarmed by the worst of the worst, and all I wanted was some room to breathe.

I wasn't getting it.

My parents thought I was a danger to myself and to their pristine reputations. They didn't want to leave me to my own devices. They didn't trust me . . . and I couldn't blame them. But that didn't mean I wasn't queasy about the idea of having someone watch my every move while I tried to make my way back to a place where my feet touched the ground. I resented the thought that I needed a babysitter, and I hated the idea that anyone would be close enough to me to see the fractures in the mask I wore day to day. They would see the true ugliness I wasn't sure I had the ability to hide anymore. If I wanted to stay out of prison and get any kind of independence back, that meant no more leaning on the crutch of drugs to keep all that darkness at bay. No more pretending like I was fine, that life was nothing more than a party that didn't start until I showed up.

I'd been steadily working my way through a bottle of shitty, cinnamon-flavored whiskey for the last couple of hours, and I had hoped it would take the edge off the bubbling irritation that was already under my skin. I wasn't supposed to be drinking. I wasn't supposed to be doing any of the things I'd always done. No booze.

No drugs. No sex. Pretty much no fun.

The vices were a distraction; I knew that even before the prison shrink tried to enlighten me. I'd never wanted to focus on myself, on the fact I was inherently unhappy with no real reason to feel that way. I had everything anyone could want. I was privileged . . . special . . . but none of it mattered. I couldn't remember a time when I woke up satisfied and content with my life. I was always getting sucked under, lungs filling with dissatisfaction; but the girls, the partying, all helped to make the feeling of suffocation less powerful. I wasn't thinking about myself either; I was thinking about making the girls feel good, or I was too impaired to feel at all. I felt like I was treading water. Admittedly, the more I used, the more I took from others, the farther out I drifted. Every day I could see the shore getting farther and farther away. By then, I was caught in a current and there was no fighting my way back. I let it suck me under without struggle . . . without complaint.

I made a face as I took another pull on the bottle. I couldn't figure out why the whiskey needed to be candy-flavored, but considering I'd conned it off a group of underage, high school girls, it didn't surprise me they'd been drinking this. They were probably only a couple of years younger than me, cute and inviting in their tiny bikinis. They wanted me to join them, and if I wasn't expecting a very unwanted visitor, I probably would have. I didn't have much of a choice when it came to giving up drugs and booze, but no one was going to be checking up on my sex life. The only person accountable for my dick was me. That was a vice I could still hold onto, and I had no doubt I would. Of all the things I'd ever indulged, girls were always the easiest to score.

I took the bottle when it was offered, told the girls I would be around for the summer, and proceeded to chug the vile stuff as the sun went down. I was going to be screwed if I got called in for a surprise screen tomorrow, not just because I was violating my parole, but because I was still technically underage as well, even though I was staring down the barrel of my twenty-first birthday. Every time I took a drink, I was risking my neck. The judge who sentenced me would love nothing more than to tack on time to my original sentence. I couldn't bring myself to care too much. I didn't want to go back to prison, but the need to numb all the emotions rioting inside of me outweighed any fear of the consequences. I never gave a shit about the consequences . . . that was how I ended up in this mess from the get-go.

I never cared what the drugs were doing to me, what they were doing to my life, what they were doing to the people around me. All I cared about was the way I felt when I was high. I was free. I was above all the things pressing down on me. I was out from under the weight that was always there sitting heavy on my chest. I wasn't happy . . . but it was as close as I'd ever been, which was why it was so easy to let the current carry me so far out.

I knew my mom blamed herself.

I also knew she loved me and wanted to help. It wasn't her fault she married a serial philanderer and an all-around asshole. If I'd given a shit about my father, I would have been caught up in all the ways he was ruining our family. It was impossible for her to hold together her marriage, and me, at the same time as her career. Ultimately, she was forced to let both of those things go, but now that I was out, on my way to being clean and sober, and with my dad out of the picture, she was on a mission to make amends.

Her overzealous need to apologize, to shoulder the blame for all the things I had done, and to hold herself accountable for all the ways I had failed was too much. Her guilt felt heavier than my own, and that wasn't fair. She shouldn't be suffering more than I was. Her hurt had no right to be bigger and badder than mine. I couldn't take it. Even after everything she'd done to make sure I got the minimum sentence possible and the money she'd tossed around to make sure I got into the best after-care facility the state had to offer, I couldn't take her remorse and regret. My own was choking me every time I breathed. Hers was liable to crush me. I shut her out and since she was wallowing in blame—no matter how many times I assured her my actions were all on me and had nothing to do with her—she insisted on taking care of me. If I wouldn't let her do it, then she was going to send someone in her place.

Someone I had thought about every single day since she told me she hated me.

Someone I watched from the moment she showed up in Loveless looking as lost and alone as I felt.

Affton Reed.

I could see in her pretty blue eyes that she meant it. She hated me. She hated what I did, and it was like she knew the things I was going to do and hated those, too. She hated that she was standing in front of me giving a shit if I lived or died, and it was clear she hated that she knew she was the only one who dared to say something. She hated that she cared when I was incapable of feeling a damn thing.

I wasn't lying to her when I told her she should join the "I Hate Cable Club."

My teachers hated me.

Most of my fake friends hated me.

The girls I blew through, used, and left, hated me.

My father hated me. This was clear. Despite every effort my mother made, all the ways she's shown up since *the incident,* my father had been absent. He took the opportunity to wash his hands of me entirely and ran with it. He left my mom, and he left me. Now that I was sober and thinking somewhat more clearly, I realized it wasn't much different than when he'd been around. My mom was still sad about it. I was not. But then again, I was never much of anything. It bothered me that she was hurting, but I could barely take care of myself; there was no way I knew how to be here for her.

And really, I was the president of that particular club.

I hated myself. I hated myself more than anyone else ever could. I didn't bother to hide it the way everyone else did . . . everyone but Affton.

I was just trying to get under her skin the day she stopped me, tried to save me, and eventually sold me out. I was the one who was supposed to be untouchable. My parents' money and influence made me bulletproof, but Affton Reed was really the one who was unmatched and unattainable. She showed up one day and seemed to know instinctively that every single person in Loveless was beneath her. She walked through the halls immune and insulated from all the regular high school bullshit that made teenage years miserable and exhausting. She did not engage. Not in the same way I did. I kept my distance because I didn't want anyone close enough to see my secrets. She kept everyone at arm's length because she didn't want anyone to hold her down or keep her from moving forward.

I was being a dick to see if anything could rattle her cage when I told her that she needed to take care of herself before she worried about taking care of someone else. I was shocked that she had seen through all the bravado and smoke screens I threw up day in and day out. I was in trouble, getting deeper in every day, and no one noticed that I was drowning. No one except for Affton. I hadn't even noticed her watching me even though I was constantly watching her. If I had noticed, I would have done something terrible, something outrageous and unforgivable so that she couldn't stand the sight of me. I couldn't have someone as perceptive and honest as her looking too closely at my demons. Especially not someone who recognized them like they were old friends.

I was surprised that my dig about her appearance had done the trick. She didn't come across as self-conscious or insecure, but she obviously bristled when I pointed out she could put forth a little effort in the looks department. She had a soft spot after all, and because I was a fucking terrible person, I poked at it, hoping she would leave me and my monsters alone.

As far as being attractive went, she didn't need much help. She was tall for a girl and built with a lot of curves that would fill out stunningly as she got older. Her eyes were a spectacular light blue that hovered on the edge of violet. They were unusual and missed very little. Those eyes saw right through me and picked me apart. Her blonde hair was a million different shades of white and gold. It shimmered like something expensive in the sun. It was messy, but that suited her. If she was put together and polished, it would make her too perfect and completely unapproachable. Her skin was a mellow honey color from the sun, and she had freckles across the bridge of her nose. All of it made for the perfect girl-next-door, the one who half the boys in school fantasized about when they were beating off in the shower. We always wanted what we knew we could never have. What we knew was too good for us.

When I drove away from her that day, I thought it was all said and done. She hated me, but I was nothing to her so I assumed she would let it drop. Imagine my surprise when, the following day, I went home after an all-night party and found my entire room tossed and my mother on my bedroom floor in tears surrounded by my stash. The blonde bitch had ratted me out and had taken her concern to my mother when I wouldn't listen. I wanted to be angry at her, but I was impressed. No one in Loveless went against a McCaffrey. No one wanted me as an enemy.

Mom broke down. She said she should have known, that my behavior had been erratic and hostile for a long time. I thought I was in for a slap on the wrist and maybe some tough love but no . . . she went nuclear on me. She pulled me out of school and told me I was going to a treatment center. There was no argument and no choice. She was locking me down and forcing me to get help. Now, I could look back and see she was doing what she thought she had to do. At the time, I wanted to grab the stash and run. The idea of losing my only relief from the ever-present disgust and discontent made me panic. I said things to her I would never be able to apologize for. What happened when I told her to 'fuck off' and escaped in a huff the day before I was supposed to leave is something I would never be able to make amends for. I ruined a lot of lives simply because my mother was trying to save mine.

I took another swallow of cinnamon-flavored booze and made a face as it burned down my throat. Maybe I could breathe fire. I needed to be able to if I was going to make it through the summer with Affton Reed looking over my shoulder. She had some of the strongest shields I'd ever seen. If my fire wasn't hot enough, it would bounce off her and burn me to a crisp.

The sun was down, and I was pretty much sitting in the water now. I thought about lying down and letting it lift me up and carry me wherever it wanted. I wasn't drifting anywhere good on my own. I heard splashing and felt the air behind me stir. No longer alone. No longer left to my own devices and bad choices.

I took another swig from the bottle, draining it, and looked over my shoulder at the girl making her way toward me. Her hair looked silver in the darkening light, and there was no mistaking the annoyance on her unmade-up face. She looked at me then shifted her gaze to the empty bottle in my hand. Her lips pulled into a frown, and her eyebrows tugged down into an angry V over the top of her nose.

"You aren't going to make anything about this summer easy, are you, Cable?"

I had a thing for her voice. It was a little bit husky and a lot sweet with that slow, southern Texas twang in it. The way my name sounded when she said it, all exasperated and frustrated, was fucking sexy. It made me wonder what it would sound like when she whispered it in the dark while I was inside of her. I'd imagined that more times than I could count over the last eighteen months.

"I don't really do easy, Reed." I looked at the empty bottle in my hand and contemplated tossing it into the Gulf. Knowing my luck, I'd hit some endangered marine life and give the judge one more reason to add months onto my sentence. Instead, I reached up and handed it to the leggy blonde who was now standing next to me, the water well above her ankles.

"Jesus. Did you drink this whole thing?" She sounded incensed, and when I rolled my eyes up to look at her, it was clear she was contemplating hitting me over the head with the very weapon I'd just handed to her.

I shrugged. "Pretty much." The bubbly teen girls barely had the chance to put a dent in it before I swooped in and snagged their stash.

She sighed from where she was hovering above me. I jolted in shock when she suddenly lowered herself to the wet sand next to me, the water immediately soaking into her frayed cutoffs and swirling around her ankles and hips as she copied my pose, my empty bottle caught between her feet. She leaned forward, rested her cheek on her knee, and gazed at me steadily out of those mesmerizing eyes. "I tried to tell your mother this was hopeless. I warned her there is no helping someone who doesn't want to be helped. I don't want to be here, Cable." Her voice was hard, and I was surprised that her admission hurt a little bit. I didn't want to be around me most of the time, but I was used to other people flocking to me, vying for my attention. "I don't want to be here, but I have to be, so that means you're stuck with me no matter how difficult you decide to make the next couple of months. I don't have a choice."

I wanted a cigarette. I needed something to occupy my hands and my mouth. I'd left the smokes and my t-shirt on the steps of the deck off dad's house. The steps led to the beach, just a few feet from the water. It was a beautiful house on a prime piece of property. With Affton here, it was nothing more than an expensive jail cell.

I knew exactly what means my mother had gone to in order to get Affton to agree to this madness. She told me outright she was blackmailing my former classmate, I think in a thinly veiled attempt to make me care about someone else's future if I wouldn't care about my own. I knew if I drove Affton away, her father would lose his job. It wasn't fair, but my mom had been nothing short of ruthless in her pursuit of my sobriety. "My mom can be very convincing when she puts her mind to it." She could also be tough as nails and immovable when she wanted something.

Affton snorted and shifted so her chin was resting on her knee instead of her cheek. She looked out over the endless landscape of water and sky, and I shivered even though it wasn't cold. I lifted a hand to run it through my hair. My unease lived inside of me, crawled all around my bones and under my skin. I wasn't used to it making its way to the surface because of someone else. There was a lot unsaid between me and this girl. The few words we'd exchanged were powerful, important ones that hung heavy between us. It was so much easier when I looked at her, and she refused to look back.

"I don't think convincing is the word I would use . . . more like conniving. Either way, she tied my hands, so succeed or fail, you are stuck with me until the end of summer. Let's get you into the house so you can sleep this bottle off and pray you don't get popped for a piss test tomorrow." She grabbed the bottle from where she had plunked the base in the sand and lifted a pale eyebrow at me. "You should have picked something . . ." she trailed off and gave me a shrug. "Less wussy to enjoy your last binge with. This stuff tastes like toothpaste."

She offered me her free hand, and for a second all I could picture was grabbing it and pulling her under with me, letting the water cover us both and take us somewhere we would both rather be. I didn't. I took her hand and struggled to my feet. Months of forced sobriety tumbled away under the wash of cinnamon whiskey. I wobbled and almost went back down, but before I could nose dive into the shallow water, Affton was there, arm around my waist, empty bottle pressed into my side, a chilly reminder that I'd already fucked this up and it was only the first day.

I had no idea how either one of us was going to survive the summer, and if we did, I had no idea how I was supposed to survive beyond that when I was once again left to my own devious and duplicitous devices.

three

AFFTON

THE HIKE ACROSS the sand back to the towering beach house was no easy task. The sand sucked at our feet and Cable was anything but steady as I struggled to keep both of us upright. He smelled surprisingly good—part salt water, part cinnamon. He looked ragged and scruffy. He sounded despondent and disappointed. For all the things that had changed since I last spoke to him, an alarming number of things had remained the same. I wasn't sure how I thought *the incident*, then a year and a half in prison, plus a stint in forced rehab, would change him, but I was shocked at how familiar he seemed and how similar he was to the Cable who always got under my skin.

His dark blond hair was a little shorter, his face a little harder, and his mouth set tighter in the frown that seemed to be his default expression. His dark eyes still appeared fathomless and void of any kind of basic human emotion, but there was a vulnerability about him that was new. The disaffected shell he'd always been wrapped in before seemed to be missing pieces, and the tender, torn parts that reminded me Cable was, in fact, a human being were peeking through.

I thought the old hatred that burned through me would flare to life, but instead, all I felt was sympathy. Neither of us wanted to be here. Neither of us wanted to be in charge of saving him.

When he staggered to his feet, I noticed he was taller than he had been the last time I saw him. He was also bigger . . . everywhere. His shoulders were broader. His muscles were no longer lanky and lean. They were hard and solid, obviously his time locked up had been spent improving his body instead of his messed-up mentality. The hand I was holding as he leaned heavily into my side was wide and rough. It wasn't the hand of a teenager who never had to work for anything and was given everything he'd ever wanted on a silver platter. The hand in mine belonged to someone who had not been living the good life for quite a long time. It had struggled. And suffered.

When we reached the back stairs that led up to the sweeping deck circling the entirety of the beach house, Cable pulled away from my grasp and almost face-planted onto the wooden steps. He lost his balance when he bent over to grab his shirt and the pack of cigarettes laying on top of the crumpled cotton. The moonlight highlighted the stretch and pull of his back muscles as he worked to regain his balance. It also illuminated the intricate black and gray tattoo that covered one of his shoulders and circled down around his bicep. I wasn't sure if that was something he had when we went to school together since I'd never been in a situation where I would have seen him without a shirt, but whenever and wherever he got the tattoo, it was beautiful and impressive. He also had an elaborate and delicate looking spider web inked right where his thumb bent, crossed the back of his hand, and spread down his middle finger. I was sure that one was new, as was the skull and crossbones he had inked on the knuckles of each of his index fingers. He was too blond and refined to really pull off the ex-con look, but the tattoos helped give him a dangerous edge that hadn't been there before he got locked up.

He'd changed. And so had I. It had been almost two years since I'd seen him last, enough time and distance for me to really reflect on the terrible last words I lobbed at him. I told him I hated him, and then he'd gone away. There was no getting around the fact that I was the one who set those wheels in motion. I was partly responsible for the fractured shell he was still trying so desperately to hide inside.

"I need a smoke." He awkwardly lowered himself to the step next to my feet and worked at getting the cancer-stick between his lips. It took three tries, since he kept dropping the stupid thing, and he tried to light the wrong end. I sighed, took the lighter from him, and touched the flame to the right end.

I took a step back as he blew out a cloud of the acrid smoke. I waved a hand in front of my face and told him, "That's a disgusting habit." I preferred it to the gnarly wads of chew that were so popular among boys my age in the heartland, but really, it was all gross. Why anyone would want to turn their teeth yellow and shorten their lifespan on purpose was beyond me.

He puffed out another toxic breath and tilted back his head so that he was looking up at the night sky. "It's the least disgusting habit I happen to have at the moment."

His words were slow and slightly slurred together. It was a stark reminder that he was already doing exactly what he wasn't supposed to be doing. This summer—and his mom's wishes for his miraculous recovery—were already in the toilet. I wasn't surprised, but I was unexpectedly disappointed. I wanted to believe when something terrible happened, when tragedy struck, it had the power to change someone for the better. There were a lot of lessons Cable should have learned after *the incident,* and it didn't seem like he'd opened his eyes to any of them.

"Is there a particular room you want me to take?" I sounded annoyed because I was. I wanted to be compassionate and understanding for all that he's been through, but the boy still had the ability to rub me the wrong way without even trying.

The house was huge: three levels of designer furniture and expensive design. There was no shabby, beachy goodness to be found, and I was terrified to touch anything. I had no clue how many bedrooms there were, but I assumed he already had one he used and he would want me in the one that was farthest away. I hadn't broken the news to him, but I was going to be regularly tossing the entire waterfront mansion for any kind of contraband he might try to hide. I was a pro at finding a secret stash—years of practice for a competition no one would win.

Thanks, Mom . . .

He inhaled on the cigarette and let his eyes drift closed. He was silent for so long. I thought he was going to ignore me, so I took a step around him and went to move toward the massive accordion windows that folded in and opened to the stunning view of the Gulf. Wherever I ended up in this giant house, I was going to have an amazing view—not that it made up for being blackmailed out of my entire summer.

I froze when his hand curled around my knee, his rough fingers brushing along vulnerable skin on the back of my thigh. When I shivered, I blamed it on my wet shorts because there was no way in hell I would ever admit to being affected by Cable James McCaffrey. He embodied everything I never wanted in my life again, and he had no self-control. I looked down at the empty bottle of whiskey I still held in my hand and gave my head a little shake to get my thoughts back in order.

"My room is on the lowest level. It faces the pool. My dad's room is on the top level. It's the one that looks like a suite at Caesar's Palace and smells like infidelity and alimony. I would avoid it at all costs in case STDs have suddenly become airborne." He let out a sharp laugh that held zero humor and his eyes burned with black fire as he looked up at me under the fall of his wheat-colored hair. "I would suggest you take one of the rooms on the main level, that way you won't be subjected to any of my other disgusting habits when I indulge."

His eyebrows arched up, and he let go of my leg as he smirked at me. He was talking about sex. He wanted me to find a room in the house that had enough distance between where I was sleeping and where he was planning on doing anything but. I was there to keep him sober, not celibate. The idea of sharing a house with the types of girls who had driven me nuts in high school because they were content to be his playthings, made my teeth clench.

"Fine. I'm going to grab my bags and get settled in. It was a long drive from Loveless, and I didn't think I was going to have to start with an intervention as soon as I got here." I lifted the whiskey bottle and finished climbing the steps. "If you pass out on those stairs, I'm leaving you there, and I'm gonna laugh my ass off if you're covered in seagull shit in the morning."

He snorted and turned back to face the dark water, smoke billowing over his head. "Live my life swimming in shit, Reed. A little bird poop won't kill me."

I didn't have anything to say to that, couldn't think of anything witty or sympathetic enough, so I slipped through the dark and empty house and practically ran to my car. It was the only thing that felt familiar and safe in the current state of my life. I unlocked the door and slid behind the wheel; the urge to crank the motor and drive until I was anywhere but here was so strong that my palm hurt from clutching my keys so hard.

My phone was glowing with messages and missed calls. I'd left it on the dashboard when I first got to the house, but I regretted that now. I could have used the distraction while dealing with Cable. I told my dad I would call him when I arrived. He had no idea why I was in Port Aransas for the summer. I didn't want to tell him that he was hanging onto his job by a thread or how Melanie McCaffrey had me over a barrel. He would quit in a heartbeat, but then he would struggle to find work if he stayed in Loveless, and there really was nowhere else for him to go. I was headed to California in a few months, and his entire family was in that small Texas town. So, I lied. Something I never did. I told him that Melanie had set up an internship for me over the summer that would help me not only earn money before college but would look great when I applied to grad school. He didn't question any of it, and was, as always, so supportive and proud of every little thing I did. It made me feel awful.

Jordan had also called several times. She was dying for a rundown of the McCaffrey's beach house, and she was chomping at the bit for an update on Cable's condition. The rumor mill had started grinding away now that the news that he was out of prison and on parole was making the rounds. Jordan told me she had heard that he was horribly disfigured after *the incident*. She told me people were speculating his time in prison had been brutal and he had come out a changed man. Some were saying he had joined the Aryan Brotherhood while he was behind bars, and others were saying the feds had put him in witness protection and that's why he wasn't coming back to Loveless. I told her it was all ridiculous, but small-town gossip was a living, breathing thing, and without Cable there to deny any of the things being said about him, the stories grew wilder.

Needing a minute of normalcy, I touched the image of Jordan's smiling face and called her back.

Jordan was as opposite from me as could be. She was dark where I was light. She was born to stand out when all I wanted to do was make my way unnoticed. Her parents were happily married and everything in her home centered on family. Her mom and dad had been together since they both went to Loveless High and neither one of them knew the first thing about having their family ripped apart by addiction and dishonesty. She was loud, outgoing, bubbly, and vivacious. She was friends with everyone, but I was the only one she kept close. She told me early on, when we first started hanging out, the reason she liked me so much was because I didn't *try* to get her to like me. I laughed and told her it was because I didn't want her to befriend me . . . I wanted to be left alone. But Jordan was persistent, and she didn't have a mean or spiteful bone in her body, so there was no way I could resist her. We'd been inseparable since seventh grade, which was another reason I could gladly scalp Melanie McCaffrey. This was the last summer I had with my best friend before our lives inevitably split in different directions, and Cable's mom had snatched that time away from us by forcing me to babysit her son. I was going to Berkeley; Jordan was staying in Loveless and learning all about her parents' event planning and catering business.

Her older brother, Johnny, was supposed to take over when he graduated a couple years ahead of us, but he'd met some girl on spring break in Cancun and had followed her to Arizona. He shocked everyone by enrolling at Arizona State. Jordan, on the other hand, was made to show people how to have a good time, so she couldn't wait to dive into learning the ropes of event planning. I was sad she was set on staying in Loveless. I wanted her to want more. But I understood why she was staying, and I couldn't say I wouldn't be more willing to stay if I had more to look forward to than watching my dad get older while things stayed the same as they were now.

I couldn't bring myself to lie to Jordan when I told her why I wouldn't be around for the summer. I owed her the truth, and I needed someone to commiserate with. She knew how I felt about Cable. She was also the only person who knew I was the one who had ratted him out to his mother about his drug use.

"OMG! I've been calling you all night. I thought you might have been abducted at a truck stop. Are you okay? How's the house? Does it look like something from a magazine? How's Cable? Does he look like a felon?" The questions came so fast and furiously I could barely keep up with her.

I tugged on my bottom lip and closed my eyes as I rested my head on the back of my seat. "The house is just as impressive as the one on the ranch. It's big and has a wraparound deck. The beach is right off the back steps, and the water is within throwing distance. It's all fancy. It reminds me of a luxury hotel. I'm scared to touch anything." I blew out a sigh and ran a hand over my face. "He was drunk when I got here, Jordan. Trashed. He's not supposed to be drinking or using any kind of narcotic. He didn't even wait a day. This is going to be a disaster. I'm already annoyed and exhausted. This wasn't how I wanted to spend my last summer before school starts."

She made a sympathetic sound. "I know it wasn't, but what can you do? If Cable is already on his way to screwing up, all you have to do is wait him out. Once he messes up, he'll go back to jail, and you can come home and party with me until you leave for Berkeley."

I rubbed my temples with my free hand and sighed again. "Yeah, but then I have to worry about Melanie firing my dad anyway because I couldn't help her son. She's desperate and unpredictable. She might blame me if Cable fails."

"You need to tell your dad what's going on and let him handle her." She'd been saying that since I told her about the ultimatum from Cable's mom.

"If I can't keep Cable on the straight and narrow for even a day, I might not have any choice. I wasn't sure what to expect when I showed up. I knew he wasn't going to be happy to see me, but I didn't expect him to be three sheets to the wind already." I also didn't expect him to seem so broken and battered.

"How did he seem, besides hammered?"

I knew she was asking about guilt and remorse. Anyone else would be lugging around a truckload of both those things after *the incident*, but I couldn't tell if Cable was any heavier emotionally than he was before that night. "He seems miserable."

He really did. There was no light anywhere in those dark eyes.

She made another noise, and I could hear her typing on a keyboard in the background. "Well, I guess going to prison didn't change much. He's still drinking. I swear that boy's face would crack in half if he ever smiled. It's a total bummer you're stuck with such a gloomy Gus all summer, especially since you're in such a beautiful spot. You should be out chasing cute surfer boys while you're there, not babysitting a grouchy, drunk, pain in the ass. This should be the summer you let your hair down and finally have some fun."

She was always telling me I needed to loosen up and live a little. She never understood why I never went with her to parties or school activities. She swore I was missing out on making memories that would last me a lifetime. I tried to explain to her there was nothing about this time in my life I was interested in remembering. I had a destination in mind, and I was focused on the road, not the surroundings I was passing.

"I'll take it as a win if I get through the next few months with my sanity intact." No one had ever pushed my buttons as violently as Cable did. "One of these weekends you'll have to grab Diego and come down for a few days. It won't be the kind of fun you're used to since the house has to stay an alcohol-free zone, but you can come play in the water, and we can go shopping and lie around in the sun."

She hummed a little bit; the clicking of her keyboard halted. There was a long moment of silence that grew weighted and drawn out until she quietly told me, "Diego and I broke up a few days ago. I didn't want to tell you because you were dealing with your own crazy stuff and packing up to leave."

I gasped a little and sat up straighter in my seat. I wrapped my free hand around my steering wheel and asked, "What happened?" She and Diego had been together for the entirety of our senior year. She was smitten with him after their first date, and he treated her like she was his entire world. I couldn't imagine what could have come between them and caused such a major break.

I heard a shuffle as she shrugged on the other end of the line. "Real life happened, I guess. I'm spending the summer working, and he's going to visit his mom and brother in El Paso before he leaves for college. We'll see each other for a week before he leaves for good. I wasn't invested enough to work at keeping things together, and he wasn't either. I don't think he wanted to start college with his high school girlfriend holding on back home."

I bit the inside of my lower lip to keep from blurting out, "I told you so." What she was going through right now was exactly why I didn't get attached or go out of my way to bond with anyone besides her. "I'm sorry. That sucks."

She laughed a little bit, and I could practically see her wrinkling her nose at me. "How badly are you biting your tongue right now?"

I snorted. "Hard enough that it might bleed."

She laughed again. "One of these days you are going to meet someone who gets in, Affton. They're going to ignore all those 'No Trespassing' signs and all the barbed wire you have your insides wrapped up in, and they are going to get in so deep you won't be able to get them out. You aren't going to know what to do with yourself. They're going to knock you so far off course there won't be any finding your way back."

That was never going to happen. After my mom, after the loss and confusion that followed, I made sure the path to my heart was pretty much impassable. I functioned by keeping my soft spots unreachable.

"Well, you found your way inside, so I guess anything is possible. I'm going to go make sure Cable didn't suffocate in a pile of his own puke and try and get some sleep. If you're flying solo, maybe you can get a week off and come down to visit me. I'd love to see you." I'd love to see anyone who wasn't Cable, but she was at the top of the list.

"I'll see what I can do. Keep your chin up and don't let that boy get to you."

"Same. I'm sorry I wasn't paying attention and missed you going through a breakup. I'm a terrible friend."

It was her turn to snort. "No, you're the best friend ever. Cable McCaffrey is simply too distracting. He always has been. Check in with me periodically."

I hung up and tapped the phone against my thigh.

She was right . . . he was distracting. I could still feel the touch of his fingers on the back of my knee and the heat from his body as he leaned into my side all solid and strong . . . and sloshed out of his mind.

He was distracting, and it was just one more thing I hated about him . . . or maybe it was the fact I allowed myself to be distracted by him that I hated. Hating him didn't seem to be as important as it once was. Either way, it was going to be one looooong summer.

four

CABLE

NEVER MADE it to my bed.

The whiskey and melancholy proved too powerful of a combination to combat, so the farthest I managed to make it was to one of the reclining Adirondack chairs that dotted the deck. I woke up when a seagull squawked, and a family with several small kids who couldn't wait to get into the water came screaming by.

My eyes felt like they were coated in sand and laced with fire. My mouth was dry, and there was a charming combination of something that tasted like ash and asshole on my tongue. Everything from my neck down hurt, and my shoulder throbbed from where it had been wrenched at an awkward angle all night long since I used my arm as a pillow. All my joints popped and creaked as I slowly got to my feet and tried to stretch out all the kinks. I cringed as my stiff, crunchy jeans scraped across my skin. I should have at least climbed out of them before I passed out. The saltwater had dried, and the residue was flaking off in white chunks with each of my slow, hesitant movements.

I scratched my chest and lifted an eyebrow as the mom, who

was chasing after the noisy kids, stopped suddenly and gave me an obvious once-over. I snorted in amusement when her husband turned his head to see what was holding her up. He was loaded down with towels and toys. His look screamed that he wanted to drop all of it on the sand and walk away from her and the rugrats when he caught sight of me. He was doing the heavy lifting while his wife checked me out. I would be pissed if I was in his shoes. I lifted my hand in a jaunty little wave and heard the man swear loudly. It made me chuckle as I grabbed the t-shirt I'd never bothered to put on the night before and headed inside to find something that might knock my hangover back a few steps.

The massive wall of glass slid open easily and I squinted into the interior. I was not surprised at all to find my unwanted houseguest already up and ready to face the day. She was banging around the kitchen in another pair of frayed cutoffs and a t-shirt that had been black at one point but had faded to a much-loved gray. It had a picture of Johnny Cash flipping the bird on it, and in places, the white print had cracked and peeled away. I told myself not to look where the fabric was tied in a knot at the small of her back, exposing a swath of tanned, smooth skin. It was impossible not to stare as she stood on her tiptoes, opening all the different cabinets, and as she bent over to search through the fridge.

"Are you looking for something in particular?" I asked the question mostly because she gave me a look of utter disgust but didn't say a word as I stumbled through the living room.

"Food. I'm looking for food. Haven't you gone to the grocery store? What do you plan on eating for breakfast?" She slammed the fridge shut with more force than necessary and gave me a once-over that was nowhere near as appreciative as the one the mom had given me. "You look like shit."

I rubbed a hand over my face; the stubble on my chin scraped against my palm. "I feel like shit, so that's not a shock." I rounded the massive, white leather couch in the family room right off the kitchen and flopped down across it. My dad would have a fit if he knew I was sprawled across the thing in dirty jeans and sandy feet. Everything the man possessed was for show and nothing else.

I closed my eyes and tried to rub some of the grit away. "My dad has a lady when he's here." He had several. "A woman named Miglena comes in every other day and stocks the fridge and the pantry. She makes enough food to last a few days, and she cleans up the house. She should be here sometime this afternoon."

I cranked my head around so I could look at Affton as she made a strangled sound and glared at me from her place in the kitchen.

"You've got to be kidding me." Her words snapped out. She was pissed . . . she always seemed pissed. I could tell she was ready to explode. "You're too precious and perfect to get off your drunken ass and go to the store so you can feed yourself? You're so delicate and fragile you can't be bothered to pick up after yourself and keep this place clean for a couple months? You managed to land yourself a bottle of booze, but something practical like breakfast eludes you?"

She was scathing, and her sarcasm was thick enough to cut with a knife. She put her hands on her hips and narrowed her eyes at me as I tried to formulate a response.

"What are your plans for the summer, Cable? You can't party. You won't be able to work with the random drug screens that will be thrown your way, no boss will understand you having to run out in the middle of a shift to pee in a cup. You aren't getting ready to go off to college. So, what are you going to do with yourself? Were you planning on lying around, feeling sorry for yourself while someone else takes care of you?" Her eyebrows shot up, and a furious flush stained her cheeks hot pink. "You've already lived your life that way and look where it landed you. I think it's time you figure out how to be self-sufficient."

I tried to roll my eyes but it hurt too badly, so I ended up squinting at her from the couch. "I don't even know where the grocery store is." I would rather have her pull out all my teeth with rusty pliers before admitting I also had no idea where the laundry room was in this sprawling house or which of the stainless steel appliances in the gourmet kitchen was the dishwasher. I closed my eyes and laid my head back as an army of elephants started doing the tango in my brain. "Besides, I've spent the last year and a half being told when to eat. When to go outside. When to shower and shit. I haven't been living in the lap of luxury." And as soon as I'd left prison I'd gone right into the sober living facility, which had been as far from extravagant as could be. The place was only a couple of steps up from a slum, as far as I was concerned.

Affton started slamming the cabinet doors for no other reason than to irritate me. I swore and grabbed one of the designer pillows decorating the couch to cover my head.

"You're unbelievable. You know that, right?" I didn't answer her, but I felt the tension that seemed to snap and pop from her move closer to where I was doing a pretty good impression of a beached manatee. "There is only one person you can blame for your recent, less-than-stellar accommodations. Speaking of which, did your parole officer call this morning?"

"Fuck." I threw the pillow off my face and moved faster than I thought my sore, hungover body could move. I could get called in for a piss test anytime between eight and five. I only had an hour to get to the facility, and if I didn't show or pissed hot, I was on my way back to lock up.

I'd left my phone on the imported marble countertop and put it on silent so I didn't have to listen to it ping with notifications from my mom. She wanted to know if I was doing okay and make sure I didn't do anything to chase off Affton. If I was speaking to her, I would have told her Affton didn't scare easy. She proved it the day she confronted me in the parking lot, and she kept proving it as she refused to move out of my way as I bolted for the phone. She wasn't someone I could roll over with manipulation and intimidation. She stood her ground.

The screen had a multitude of missed messages. None were from my dad, which wasn't surprising. Most were from my mom, a few were from girls who wanted to touch base now that I was out, and several were from a blocked number I knew belonged to a reporter who had been all over me since I was released early. The last thing I wanted was my face plastered all over what passed as the news in Loveless. I wanted that almost as little as I wanted to talk about the night I had gone from a fuck-up to a felon.

I didn't want to talk about it.

I didn't want to think about it.

I didn't want to remember it.

And I really, really didn't want to relive it every single second of every single day. I could feel familiar pressure starting to weigh down the center of my chest. My lungs squeezed tight as my breath whooshed in and out and my blood turned to ice and struggled to move through my veins. All I wanted was a drink, or a line, or a smoke. All I wanted was everything I couldn't have to get out from under all the things that I was sure were going to bury me.

"Did he call?"

I forgot Affton was there until her question snapped me back to reality. I scrolled through all the messages and shook my head at her. "No. I'm in the clear." At least I was this morning. If I did something stupid like getting wasted and passing out without my phone again, I might not be so lucky. The expression on Affton's

face clearly indicated that she was aware of the truth. I tended to
be one lucky bastard.

She pointed to the phone. "Call your dad and tell him you
don't need the housekeeper while you're here this summer."

I let out a startled laugh and lifted my hands to rub my aching
temples. "Why would I do that?" I usually enjoyed the sound of
her voice, but I would be really happy if she stopped using it until
I had my headache under control.

"You're going to do that because you and I are perfectly capable of keeping ourselves fed and this house in order. You might
be comfortable being waited on hand and foot, but I'm not. And
since you have to go where I go for the foreseeable future, that
means you are about to find out where the grocery store is." She
sounded unwavering and firm in her decision.

She was an anomaly. Who wanted to pass up the chance to
spend a summer at the beach being catered to and pampered?
Who didn't want to exploit all the wealth she currently had at her
fingertips? This girl was different than anyone I'd ever met, and I
wasn't sure what in the hell I was supposed to do with her.

"I'm not calling my dad." Hell would freeze over before I gave
that bastard the time of day. I tapped my phone on the counter
and watched as she bristled at my words. "Miglena is a nice lady.
She doesn't make a ton of money and she has a buttload of kids.
I'm not going to take an entire summer of pay away from her
because you're all fired up to teach me some bullshit lesson about
independence and responsibility."

I watched as some of the fight drained out of her. Her shoulders fell and some of the heat wilted out of her eyes. She crossed
her arms over her chest and tapped her fingers in agitation as
she considered me thoughtfully for a long moment. Finally, she
shrugged, turned on her heel, and headed toward the guest rooms.

"Fine. She can cook and clean for you, but I'm not letting her do anything for me. That means you need to take a shower and wash the stench off yourself because I still need to go to the grocery store and I'm not supposed to leave you here alone."

I wanted to tell her I had been here alone all day yesterday, but I lost that argument by getting wasted before she showed up. I was a twenty-year-old man. I shouldn't need a keeper, but nothing I had done proved that to be the case. Forever a fuck-up. Forever finding new ways to fail.

Annoyed, I smirked at her disappearing back and drawled, "The MILF on the beach this morning didn't think there was anything wrong with the way I look." Most women didn't.

Affton stopped and shot me a look over her shoulder. It didn't take her longer than a second to fire back, "She obviously wasn't close enough to smell you. Go take a shower, Cable."

I scowled as she swept out of the room leaving me alone so I could discreetly sniff under my arm. I made a face and dropped my arm when I caught a whiff of the less-than-pleasant odor.

I smelled like a drunk.

I smelled like a bum.

I smelled like bad choices and regret.

I thought about stubbornly refusing to do anything she asked. I didn't want her here, and I didn't want to be stuck on the end of her leash; I also couldn't imagine sitting around the house, both of us pissed off and hungry because I was acting ridiculous. That behavior had landed me in the deepest, darkest hole I'd ever been in, and I was just starting to make the slow climb back to where I used to be. It wouldn't kill me to tag along with her to the store. After all, she was going to have to be my chauffeur to and from my check-ins. That meant she was going to know firsthand if her efforts to keep my nose and veins clean had paid off. There would be no hiding my failure from her.

I hit the shower, and it took about a second for me to realize this was where I should have gone instead of searching for a drink yesterday.

Showers in prison were anything but relaxing, and the shower at the group home had hardly worked. I knew my soul would never be clean, but standing under the scalding water in a real shower, it started to feel slightly less filthy. The water did wonders. It washed away a plethora of bad things, and it zapped some of my hangover down the drain. My head was still throbbing, and my eyes still felt like they were being rubbed raw by sandpaper each time I blinked, but the aches from my night and the stiffness in my limbs loosened.

It also only took a second for me to regret not taking the beach babes up on their offer to hang out. I enjoyed being alone, but I also tended to lose my loneliness inside of a warm and willing body. I'd lost my virginity by the end of my freshman year and hadn't spent many nights alone until I got locked up. Now, I'd been without someone else longer than I'd been without any of my other vices, and my body was noticing the loss. My dick went hard at the wayward thought of just how long and tanned Affton's legs were in those shorts of hers, and it throbbed when I recalled that sliver of skin at the curve of her back.

I let out a string of explicit words and lifted one of my hands to the tiles in front of me. I squeezed my eyes shut and tried to pull up an image of any of the girls who passed in and out of my life who weren't Affton Reed. There had been plenty of them. Most of them a lot more welcoming and friendly than Affton. At least until I ghosted them after I got the few, stolen moments of peace and quiet being inside them offered.

But, because I was broken in all kinds of terrible ways, it was only her messy blonde hair and those lapis-colored eyes I could conjure as I slowly started to work my fist up and down the length of my straining erection. Sure, back when we were nothing more than strangers who passed each other silently in the hallways during school, I'd imagined Affton doing all kinds of dirty, raunchy things I doubt she had ever experienced. There wasn't a guy in the school who didn't have a passing fantasy about ruffling her seemingly unrufflable feathers. Jerking off to the idea of her legs and her sweet, golden skin when she was just a few doors away seemed more illicit and wrong. I enjoyed it even more.

The idea that she might find out, that she might catch me and demand to know what I was doing made me even harder and had pleasure coiling tighter around the base of my spine. I wanted to tell her I got off thinking about her. I wanted to scandalize and outrage her. I craved a reaction from her. It made it seem like maybe we're more similar than I thought. Both of us reacting against our will. Both of us responding because we had no choice.

I was so hard that it hurt, and when I finally found release, I had to bite back a sound of satisfaction that sounded suspiciously similar to Affton's name. I ended the shower feeling a little bit dirtier than I had when I went in, but at least I smelled a whole lot better.

five

AFFTON

"**R**EALLY, WHAT ARE your plans for the entire summer, Cable? You can't just sit around feeling sorry for yourself day in and day out."

Well, he could, and he seemed perfectly content to do exactly that, but if I had to watch him wallow in self-pity all day, every day, I was going to lose my mind. Actions had consequences, and clearly it was the first time in his life that Cable had to face those nasty little fuckers head-on.

He looked at me out of the corner of his eye from where he was folded into my passenger seat, an unlit cigarette dangling his lips. I refused to let him smoke in my car, and I stuck to my guns even though the car was a thousand years old and already had a distinct smell of its own. His hair was still wet, and his attitude was piss poor and prickly. Being trapped in a small space with him was unnerving, and I was disturbed by the way the space between us seemed charged and electric. If I moved in any direction, I worried there was a risk of getting shocked. I didn't want to have any kind of reaction to this sullen, spoiled boy. I wanted to be immune.

Numb. Frozen.

He plucked the cigarette out of his mouth and put it behind his ear. His wide shoulders lifted and dropped in a bored shrug. "You're here to ensure I can't do all the things I normally do, so I guess I'll have to find other ways to entertain myself."

The suggestive drop in his tone made me blush as I cast a narrow-eyed look in his direction. It bugged me that every time he insinuated something sexual, I couldn't control the way my blood heated and my heart rate sped. I tried to convince myself it was from embarrassment and awkwardness, but I'd never been a very good liar.

"You know that anyone who comes into the house has to go through me first, right? You can't waltz any party girl you want through the door without me making sure she's not carrying any-thing for you." I couldn't hold back a cringe at the idea of having to shake down strangers just because Cable couldn't make good choices. It was going to be terrible and ruin my entire summer, but I told his mom I would do my best to keep him sober to save my dad's job, and I meant it.

He let out a low grunt and turned his head so that he was looking out the window when I wheeled into the parking lot of the small grocery store.

"That's going to be a bit of a buzzkill, Reed, but that's nothing new with you, is it?"

I didn't respond. Instead, I threw open the door and stepped out. It was hot and muggy out, so I instantly felt wilted and sticky. I lifted my hair off the back of my neck and continued to glare at Cable as he took his time getting out of the car. The cigarette was back in his mouth, the tip glowing before he had the passenger door shut.

A plume of smoke drifted between us as he told me quietly,

"I was actually thinking about working on my GED while I have nothing else to do this summer. I started studying for it when I was locked up, but it was too hard. I couldn't afford to have my attention on anything other than keeping my ass safe and not pissing off the wrong people." His tone was deeper than usual. Thoughtful, even. There was honesty and reflection there I would bet he didn't mean to share with me. His time locked up hadn't been easy, and once again I was reminded that I was the catalyst for that. It made my heart drop and my throat feel tight. Compassion was so much harder than the hate I was comfortable with.

I stood silent, mouth open in shock, brain whirling in circles the entire time it took him to finish his smoke. I had to shake my head to wrangle my thoughts into order.

"I . . . well . . . that's a great idea. You should totally do that." I never stuttered. I never tripped over my words. I never stumbled. I detested that this boy was the one who knocked me off kilter and made me unsteady. I hated that he was the one who tripped me up over and over again.

"Don't get too excited. I still plan on fucking myself stupid and spending my days surfing. I just thought I might as well do *something* productive for once in my life while I have all this time on my hands." His blunt statement shook the last of my surprise away. I wanted to kick myself for believing—for even a second— that Cable James McCaffrey had learned a lesson from all the destruction he had caused.

I cleared my throat and adjusted the strap of my purse on my shoulder. "If you stay on the wagon, I really don't care what you do with your free time." But because I was a glutton for punishment, I couldn't hold back the offer to help him do something right. "If you're serious about the GED, let me know, and I'll help you study. I was valedictorian." I'd accepted the honor and given a speech to my graduating class only a couple of weeks ago. I was sure a lifetime had passed between then and now. I cocked my head to the side and studied him as he fell in step beside me, his handsome face set in familiar, disinterested lines. "Do you really surf?"

He looked like a surfer with his shaggy, dirty blond hair and the careless scruff that darkened his chin and cheeks. He had on a light gray t-shirt featuring the logo of his parents' brewery and a pair of jeans that were in far better shape than the ones he'd dipped in the Gulf last night. He was wearing faded black Converse that were almost identical to mine. Looking at him, it was impossible to tell he was the privileged son of a couple of millionaires. He didn't look like an ex-con or a recovering addict. At least he didn't until you got to his eyes.

Those dark orbs were perfect for hiding secrets, but if you looked hard enough, you could see the storm raging inside of Cable McCaffrey. There were shadows in those dark eyes, and they were at war with him.

They were winning.

I stiffened as his hand landed on the small of my back where my shirt was tied so it fit instead of hanging down around my thighs. It was one of my favorites. I stole it from my dad and re-fused to give it back even though it was three sizes too big. The bare skin where his palm landed tingled, and I quickly took a step forward to break the contact.

"Yeah, I can surf. We've had this house since I was little. I learned how so I didn't have to be stuck inside while my parents did their best to eat each other alive. I never particularly looked forward to summer vacation, but I always loved being on the water." He took the cart from me and immediately put his feet on the bar and rode it like a scooter as we started through the store. "I was into the girls in bikinis who liked surfers even more."

I bristled and was going to snap at him that he was into anyone who had a willing vagina when I realized by the smirk on his face and quirk in his gold-tinted eyebrows that he was baiting me. He knew it ruffled my feathers when he brought up sex and his vast experience with the opposite sex. He was purposely rattling my cage just to get a reaction.

Onto his game, I changed the subject and obediently followed as he swung the cart away from the vegetables and fruit and headed toward the center aisles. I never shopped from the center of the store. That was a luxury my dad and I could rarely afford. I figured Cable would get bored after the novelty of wandering up and down the aisles wore off, and I could get what I came for.

"If you're thinking about a GED, does that mean you might be interested in college next year?"

He gave me a look over his shoulder that made me shiver. "I'm not really the sit-in-a-classroom-all-day type. I get bored and distracted, and when I'm bored and distracted, I find things that aren't any good for me to entertain myself."

I huffed a little and reached into the cart to pull out the bag of Doritos he had just thrown in. Spicy Nacho was my favorite, but if he wanted them, he could have his dad's housekeeper bring him some. I wasn't paying for his munchies. "College isn't the same as high school. You're more in control. You get to focus on the stuff that interests you, not the stuff everyone else thinks you should know."

He made a noise and tossed a bag of licorice in the cart I also had to pull out. "I've had enough of being on someone else's schedule and being confined to four walls." He shrugged and I couldn't help but admire the way the cotton of his shirt pulled across his broad shoulders when he did it. "Besides, I don't really have anything that interests me, so paying for college would be tantamount to throwing money in the trash."

I jerked to a stop in the middle of the cereal aisle, my Chucks squeaking on the linoleum. It took Cable a minute to realize I was no longer walking next to the cart, and by the time he did, he was at the end of the aisle. He was too far away for me to fish out the Cap'n Crunch he had added to the cart. When he finally noticed I stopped, he turned around and stared at me with a questioning look on his face. "What?"

I frowned at him and asked, "How can you not have anything that interests you, Cable?" He had the means to have anything, experience everything, and yet none of it held any appeal to him. That was one of the saddest things I'd ever heard.

It seemed he could sense the direction of my thoughts because his reply was smooth and laced with that silky innuendo I was starting to hate. "Well, there are things I'm interested in, but I don't have to be in college to have sex with college girls. They take me just the way I am."

It was deflection at its finest, but now that I could see what it was, I could walk around it with no effort at all. I made my way toward him and put my hand on the side of the cart. I decided to leave the cereal alone as I stared at him intently. "You should take the time to find something real that interests you, Cable. You should find the thing that keeps your mind occupied and soothes you when all those cravings and demons rise to the surface. If you have something that matters to focus on, then it won't be as easy for your bad habits to clamor for your free time."

I sighed and grabbed the end of the cart, so I could pull it toward the dairy section in search of eggs and milk. "Unless you plan on living off your parents' money and your inheritance for the rest of your life. If you do, I guarantee you won't manage to maintain your sobriety. You should figure out what you enjoy doing so you can leverage that into some kind of career." He opened his mouth, but before he could give me his sarcastic reply, I held up a hand and told him flatly, "And I don't want to hear about your lofty dreams of being a porn star."

He chuckled and made a sound of approval when I added a package of bacon to the cart.

"What interests you, Reed? I'm sure you have the next twenty years all mapped out." He said it jokingly, but I bet he wouldn't be at all surprised that he was exactly right.

I refused to look at him as I added bananas and oranges to the cart. "Understanding why people hurt other people interests me. Helping people who can't control themselves when it comes to hurting the people who love them the most interests me." Why my mom couldn't pick me over her addiction was the question that took up the most space inside of my mind, and I often wondered if I would ever find a moment's peace until I found an answer.

"Saving lost causes? That's your thing? That's what you want to focus on when you finally get the choice?" He shook his head at me and suddenly veered down the school supply aisle. I watched wordlessly as he tossed a notebook and a pack of colored pencils into the cart. Before I could object he told me, "I'll pay you back for those when my mom releases the freeze on my bank accounts. Idle hands and all that."

I followed him to the checkout and tried not to roll my eyes in an obvious way as the cashier, who was easily his mother's age, openly flirted with him as she scanned our items. There was something about Cable that made it so easy for people to overlook all the warning signs those tumultuous eyes flashed between each blink. I couldn't figure out why I was the only one who heeded them. He might make my body react in ways I found unsettling, and he might challenge all the preconceived notions I had about him at times, but everything inside of me shook against the ways he was trying to slide under my skin. He would never get through my iron shell. I would never allow that.

I was back behind the wheel and headed to the beach house when I finally responded to his question about why understanding addicts was my thing. I turned my head to look at him and noticed he was scrolling through messages on his phone with a sour look on his face.

"It's not about saving them after they're lost. It's about getting to them before they lose their way in the first place." I always wondered if there was a way to help my mom before she started relying so heavily on the pills.

He went still next to me, and I felt his big frame stiffen. That electric charge that sparked between us crackled with a life of its own. It felt powerful enough to burn and hot enough to leave lasting scars.

"Is that why you confronted me that day in the parking lot? Were you trying to save me before I was lost, Affton?"

It was the first time he used my first name. The way he said it, almost as if it was sweet on his tongue and something special to savor, made me tingle in places that had no business feeling a damn thing around him.

I shrugged, uncomfortable heat staining my neck and cheeks. "Maybe. Probably. I don't really know why I did it. You were headed somewhere bad, and I didn't want you to go down that road. Someone needed to try and stop you."

"We were in school together for years. You never so much as looked in my direction. How is it that you ended up being the someone who intervened?" He didn't sound mad about it. Curious and puzzled, but there was no anger in his tone.

It took me a minute to think up an answer. I'd told him I was no fan of his, so I had a hard time explaining why I felt like I was sucked into his downward spiral right next to him. "I didn't want addiction to win."

He gave a sharp, jagged bark of laughter. I felt the pointy edge of it against my skin. "But it did."

I blinked at him and had to swallow down the fear that it would win again if he let it take control of his life. "It doesn't have to. You can win if you play the game. If you're planning to forfeit, if you aren't even going to step on the field, then you might as well resign yourself to serving the rest of your prison sentence. Consider this halftime, Cable. The game isn't close to being over yet."

This time when he laughed there was a thin thread of humor laced throughout it. "Leave it to a Texas girl to throw out a football analogy when talking about overcoming drug addiction."

I couldn't help but grin at him, and when he gave me a lopsided smile back, the cage I kept my heart in rattled loud enough I swore I heard the ringing in my ears.

Luckily this was Cable I was dealing with and the shared moment of levity was quickly torn apart by his softly spoken words.

"Some souls were never meant to be saved. They might end up on the right path, but without fail, they will veer off. It's all they know how to do. No matter how badly they might be hurting other people, they still lose their way. Honestly, the hurt they cause will never compare to how much hurt they inflict upon themselves." He lifted his hand to the center of his chest and dug the heel of his palm into the place where his heart sat. He was trying to hold back whatever that tender place inside of him was bleeding out.

I wanted to tell him that sometimes the only way to excise an infected wound was to slice it open and let all the poison out. However, I was the only one around, the only one close enough to him to stem the bleeding. I was having a hard enough time playing his babysitter—and it had been less than twenty-four hours. I didn't think I could play his spiritual guide on top of it.

We rode the rest of the way to the house in silence. He helped me carry in the groceries, then he disappeared out on the deck with that pad of paper and the colored pencils. I didn't go after him.

He had asked me why the someone who tried to catch him before he fell had to be me.

I would die before I told him it was because it was more than his addiction that interested me. Cable James McCaffrey interested me in a way no one else ever had . . . and obviously, I hated it because I couldn't lie to myself and say that I still hated him.

six

CABLE

"HAVE YOU SPOKEN to anyone about that night, Cable?"

The shrink was talking about the night everything changed.

He was talking about the night that turned me from an addict into a killer.

He was talking about the night no one in Loveless ever talked about, so I thought his question was stupid because he knew the damn answer already. Maybe because he wasn't from where I was from, he thought talking about that night was an option. Maybe he really believed talking about it was something I wanted to do.

It wasn't.

I kept my gaze trained on the tips of my Chucks and stayed silent. I was supposed to meet with Dr. Howard twice a week as long as I was in Port Aransas. If I went back to Loveless after my wasted summer was over, he was going to transfer my care to a therapist there. One who would more than likely know all the gory details of that night. One who believed I'd gotten off light. One who looked at me and saw a killer.

This was my second meeting with the doc and the second time I sat in his office, eyes trained on the ground, not adding anything to the conversation. I didn't need a professional to tell me I was fucked up. Every morning when I opened my eyes and regretted that I had another day, more opportunities to screw up everything, I knew something was wrong with me. I shouldn't feel like I was drowning before the day even began, but I did. Every morning it was harder to breathe. Every minute the weight got heavier, and it was harder to move.

"What about your pretty, blonde friend who comes with you to your appointments? She seems fairly invested in your well-being. Have you talked to her about any of the emotions you may be struggling with because of that night?"

I was so surprised he mentioned Affton that I lifted my head to look at him. He looked more like a beach bum than an addiction counselor. He had on a garish Hawaiian shirt printed with parrots and palm trees. He also had on baggy cargo shorts that were frayed at the hem, which went perfectly with the flip-flops on his feet. He had several woven bracelets wrapped around his wrist and a pair of Oakleys pushed up on the top of his head like he was waiting for our meeting to be over so he could head out to the beach.

I wondered if he thought dressing that way made him more relatable. I thought it made him look like a character out of some sappy teen movie where he was the only cool adult, the one all the kids confided in. I wasn't buying it.

"Reed? She's not my friend, and isn't it unethical or something for you to notice that she's pretty?" It was the first full sentence I had spoken in our two sessions, and I saw his eyebrows twitch in response.

"Reed? That's an unusual name for a girl." I tried not to fidget as he started scribbling on the pad of paper in front of him. I couldn't imagine what in the hell he got from me talking about the bothersome blonde.

"Her name is Affton; her last name is Reed. I told you, we aren't friends, so I usually just call her Reed." It was a way to keep some space between us while we were practically living in each other's back pockets for the summer. It was a way to remind myself that I shouldn't be noticing all the parts of her I thought about when I was alone.

"She's come to both your appointments and waited patiently for you both times. She also doesn't seem phased by your less-than-sunny disposition."

It was my turn to lift an eyebrow at the doc. "Did you just call me an asshole?"

He chuckled and gave me a lopsided grin. "I'm a medical professional. I would never do that."

But he had, and he was right. I was less than sunny; that was the problem. Every day was darker than the one before. "We went to high school together, so she's familiar with my lack of charm. The only reason she's here is because my mom hired her to keep an eye on me for the summer. She's making sure I actually show up to these appointments. And she's making sure I don't disappear after them. She's my babysitter." I couldn't keep the twist of resentment out of my tone.

The shrink leaned back in his chair and rested his flip-flopped foot on his knee. He made a noise in his throat and scribbled some more on the pad in front of him. "So, if the pretty blonde weren't here, would you be in this office, Cable? Would you be doing what you need to do in order to maintain your freedom?"

I leaned back in the chair and crossed my hands over my stomach. The truth was, probably not. I didn't want anyone peeking into my head. That was why I was doing my best to avoid Affton. For the last week, I'd spent my days on the water and my nights holed up in the media room watching old horror movies. I'd brought a couple girls back to the house with me, and I was right that having Affton practically strip search them before they could come through the door was a major cockblock. But that wasn't why I couldn't seal the deal with any of them. Something went wonky in my brain as soon as I got them naked and underneath me. My body was more than willing to get lost in the familiar comfort of the female form, but my mind . . . it was a million miles away and totally uninterested in the soft skin and warm lips that were available. I did my best to send them on their way with a smile without getting my dick wet, but I didn't feel good about it. Oblivion was never within reach. I couldn't figure out what was wrong with me . . . well, what was wrong with me *now*. I'd always been able to fuck my way into welcome numbness. It was the last escape I had left, and now it seemed as if that door was closed firmly in my face as well.

"No. Honestly, I'd probably have shown up for the first one and then blown off the rest. I don't want to be here." I never really wanted to be anywhere.

"Do you think going back to prison and serving out the rest of your sentence is preferable to spending a couple hours a week with me?" He made my options sound ridiculous, and I knew he was right.

I sighed and bent forward so I could rest my elbows on my legs. I lowered my face into my hands and rubbed my forehead. "No. I don't want to go back to jail, but I don't want to talk about that night, either."

"We don't have to talk about that night, Cable. However, my professional opinion is that you *should* talk about it with someone. It happened. You are bound to feel some kind of way about those events. If you don't address those feelings, you're going to be right back to self-medicating to deal with the inevitable, emotional build up."

I snorted and lowered my hands so I could look at him. "I was using way before that night, doc."

"I'm aware of that. So, we could start with why you started using. No one wakes up one morning and decides they want to be a drug addict." He didn't say 'someone like you' doesn't decide to be an addict. He said *no one* decides.

I blew out a breath and laced my fingers, pressing my palms together. The spider web on the back of my hand flexed, and the black widow tattooed on my wrist tensed. "I can't really remember ever being happy. I know I didn't particularly have a reason not to be, but no matter what I did, or whom I did, I never felt good. I wanted to party. I started drinking and messing around with girls my freshman year. My folks were never around, ya know? When they were, it was a lot of bickering. They were so focused on making each other miserable, they forgot I existed."

I shook my head, drifting back in time to when I lost control. At the start, I was so sure I was using to feel better. But at some point, when I used, I felt worse than I ever had before. "It was always easy to score, and before I realized it was happening, I needed more and more of whatever I was using to chase the sadness away. It never lasted for very long, that false sense of happiness, so I started using even when I wasn't partying. I was always chasing after something that felt good, trying to find a way to feel right." I let out a dry laugh and closed my eyes. "I think at the start I honestly believed my parents would notice, that someone would ask me what was wrong. They never did." Not until Affton pointed out that I was fading away right in front of their eyes.

"You were hurting, and you wanted someone to see it, to try

and take the hurt away. That's far more common than you think, Cable." He leaned forward and stared hard at me. "And once your mother was aware of your pain, it sounds to me like she did everything in her power to help you with it. She arranged for treatment. She helped you with your legal troubles. She went to extreme lengths to make sure you don't screw up this second chance you've been given. You wanted her attention; you've got it, kiddo."

The bite of resentment that nibbled on my insides gnashed and growled when I thought about her intervention when it was too late. "I needed her attention when it could have done some good."

He made a noise and scribbled something in his notebook. I wanted to grab it from him and throw it out the window. I didn't appreciate my inner turmoil being reduced to nothing more than scribbled words on a page. It felt so much bigger than that. So much harder to control.

"You're a smart kid with some pretty nasty habits, Cable. I think we both know that even if you had your mother's attention, you were still on a rocky road. She may have forced you into treatment, but it wouldn't have done any good unless you wanted the help. That night might not have happened, or it may have had different results. Do you ever stop and think that you very well could be the one with a grieving mother and father instead of the young lady who was with you that night? Do you take the time to think about what life in a wheelchair would be like? Because that could have been you instead of the man who was in the other car."

His words made everything go fuzzy and dark on the edges.

Suddenly I was struggling to breathe, and I felt too hot and too cold at the same time.

I could hear my blood rushing between my ears, and I could feel every thudding beat of my heart. It felt like there was a stomping foot wearing combat boots inside my chest.

I started to shake as all those horrific and gory images from that night started to play behind my eyes.

There was so much blood.

I could smell the metallic scent and see the brilliant crimson as it spread everywhere.

There was twisted metal and broken glass. I remembered hearing the crunch and feeling the shards of glass poke into my skin as I was thrown from the vehicle. I remembered the lights and sirens. I remembered the sheriff and the paramedics. I remembered the body bag and the sensation of having a million fingers pointed in my direction while I was mostly unconscious, the residual effects of a bump of coke swirling through my blood. All of it was so wrong, but I couldn't tell anyone that. All I could do was lie there, bleeding, broken, and wondering if everything that hurt was finally . . . finally going to stop hurting.

"Cable. Son . . . hey, kiddo, I need you to breathe." I heard the doc's voice from far away, almost like he was talking in a tunnel. I felt someone grab my shoulders and give a shake, but I was so gone it was as if none of it was happening to me. I heard my name again and then the sound of the door opening. A whoosh rushed between my ears as loud as the ocean roaring. Everything inside of my head was scrambling to overtake each frantic thought before it. I was a jumbled mess, and all I could see were blood and bodies.

"Cable." It was my name, just my name, but it was said in that husky voice with the slow, southern drawl that I enjoyed so much. She said she hated me, but there was worry and concern in her voice, and something about it pulled me back from the brink. I managed to blink until her freckles and almost purple eyes came into focus. She put a shaking hand on my cheek and said my name again. "Cable, are you all right?"

Vaguely, I realized that I was on the floor on my knees. I was bent over, head in my hands, and I was crying or at least I had hot, furious tears leaking out of my eyes. It took every ounce of strength I had to lift my hand and wrap my fingers around Affton's wrist. Her pulse was pounding against my touch, and her skin was silky soft.

I shook my head slowly to try and marshal my thoughts back into order.

This was exactly why I didn't want to talk about that night. It destroyed me. It took me apart. It ended me.

"What did you do to him? Aren't you supposed to be helping him?" Affton sounded pissed, and I had to admit that I reveled in the fact that she was pissed for me instead of at me, for once. She looked good when she was riled up, which was why I did my best to work my way under her skin. Now, she was riled on my behalf, and I was sure I had never seen any girl look better.

"Panic attack. I had no idea he was prone to those. That's not in his paperwork anywhere. Is this a common occurrence, Cable? Are you on any kind of medication for these kinds of episodes?" The shrink hunched down next to Affton who was on her knees in front of me, concern radiating off every line of her lithe body.

I latched onto that, onto her, like a lifeline. She was the only thing that seemed solid and real in all the confusion and disorder tumbling around in my brain.

"I'm okay." It was a lie.

I was very obviously not okay.

Affton's pale eyebrows pulled into a pinched V, and she lifted her other hand to my cheek so she was holding my face. Absently, she used the pad of her thumb to wipe away the wet tracks on my face. If only it was that easy to erase the things that sliced me open repeatedly. "Are you sure? You're shaking, and you're on the floor. Has this happened before?"

I tried to shake my head in the negative, but all I could manage was a stiff jerk. "No. This is a first."

She looked over her shoulder at the doctor and switched her frown to him. "What did you do to him?"

The shrink got back to his feet and tilted his head to the side, considering me intently. "I was asking him about the night of his accident. I told Cable he needs to talk about that night, if not with me, then with someone else he trusts. I told him all his emotions relating to that incident were going to find their way out, one way or another."

I expected the sympathy on Affton's face to falter, but it didn't. Her mouth tightened in a line of disapproval, and she pulled back from me so she could climb to her feet. She reached out a hand for me, and selfishly I grabbed it and allowed her to help me to my feet. Since she invaded my space at the start of the summer, I seemed to find myself leaning on this girl, giving her the weight I couldn't carry alone anymore. She made me feel lighter than ever before.

"After two sessions, you decided he was ready for that?" She gave the shrink the evil eye and bumped my hip with hers to get me moving in the direction of the door. "There is such a thing as pushing too hard, too fast."

The doctor gave her an odd look and reached for his discarded pad and pen. "I get the distinct impression that Mr. McCaffrey is very rarely pushed and is used to getting his own way far too often. I'm not going to justify my methods to a teenager, but I will apologize for not realizing a panic attack might be an option. I didn't have all the information I should have had before we started treatment." The doctor gave me another lopsided grin as Affton practically dragged me toward the door. "The good news is that I think you have every single tool at your disposal you will need to make some serious improvements in your life, Cable. I'll see you next week."

Affton slammed the door shut behind us and hustled me out of the office into the parking lot. Her shoulders were stiff, and it was obvious she was incredibly agitated as we approached her ratty old car. I hated the thing. But I didn't have a license or a car anymore, and I was learning beggars couldn't be choosers.

"You all right over there, Reed? You look like you're ready to take someone's head off." I was still a little wobbly and unsteady, but now that the memories had retreated into the dark where I would prefer they stay, I could slam some of my usual deflection and diversion methods back in place.

She cut me a look out of the corner of her eye, and I could practically see the way she was deliberately picking the words to respond to my question.

When she spoke, her raspy voice was low and huskier than usual. "You scared me, Cable. That was scary." She pulled her gaze away from mine and walked away from me. "When that doctor came out of his office and told me something was wrong with you, all I could think about was what happened with my mom. I might not enjoy the time I have to spend with you very much, but I really don't want you to die."

She sounded on the verge of tears, and a wave of self-loathing slammed into me. This was hard for her.

I was hard for her . . . and I was purposely going out of my way to make myself even harder to handle.

I cleared my throat and ran my hands roughly through my hair. "Don't worry about me, Reed. I'm not worth it."

She lifted her eyes back to mine, and this time she was the one with tears running unchecked over her freckled cheeks. "I wish that was true, because if it were, this summer would be so much easier."

Her pale head disappeared into the car, leaving me turning her words over in my head as I slowly followed suit.

Before the night that changed everything, I was already struggling with what purpose I served other than to take up space in my parents' lavish home. After the accident, I was convinced my only purpose was to suffer and to make others suffer even more. I was already raw and hurting on the inside. Now I couldn't take a breath without being reminded that I had managed to hurt others infinitely more than I ever hurt myself.

Pain was my purpose; how Affton could think I was worth anything was something I'd never understand . . . but there was no denying I was overwhelmingly grateful that she did.

seven

AFFTON

AFTER HIS BREAKDOWN and my admission that it was terrifying to watch him fall apart—that it was scary to see his vulnerable underbelly he hid so well—Cable kept his distance even more than he had been.

He was typically gone when I got up in the morning; a hastily scrawled note telling me he was on the water was my only hint that he was going to be gone for most of the day. At first, it annoyed me because he wasn't supposed to be out of my sight, but so far, all his drug tests had come back clean, and he never showed back up at the house bleary-eyed or obviously strung out. All the hours he spent in the sun and sand while he was surfing had him looking healthier and sturdier than I'd ever seen him. Which I was happy to report back to his mother. It was nice to give her some shred of hope that there was redemption waiting for her son. She called every other day to check in and lately I'd had nothing new to report. She didn't need to know that his blond hair now had streaks almost as white as mine. Or that if he wasn't spending the day on the water, he holed himself up in the media room or perched himself in the shade of the deck with his sketch pad. He seemed a million miles away. I'd never spent so much time near someone who felt so out of reach. It was unnerving, and I found myself trying to bridge the growing gap that yawned wide between us.

I asked him if he wanted company during his gore movie fests and got no response.

I asked him if he wanted to study for his GED and was blatantly ignored.

I suggested he wait for me one morning and he could teach me how to surf, and wasn't surprised when I got up that he was once again gone until the sun came down.

I was living with a very attractive ghost. One who couldn't see, hear, or interact with me at all. One who was haunting me. The more he vanished into himself and got lost inside his own head, the harder I tried to grab ahold of him, but it was like trying to clutch smoke between my fingers. He drifted away as soon as I touched him.

In a last-ditch effort to figure out a way to pull him back from whatever brink he was standing on, I had started peppering Miglena with questions. The housekeeper was much younger and far more beautiful than I expected her to be. The first time I encountered her in the kitchen, I thought she was one of the beach bunnies who followed Cable around like he was the Pied Piper of sex and satisfaction. I was going to run her off and chew Cable a new asshole for sneaking in a piece of ass I didn't thoroughly check when the woman offered to make me an omelet and told me she really didn't mind cooking for me while I was Cable's keeper.

She resembled a super sexy Bond villain with her sleek, dark hair and milky white skin. She sounded like one as well with her thick Eastern European accent. In our chats, she told me she was from Bulgaria originally and that she had been working for the

McCaffreys since she was a teenager. She was extremely friendly, super chatty, and it was obvious she had a soft spot a mile wide for Cable. She indulged him by buying all the crap I refused to get for him and not once did she scold him or seem annoyed at his careless, sloppy ways. I couldn't count the times I tripped over his discarded shoes or found myself picking up items of clothing he had left lying haphazardly around. The boy couldn't seem to keep a shirt on . . . not that I really could complain about it . . . and his wet board shorts were always draped over the deck railing or one of the chairs that dotted the kitchen island. It bugged me on principle since I was still scared to touch anything in the overly extravagant house. But Miglena didn't seem phased. When I asked her about it, she told me, "Cable's a sweet boy. He's always gone out of his way to get his parents' attention, but they never noticed. I don't mind cleaning up after him. It lets him know someone is watching out for him."

I wondered if Cable had it in him to recognize that the simple act of someone throwing his wet clothes in the wash was still someone taking care of him, showing him that he wasn't as alone as he seemed to think.

It was an afternoon after one of his random drug tests, one that seemed to put him in an irrationally sour mood, that I made the mistake of pointing out he had people on his side even if he was choosing to ignore them.

We got back to the house after an incredibly tense and silent ride home, and I followed behind him as he not only stripped off his shirt but kicked off his shoes into the middle of the entryway. He was running his hands through his hair in aggravation, and every line of his tattooed back was tense. He resembled a wild animal poised to attack, and I should have known that I was the only prey available as I picked up one of his Chucks and tossed it at him. It hit his arm and fell to the floor with a thump. I immediately regretted my actions as he turned on me, nearly black eyes blazing with too many different emotions to name.

I gulped down the sudden spurt of fear that burst across my tongue and crossed my arms over my chest because I was subconsciously trying to protect my heart. "It won't kill you to take those with you or to leave them neatly by the door, you know." I wasn't sure what kind of reaction I was going to get out of him, but I knew the second I threw the shoe at him I was going to get one. Whatever it was going to be had to be better than the deep freeze he'd been giving me lately.

He scowled at me and copied my pose, though his had a definite aura of menace to it. "Why do you care? Miglena will grab them and toss them wherever they need to go."

I scoffed at him, bravado I didn't really feel, but made my words sharp. "Miglena isn't always going to be around to take care of you. At some point, you need to start taking care of yourself, Cable."

It had been a little over three weeks, and so far he had gone to all his counseling appointments and hadn't missed one of his mandatory drug tests. In the great scheme of things, he was doing far better than I thought he would be after finding him plastered and pissed off that first night. He was sloppy and inconsiderate, but he was taking care of himself better than he had been back in Loveless. I should give him credit for that, but I wasn't. Instead, I was purposely needling him, pointedly aggravating him, because I hated how easy it was for him to move through and around me. I'd gotten used to him looking at me. I couldn't stand him looking through me.

He glanced down at the fallen shoe and then back at me. An ugly smile twisted his face as he lifted a brow at me. It was a nasty look, one that made me shiver and fall back a step.

"Miglena isn't going anywhere." He scoffed a little bit and lifted his chin defiantly. "She treats all my dad's kids the same . . . even the two he left her with before moving on to someone else."

I let out a startled gasp that made his grin darken. I was the one angling for a reaction, but without any effort, he was ripping one from me. He always seemed to have the upper hand, which wasn't fair. He was the one who was a mess. I theoretically had my shit together, had a plan and purpose that never failed me. I shouldn't be the one scrambling to keep up with him all the time. It should be the other way around.

"That's right, Reed. Miglena doesn't just take care of this house and me because she's a sweetheart. She does it because once upon a time she got to play house with my old man here. All those kids she has, two of them are my half-sisters. Sisters I've never met because my mom pays Miglena to keep them away. Sisters my dad has never claimed and never mentioned. Not once. My dad knocked her up when she was barely legal. Promised her the sun and the moon until a younger, prettier distraction came along. She did her best to prove she was perfect wife material, which included taking care of poor, unpredictable Cable. She's a nice lady, one in a long line that my old man has fucked over, but don't, for a single second, think she actually gives two shits about my well-being."

I let my hands fall and stood there in the hallway staring at him with my mouth hanging open. I always thought my home life was tragic and complicated, but it didn't have anything on the soap opera happening in the McCaffrey's household. No wonder his mom and dad had missed his headlong slide into addiction. They were too busy fucking other people and each other over to have any time to help their son. It was all so tragically preventable if anyone bothered to put in the effort.

"You're wrong." I shifted and took a step toward him so I could pick up both discarded shoes. "She may have ulterior motives, but she does care about you." I was sure of it. Her voice softened when she talked about him, and she watched him with the same kind of watchful concern I found myself watching him with. "You make it really hard, Cable, but you can't stop someone from caring about you. You can't stop them from wanting what's best for you."

I let out a startled yelp when he was suddenly standing directly in front of me, his rough hands wrapped around my upper arms. His fingers squeezed as he pulled me up onto my toes so that we were nose to nose. His black eyes burned into mine and those damn shoes that were so inconsequential fell back to the floor with a thump as his stare paralyzed me with both fear and fascination.

He didn't feel like vapor anymore.

He wasn't going around me.

He wasn't oblivious to my presence. If the way he was breathing hard and fast was any indication, my presence was finally unsettling him as much as his unsettled me.

"I can't stop them, but I can warn them. Don't care about me, Reed. Don't worry about what's best for me. The only thing I have to offer anyone is disappointment. If I start picking up my shoes and throwing my shit in the laundry, Miglena might get the idea that I'm trying." He lowered his head until his forehead touched mine. His skin was hot, and his words were scented with ash and disgust. "I'm not trying, Affton. That's not something I do."

His fingers bit into my arms, and I almost fell over when he suddenly released me and took a step back. We stared at each other, waging a war I was fairly certain neither one of us could ever win. I struggled to keep my expression blank as he deliberately popped the button on his jeans and pushed the denim down over his hips. I was used to seeing him in the baggy board shorts he wore when he went surfing, but the sight of him in nothing more than tight, black boxer briefs was enough to make me blush and swallow . . . hard. He did it to be aggravating. I would never tell him I was tempted instead.

I reached up and pushed my hair out of my face. I bent back down to pick up his shoes and his clothes. When I stood back up, I gave him a once over and told him sincerely, "Every single day you don't use, you are trying, Cable. Every appointment you keep with Doc Howard, you're trying, and as long as you try, even if you fail, that's not a disappointment. That's all anyone can expect." My mom hadn't bothered to try and that had led to something far worse than disappointment.

Clearly done with the conversation and the confrontation, he disappeared into the house, and I heard him opening the door to the back deck. He wasn't kidding when he said he loved the water. Whenever I couldn't find him inside, he was out there somewhere, feet in the water, eyes focused on the horizon, silently looking for something, patiently waiting for anything.

I dumped his clothes in the laundry room and dropped his shoes outside his partially open bedroom door. I'd been in his room enough searching for any kind of hidden stash that I knew he actually tended to keep his personal space tidy. There was an occasional t-shirt on the floor, and he always seemed to have endless packs of cigarettes scattered across every surface, but he wasn't a pig, which made the extra work he left lying around for Miglena even more irritating. Today, the black boxers he'd been sporting earlier were also on the floor from when he'd changed in a hurry. I didn't want to think about Cable naked, but I was . . . more often than I was comfortable with. He was obviously doing it to prove a point, and it made me wonder if his mom might have been right when she told me he very well might relapse just to get back at her. He seemed incapable of making the right choice and intent on hurting those who wanted to help.

I was going to pull the door closed when the spiral notebook that always seemed to be within his reach caught my eye. It was open on his bed, several colorful images dotting the previously plain pages. Without thinking too much about it, I pushed the door open and walked into the room. I was snooping, but considering I regularly rifled through his underwear drawer looking for drugs, I didn't bother to feel too bad about it.

I perched on the edge of the bed and pulled the notebook onto my lap.

For a split-second, I stopped breathing.

I was holding the ocean and the sun in my hands. The images on the paper were so realistic I could practically feel the water on my fingertips and the sun shining on my face. It didn't seem possible that cold, distant, drifting Cable could capture something so warm and real with nothing more than a few strokes of a colored pencil. He was outrageously talented. Overwhelmingly so. The skill and artistry jumped off every single page I flipped through and hit me with a punch of awe.

He said he didn't have anything he was interested in; he pretended the only thing he had going for him were his good looks and his ability to make women loopy with lust, but that was all a lie. The boy had a gift . . . was gifted . . . and he didn't even seem to know it.

The pages were full of images ranging from the stunning landscapes to darker, harder stuff. Skulls, demons, dragons, and Grim Reapers all done in harsh black and gray, and all were realistic enough that they gave me chills. There were pages full of flowers and birds. There was a handful of images of very sexy, very naked women that made me blush. Then there were the pages covered in women in a bunch of different, dramatic outfits. There was a sexy nurse, a sexy cop, a sexy soldier, and a sexy mermaid. They were all done up in 1950's pin-up style with big boobs and super tiny waists. He didn't seem to have one singular preference. The pictures he drew were all over the place, but they were all amazing and too pretty to be trapped in a cheap sketch notebook from the grocery store.

I let out the breath I'd been holding and pushed to my feet. I closed the notebook and tiptoed out of the room. Even though I knew every nook and cranny of his personal space, when I went looking through his drawings, it occurred to me that I was looking inside of *him,* and it seemed incredibly invasive and intimate. His darkness was caught on those pages, but so was the light he tried so hard to keep from shining through.

I made my way down the hallway and out to the deck through the door Cable hadn't bothered to close when he stormed out earlier. There was a light breeze whipping the salt-scented air, which immediately caught in my hair and tangled all around my face. Once I had it all wrangled and caught in a fist, I noticed that Cable was indeed down by the water and he wasn't alone.

They were too far away to make out what the girl in the water with him looked like, but there was no missing she had curves for days, and they were barely contained by an itty-bitty, teal bikini. The barely contained mounds were also pressed up against Cable's tanned, toned chest as she squealed and hollered loud enough to make my ears ring as wave after wave rolled over them. Cable wasn't smiling. He wasn't doing much of anything as the girl practically climbed all over him. His hands were on her waist, but his eyes were focused on something—or rather, someone—over her head.

That someone was me.

I hated that jealousy made me stiff. I hated that my stomach turned when the girl giggled obnoxiously and I could hear it over the wind. I hated that he watched me, that he instinctively knew the sight of him with her bothered me, and he was frolicking with her just to get under my skin. He didn't need to bother. He was way under my skin. It was the other parts of me I was worried about him getting under and inside of now.

And I hated that it made me realize I was so far from hating Cable that I wasn't sure how I got here, or if I would ever be able to find my way back.

I went inside when he started to lower his head toward the girl in the bikini, hating that he was wasting himself on her . . . and hating that I cared. I lost myself in the familiarity of it all, understanding those feelings and terrified of the ones still swirling after seeing all the brightness hidden deep inside his endless darkness.

eight

CABLE

I KNEW I was a mess.

Unhinged and hanging on the precipice of becoming someone who was beyond any kind of redemption. I teetered on the brink of making bad choices every moment I was awake, but somehow, some way, I always managed to keep myself from going completely over. It was the look in Affton's eyes when I came out of my epic freak-out that had me keep one foot on the line and one foot behind it. There was genuine concern for me in those pretty, almost purple eyes. There was worry and want she tried to hide in that gaze, as well. She tried to hate me, but she was too good of a person, too compassionate and empathetic to follow through on those emotions. She cared, and it scared the holy fuck out of me.

I had no clue what to do with these new feelings. I was sure I didn't want her to give a crap about me. I had no idea how to navigate genuine, sincere compassion. I was inexperienced in dealing with emotion that wasn't leveraged or manipulated. I was unsettled and acutely aware of her.

Every breath she took, I swore I could hear.

Every time she blinked, those eyes that saw far too much and witnessed as I ducked and dodged her. I watched them grow dark blue, blooming like a bruise as she tried to hide the way my evasion hurt her.

Every time I sidestepped and ignored her, I swore I could feel the way her blood boiled, and her aggravation made her warm from head to toe. I got hard at the way she flushed a pretty pink when I pissed her off, but I wasn't going out of my way to tell her that. I wasn't going out of my way to tell her anything.

When I opened my eyes and saw her on her knees in front of me, her hands holding my face as the memories from that night tore me apart and shredded what was left of my soul, all I wanted to do was lean on her. She always seemed so strong, so stable, and unshakable. She was the opposite of adrift, and I wondered if I got ahold of her if she would be able to keep me from sinking. But then, she told me that it was impossible for her not to worry about me and all I could see was me dragging her down, pulling her under. It's what I did. The thought of all that icy, white-blonde hair and those fantastic eyes going blank as she sank with me to the bottom of the ocean of despair and disappointment was enough to have me acting like even more of an asshole than I already was.

I thought she would heed the no trespassing signs, but I underestimated her need to save the unsavable. She danced around everything I threw at her like a goddamn ballerina. She pushed just as hard as I pulled, and as much as I wanted to pretend I could spend the summer living my life around her just to annoy her, it quickly became clear that my life was becoming *her,* and that was incredibly overwhelming.

So, I did what I always did and fucked everything up. Or, at least I tried to.

I was rude to her.

I disappeared on her pretty much every day.

I was nasty to Miglena for no reason.

I was back to refusing to talk to Doc Howard during our visits, and I blew off the idea of studying for the GED.

I didn't score or relapse, but I thought about it. I knew it was the one surefire way to get Affton Reed gone, but I couldn't do it. I was tempted. Every second of every day I was tempted, but I didn't want to see the look on her face when I failed one of my drug tests. The truth was I really didn't want to end up behind bars. Having the freedom to get in the water whenever I wanted, the liberty to talk to whomever I wanted, to frolic with and fuck whomever caught my eye . . . well, those were luxuries I didn't want to be without ever again. Not that there was much fucking taking place. It was just one more aspect of my world Affton had knocked off its axis. My body was willing, but my mind, the traitorous bastard, was still wrapped around the wrong girl and it didn't matter how much I pleaded with my thoughts to let go. There was no pretending that a stacked brunette was Affton. There was no fooling my imagination into thinking a blonde with green eyes would do when all I could think about were periwinkle ones.

And speaking of those unforgettable eyes, they clocked me as soon as I stepped in the house off the deck. I was wet and sandy from watching the sun go down over the water as I smoked and contemplated how I was supposed to keep the distance between us when all I really wanted to do was get as close to her as possible. She was in a white sundress that showed off her golden tan, and her pale hair was piled on top of her head in a messy knot. She could be the poster girl for sweet and seductive innocence. In that moment, I felt every forbidden feeling she awoke in me roar and howl in my blood. She was so bright and clean. I wanted to drag her down to my level. Dirty her up and show her how much fun we could have in the dark. She would glow there, the only spot of light allowed into that dreary place.

She watched me, and I watched the way she blushed. I ran a hand over my damp hair and let it trail across my chest. Her eyes tracked the movement as the end of her tongue darted out to slick across her bottom lip. I got off on getting her to react but hated that her reaction always caused one of my own. There was very little the wet fabric of my board shorts could do to hide the way my body tightened and hardened whenever she responded. She lifted a hand to her throat and jerked her eyes back up to mine. Yeah, she wanted to hate me, and it really bothered her that she didn't. It made her all kinds of flustered and uneasy that I got to her. It made me even harder.

"What were you doing out there for so long?" I knew she meant to sound authoritative, but I could hear the hesitancy in her tone. She hated it when I vanished. She hated it even more when I reappeared with a warm body that wasn't hers. She tried to hide the way my dalliances rubbed her the wrong way. As much time as I spent watching her, I could see through her façade. She thought it was made of iron and steel, but her barriers were as clear as glass and probably just as fragile.

I put my hands on my hips, and her gaze immediately dropped to my waist. I saw her swallow hard and bit back a grin as she whirled around and stomped toward the kitchen, her bare feet slapping noisily on the marble tile. I followed behind her, my eyes on the soft sway of her hips in that white dress. She was supposed to be the girl next door, not pure temptation and sultry seduction. She was going to have those college boys clamoring to find out if she tasted as sweet as she looked. My mouth was already watering.

The thought made me frown as we faced off over the wide island. She crossed her arms over her chest, which only served to push her very nice rack up higher and tighter against the cotton fabric. My brain short-circuited a little as I tried to determine if she was wearing a bra or not. I braced my hands on either side of the counter and leaned forward. "I was thinking."

She was surprised I answered her. "Thinking about what?"

I was thinking about all the time I'd wasted and all the opportunities I'd let slip by me. I was thinking about all the sex I wasn't having and all the sex I wanted to have with her. I was thinking about finally answering the phone when my mom called and asking Miglena if I could meet my sisters. I was thinking about drawing her, her face, her eyes, her mouth, and that led to thinking about *why* I was thinking all those things.

I pushed on the edge of the counter, which made the muscles in my arms bulge and flexed the ink that decorated my shoulder. She watched, but her eyes were wary because she knew I was leading her somewhere she didn't want to go.

"I was thinking about you."

Her eyes immediately narrowed at the confession, and her shoulders stiffened. I watched her chest heave, and I swore I could see her pulse flutter at the base of her throat. "You've been ignoring me, and when you do bother to acknowledge me, you pick a fight. You don't want me here any more than I want to be here. You've made that pretty clear."

"I don't want anyone here, Reed. You aren't special." I was lying through my teeth. She was more than special. She was extraordinary, which made me feel even more unworthy and inferior than I typically did.

I let my eyes roll over her and gave her a smirk. "You could be some kind of virgin sacrifice who's going to get thrown into an erupting volcano in that dress."

She hugged herself tighter, and her flush turned even redder.

Something hot and hungry pulsed in the center of my chest as she averted her eyes and snapped, "The only angry god I want to appease is the one standing in front of me. Can we call a truce, Cable? Whatever it is we're doing is exhausting and not very much fun."

Usually, the only thing I had to offer the opposite sex was a good time and a whole lot of fun. Nothing was typical anymore, especially when it came to her.

"Are you calling me a god, Reed?"

She rolled her eyes so hard I was pretty sure she could see the back of her skull. She let out a little huff. "You're definitely a legend in your own mind."

I grinned at her and lifted an eyebrow. "So, are you?"

She uncrossed her arms and tossed up her hands in exasperation. "Am I what?"

"The sacrificial virgin? My mom wouldn't think twice about spilling a little innocent blood in order to achieve the outcome she's after." Affton was glaring at me so hard I was surprised the impact of her gaze didn't leave marks.

"I fail to see how that's any of your business." She was uncomfortable. She always got fidgety when I brought up sex, so I did it a lot because it was fun to watch her feathers ruffle.

I snorted. "We went to school together, remember? I think it would have gotten around if someone managed to melt through all that ice that surrounds you. The guys used to talk about it all the time. There was a running joke that anyone who got close enough was going to need a blowtorch to get to the goods."

Her eyes darkened to that blueish-purple. Those eyes gave every hurt I caused away. I was just giving her a hard time, trying to rile her up, but she looked at me like I betrayed her.

Her spine stiffened so that she was arrow straight, and before she bit down on it, I saw her lower lip tremble. I felt that little quiver all the way through me. I never needed much help feeling like shit, but watching this girl who seemed unbreakable visibly hold herself together in front of me because of what I'd said hit a low that was lower than low . . . and I'd been in prison. I'd also been responsible for the death of another person and forever changed the life of another.

"Affton . . ."

She held up her hand as I started an awkward and clumsy apology. She didn't want to hear it, and I couldn't fault her for it.

"I don't know why any of those boys would say anything about me. All I wanted to do was graduate and get out of Loveless. I didn't bother anyone . . . except for you." She laughed, but it was harsh and grating. "I've regretted it every second since. If I'd just kept to myself, I wouldn't be here, and you would be . . . well, I don't know where you would be, but it would be far, far away from me."

She stepped back from the island and moved out of the kitchen. I called her name again and she stopped reluctantly. She looked at me over her shoulder, and I could see I'd finally found a way to make her as vulnerable as I was.

"Guys talk. When you look the way you do, and you ignore all of them, they talk even more."

Her eyebrows shot up. "You told me I needed to worry more about myself and how I looked, so what do you mean when I 'look the way I do'?"

Shit. Of course, she would remember that dig when she first confronted me. I turned, so I was facing her and shrugged. "I lied."

She jerked a little at the admission but kept her eyes locked on mine.

"I'm a liar. That shouldn't surprise you. Most addicts are. I lied about you needing to change anything about the way you looked for you to be hot. You're a stunner without even trying, Reed. It's actually pretty annoying."

She blinked at me a couple of times without saying a word. I couldn't tell if I had smoothed things over or not, but then she told me, "I dated Hayes Lawton for a while. He was sweet. He was smart, and I trusted him."

"He's the sheriff's son." I knew Hayes. He was the exact opposite of everything I was. He was a straight-A student. He was the captain of the football team. He was a good ol' boy who was a genuinely good guy. He never talked about Affton or any other girl, for that matter. He never got in trouble, and of course, if Affton was going to give it up it was going to be to someone who was as idealistic and as driven as she was. She was on her own level, but Hayes Lawton was almost up there as high as she was. Suddenly, I was the one feeling wounded by my words.

"He is. He was also the only guy in Loveless I ever considered having sex with, but it never got that far. He met someone else. Someone who needed him far more than I did, so, yes, Cable, I am the virgin sacrifice. Are you happy now?"

I tossed my head back so that I was looking up at the ceiling. No, I wasn't happy. That was how this whole mess started a million years ago.

"Not really. I don't sleep with virgins. It's pretty much the one and only rule I follow." Anybody deserved better than what I had to offer for their first time. I wasn't patient and gentle. I wasn't soft or delicate. I wasn't the kind of memory any girl wanted for something that was supposed to be a big deal. I never wanted to be anyone's first or their last. I just wanted to be a moment they would think about with fondness and a smile.

I was telling her she was off limits, not that I'd ever had a shot at getting a piece of her. Surprisingly, it wasn't a piece I was after. It was the whole damn thing. All of her, and that was why

I pushed. I didn't deserve anyone as good as Affton, and even the greedy, selfish part of me that thrived on knowing she wasn't immune to me knew it.

She shook her head and turned back toward the hallway. "That's okay, because I would never sleep with an addict . . . recovering or otherwise."

Ouch. That sentence stung, just as she intended.

"Tomorrow I'm ready to sit down for a few hours and start studying for the GED test." It was as much of a truce as I could offer.

It was her turn to shrug, and she did so without looking at me. "I think I'll wait to see which Cable I get tomorrow. I've learned there are a bunch of them hiding in the darkness and some are easier to deal with than the others. Right about now, I'm missing the Cable who pretended I didn't exist. He was obnoxious, but he wasn't mean."

She disappeared down the hallway, and I watched her go until she was out of sight. She was right that there were a bunch of different versions of me vying for control. There was the me who wanted to be reckless and wild, the one who got drunk and played with pretty girls in bikinis. There was the one who scared me. The one who couldn't talk about the night that things changed, or face the fact that life would never be the same because of his choices. There was the resentful me who was still pissed it took an accident and bloodshed to get my parents' attention. There was the lost me who couldn't figure out what was next. He was the one who was around the most. He was the one who pushed Affton away because he couldn't figure out how she fit in his new world, but he knew that he really, really wanted to find a place for her in it.

If she was as smart as I thought she was, she would be prepared for the different versions of Cable who wanted her. Because every single part of me did want her, even the parts that we both knew were going to be hell.

nine

AFFTON

I T WASN'T THAT I was afraid of sex or even disinterested in it. The truth of the matter was I was just as curious and confused about all the intimate workings between a boy and a girl as any girl my age. Well, any girl my age who hadn't already jumped off that bridge one or two times. I was the last one standing, and the older I got, the lonelier my place on that bridge became.

There were too many other things that occupied my time and my attention when I was in school for hooking up to be on the agenda. I wasn't the kind of girl who could get naked and romp around with someone casually. I was too intense for that. I was too careful with my time and my affection to hand it out to whoever offered me a good time. That's why Hayes had been the one and only person I'd even considered sleeping with.

He was adorable in a big, burly kind of way. He was really handsome with his dark hair and light green eyes. I appreciated the fact that he was soft-spoken and thoughtful. I liked that he had a kind heart and an honorable streak a mile wide. His dad was the sheriff, and he took the responsibility of being the sheriff's son very seriously. He was also stubborn and determined. He asked me out no less than five times before I finally relented and agreed to go on a date with him. I was attracted to everything about him except that he was a hometown boy through and through. I told him upfront that I was leaving, and once I was gone, I would only be back to see my dad. Hayes just smiled and told me there was no harm in spending time together before I left. I believed him when he said he had no intention of holding me back, and eventually, I trusted him enough to entertain the idea of having sex with him. No one wanted to go away to college untried and naïve. No one wanted to be the girl who didn't know anything about sex and seduction when she was finally on her own and free to experience all that life had to offer without the watchful eye of a parent hindering her.

Unfortunately, things never got that far with Hayes. As it turned out, he was as much of a sucker for a lost cause as I was, and when a new girl showed up at school sporting all kinds of punk rock pointy edges, it hadn't taken long for his attention and his affection to shift from me to her. I barely felt a single sting when he was gone, so I breathed a sigh of relief that I hadn't slept with him. In zero time, I was back to being engrossed in school, college prep, spending time with Jordan, and taking care of my dad. In hindsight, there was also a lot of wondering and worrying about Cable taking place in those hours. He always took up space and distracted me, even when he was locked away.

With Cable, I felt more than a sting when he pulled away and when he pushed me to the point of no return. He made me burn. I felt the familiar fiery heat of anger, but there was also a smoldering warmth of something else that lingered beneath the surface. I'd never been so acutely aware of another person before. I swore I had every line of his long, lean body memorized, and I could tell his mood by nothing more than the shift in his eye color. Being around him also made me hyper-aware of my own body and the way it responded to his nearness. I was constantly trying to cover up the way my nipples tightened around him. I was continually baffled by the heavy throb between my legs and the way my blood rushed to all the most sensitive parts of my body when he looked at me with those dark eyes, made even darker with desire. I was attracted to him despite knowing what a mess he was, despite the inevitable train wreck any kind of involvement with him would end in. I was into him when he made it nearly impossible for me to even like him, and I was worried about him when he made it abundantly clear he didn't want me to be.

He was confusing.

How he made me feel was perplexing.

How I reacted to him was terrifying.

I'd never felt so out of control, and I despised every second of it. All I wanted to do was hide in the fancy guest room with covers over my head and my sanity intact, but I wasn't given any kind of respite after a sleepless night. That night I spent wondering just how Cable's, 'I don't sleep with virgins' rule came about, because as soon as the sun came up, he was knocking on the door, sweeping into my room unannounced. He plopped down on the edge of my bed ignoring my groan, his weight making it impossible to pull the covers up to my chin.

He had a bowl of cereal in his hands and a smirk on his face as he watched me struggle to make sense of why he was in my space so early, hell, why he was even in my space at all, when he had done his best to send me running last night.

"You want to come out on the water with me this morning?" He shoved the spoon in his mouth and lifted his eyebrows at me. "You never know when I'm going to get called in for a piss test, so there's no time to waste."

I groaned again and rubbed my tired eyes. "What are you talking about?"

"Surfing. You want to come with me this morning?" He sounded so reasonable and normal. I didn't trust him for a second.

"Why do you want to take me surfing? You've been gone every day for weeks and all of a sudden you're craving company? I asked you once already to show me how to surf, and you ignored me." I sounded surly and short. All he did was grin even bigger at my irritated tone.

"You're gonna help me get my GED. I figured I could help you learn to do something. Maybe teach you how to do something fun since you seem to be allergic to it."

I wanted to yank the spoon out of his hand and smack him in the forehead with it. "I'm not allergic to fun. There just hasn't been a lot of opportunity for it this summer."

"I'll give you that. I wouldn't want to be stuck being responsible for me either, but what about before this summer, Reed? We went to high school together, remember? I know you were never around any of the parties. You never showed up for any of the school events. You barely interacted with anyone. When did you have fun?" He sounded genuinely curious, but every time I gave him the tiniest bit of myself, he ended up taking so much more.

"Not all of us have parents who own an entire town, Cable. Some of us don't even have parents . . . just a single, hard-working dad who does his very best to put food on the table and keep the lights on. There isn't a lot of time for fun when you have to pay your own way in life." I was sure that if I took a single step out of line, if I veered even slightly off the path I'd set for myself, everything would end up crumbling down around me. I didn't have the time to fail. I didn't have the confidence to get back up if I fell . . . so, I never wavered, and I never wandered. At least I hadn't until this boy and all his tragic, tormented ways sent me spinning.

He gave a little grunt and pushed off the bed. His gaze took me in from my messy hair to where the covers caught around my waist. His eyes shifted to the dark brown that was almost black as he gave a little shrug. "Fair enough. I've never had to struggle to find time for fun. The invitation is open if you want to join me. I'm headed out in ten minutes."

He left the door open when he left the room, and I could hear him in the kitchen actually rinsing out his bowl. I wasn't sure what version of Cable this was, but if he was willing to give me the truce I'd asked for, then I wanted to keep him around as long as I could. I figured it wouldn't kill me to spend the morning with him out on the water. I was, after all, in a beach town and had yet to have a single moment that felt restful or relaxing. There was no vacation in this summer vacation.

I kicked off the covers, rushed to brush my teeth, and pulled a comb through my hair. I pulled the pale locks up into a high ponytail and frantically searched through my suitcase for the one and only bathing suit I brought with me. It was a floral-patterned two-piece with a halter neck and boy short bottoms. It was far more modest than the teal number the girl he'd been frolicking around with in the water a few days ago had on, but I still felt uncomfortably exposed as I pulled on a pair of cutoffs and my Chucks before dashing down the hallway. I caught him as he was pulling open the massive glass doors.

He gave me a once over and inclined his head toward the deck where there were two surfboards resting. His was black and white. It was a familiar sight propped up against the railing, but the one next to it was baby blue and looked brand new.

"You ever done this before?" He stuck a cigarette in his mouth and squinted at me through the flame of his lighter as he asked me the question.

I shook my head in the negative and slid a pair of cheap, gas station sunglasses over my eyes. "Nope. I don't come from vacation homes on the beach type of people. The only reason I know how to swim is because my mom moved to a shitty apartment complex with a pool when she and my dad split, and my dad insisted on getting me lessons." He insisted because he knew my mom never really kept an eye on me and he was worried I would wander off and end up in over my head . . . literally.

He slid on a pair of obviously expensive sunglasses and blew out a puff of smoke that made me wrinkle my nose in distaste. "You don't talk about your mom much."

I shrugged and took the blue board when he handed it off to me. "It hurts to talk about her." Because he was so close, I felt him stiffen when he realized just how much it cost me to confront him that day at his car.

"I know all about that. Having something that hurts to talk about." I could still see him on his knees, shaking and breaking apart in the counselor's office. That night didn't just hurt him when he talked about it; it destroyed him.

I followed him down the steps to the beach below, the sand immediately sticking to my shoes. He chuckled as I grumbled and bent to take them off. I looked up at him over the top of my sunglasses and told him, "Your shrink thinks it would help if you actually talked about that night. Dealing with the fallout all on your own isn't doing you any good."

We got closer to the water, and he dropped his board on the sand and indicated I should do the same. He put his hands on his hips, and his cigarette bounced against his lips when he asked me flatly, "Who did you talk to about your mom?"

I mimicked his pose and turned my head so that I was looking out over the water. "No one. It made my dad upset, and telling your friends that your mom was a junkie who overdosed isn't exactly easy. My best friend, Jordan, knows the basics, but I never told her how bad it got or how much it hurt each time my mom left rehab early and went right back to using. That's not exactly a topic you bring up while studying for finals or talking about prom."

He made a noise of understanding in his throat and plucked his cigarette out of his mouth so that he could toss it into the water. "That's how I feel about everything that happened that night. It's not a conversation I want to have with anyone. Talking about it, going over all the details, it's not going to change anything. Someone is still going to be dead, someone is still going to be paralyzed, and I'm always going to be the bastard who's responsible."

Without thinking about it, I moved closer so I could put my hand on the center of his back. He was so warm, and the contact sent an electric shock through my arm. "Talking about it won't change what happened, but it might change how you feel about what happened. You don't have to shoulder all of that guilt and regret alone, and if you keep trying to, you're going to end up right back where you were."

That was a place I hoped he never visited again. I had serious doubts he would survive if he ended up back there.

His muscles shifted under my fingertips, and he cocked his head to the side so that I knew he was looking right at me even though I couldn't see his eyes behind the dark lenses. His voice was low and vibrated with emotion that dragged the tone even deeper as he asked, "What if I don't want to change how I feel about that night? What if I know I deserve every sleepless night and every single minute it haunts me when I'm awake?"

I sighed, but it turned into a gasp as he reached for my free hand and pulled me around so I was facing him. He did that yesterday as well, brought us eye to eye. There was no hiding from each other when we were this close, even with the barrier of our sunglasses. He was forcing his way through my walls and showing me the wreckage that lay in waste inside of his.

"You're going to have to learn how to deal with those feelings because you are going to have them for the rest of your life, Cable. You can focus on what you can do now, on the ways you can do better and be better, or you can stay caught up in what was done. That's never going to change but *you* can. The choice is ultimately yours."

His mouth flattened into a tight line as he let me go and fell back a step. "Never been one to make the right choice even when it was right in front of me, Reed."

I blew out a breath and pleaded with him, "Try, Cable. All you have to do is try."

His broad chest rose and fell as he exhaled hard enough for me to hear. "What if we make a deal?"

This was the Cable I was most familiar with. The one who manipulated and never gave anything without taking something in return.

"What kind of a deal?"

He reached up and pulled his sunglasses down the bridge of his nose so that I was confronted with something unreadable in his dark eyes. "One that benefits us both. When you're ready to talk to someone about your mom, you come to me. When I'm ready to talk to someone about that night, I'll come to you. No judgment, no recrimination."

It sounded so easy, even if nothing with him ever was. But he needed to talk, and I'd already given him the sorry ending to my story.

"Okay. That's a deal I can work with."

He dipped his chin in agreement and pushed his sunglasses back up his nose. "Good. Now we can get to the fun portion of the day if all those consequences I earned don't come calling. Are you ready to do this?"

I was so far from ready to learn any of the things he seemed so hell-bent on teaching me. But I'd always been a good student, and I wasn't about to let fear of the unknown stop me from absorbing whatever it was that I was supposed to be learning while I spent this time with him.

ten

CABLE

SHE WAS GOOD.

Not that I was surprised. Affton Reed was the type of girl who was good at everything she attempted. She listened to everything I told her to do before we got in the water. She copied everything I did to a T, and it only took one or two tumbles off the board before she found her balance and could stand for almost the entire curl of the smallish waves we were playing on. She didn't get frustrated. She didn't freak out when she went under. She simply shook the water out of her eyes, braced herself, and climbed back on the board to try again. She was graceful and agile. The truth was, if she dedicated some of her time to having fun, she would be good, better than I was. I meant it when I told her she was better than most without even trying and it was annoying, but it was also inspiring and enticing.

I was so used to people constantly *trying* to be something. Trying to be popular. Trying to be liked. Trying to be badass. Trying to be a family. Affton didn't bother to be anything she wasn't. She was unapologetically who she was and who she was just happened to be an incredibly attractive, competent, and considerate girl. I was sure a lot of that came from having to take care of herself after her mom went sideways, but it was remarkable how capable she was. It was a daily struggle to present myself as something close to a normal human. And here I was, all kinds of twisted up and confused over a chick who made life, and all its ups and downs, her bitch.

I was standing on the shoreline checking my phone to make sure I hadn't gotten a call. I had to do that every hour, and so far, this morning, I'd been lucky. I loved watching Affton move in that bikini. I could get lost in the way the water glistened on her honey-colored skin and the way her almost white hair tangled in the waves and stuck to her neck. I spent more time checking her out than I did surfing, and I honestly couldn't remember a better day. There was no way in hell I was fucking up and going back to jail, not when I now knew I could have days like this. Days when I wasn't drowning. Days I didn't float away. Affton was more than an anchor. She was gravity. She held me in place. It was hard to live in the past when she had me firmly moored to the present.

I put my fingers in my mouth and let out a loud wolf whistle as she seamlessly slid to her feet on one of the biggest waves we'd seen that day. Without thinking about it, I snapped a picture of her on my phone before I dropped it back with all my stuff on the sand. My mom had called twice, and that goddamn reporter had left four messages. Thinking about any of it was going to ruin the pleasant buzz I was feeling. The first one I'd ever had that didn't come from shooting, snorting, or smoking something I shouldn't be putting into my body.

Affton gave a little wave, and I could hear her laughter. It was husky and a little rough. She sounded out of practice, like she didn't get the chance to laugh very often. I hated that. She should laugh all the time. She deserved a break after the cards she'd been dealt. It wasn't fair that she was playing someone else's game and hadn't had the choice to walk away from the table before losing it all.

"Hey . . . Cable, right?" I jerked when a hand landed on my arm, painted pink fingernails digging into my skin.

I looked down at the brunette I'd picked up the other day when she was lying on the beach behind the house. It was a calculated move, chatting her up and putting the moves on her right after Affton and I verbally tore each other apart. I'd seen her a couple mornings when I was coming and going from the house. There was no doubt in my mind she'd staked out the prime real estate so I would practically trip over her when I came off the deck. She had a body that wouldn't quit and a face that I imagined made most men stupid. She was a looker and made it clear she was down for whatever I was bringing to the table. It worked for me that she was confident and forward. She was the kind of girl who came for a good time and nothing more. She was perfect . . . except she was the wrong girl.

All wrong.

"Last time I checked." I didn't try to hide the irritation in my tone.

I had fooled around with her. Dragged her in the water so I could cool off after my showdown with Affton. I thought a kiss and maybe a little slap and tickle would help the way my blood was boiling, but all it did was leave a sour taste in my mouth and when I saw Affton on the deck watching me watch her, whatever lust and rush I'd been feeling died a quick death. Losing myself in someone who had no interest in knowing where I'd come from or any concern about where I was headed wasn't going to work. Because of Affton, I understood it had to matter more than that. I was starting to see I was supposed to matter more than that. I didn't necessarily agree with her, but the part of me that woke up and took notice every time she told me she cared about me sure as hell did.

I squinted behind my glasses as I reached up to pull the girl's talons out of my skin. Affton was sitting on the board as it bobbed up and down on the water. She had her hand over her eyes for shade, and I knew she was looking directly at me and the beach babe. I purposely took a step to the side as the pretty brunette, clad in a fuchsia bikini that was nothing more than a couple of triangles and dental floss, landed her hand on my shoulder. She used her hold on me to pull herself up on her tip-toes so that she could plant a kiss on my cheek.

Her lips touched my ear, and her very generous breasts pressed into my arm as she whispered, "I've been wanting to pick up where we left off the other day. You never gave me your number."

She would have only been another person I was dodging calls from because I was an asshole. I looked down at her hand and sighed. "Not really interested in what happens next, babe. Sorry."

I couldn't remember her name. I thought it was Kelsey, or maybe Chelsea. But then again, it might have been Bailey or Hailey. She didn't matter enough for me to keep that information on hand, and shockingly, I was uncomfortable with that and what it said about me. While I might not be ready to embrace the whole, 'Cable deserves better' spiel Affton had been giving me all summer, I was starting to get on board with the idea that the people around me and those affected by me did. I didn't want my mom to be sad and worried about me anymore. I didn't want Affton to look at me like she was afraid of me . . . and afraid for me anymore.

The brunette let her hand fall and bit down on her lower lip. I liked it when Affton did that. I thought it was cute, and it made me want to be the one with that plump flesh between my teeth.

I wasn't a fan when this chick did it. It made her look coquettish and practiced. "Well, that's a shame. I was sure we were headed somewhere that was very naked and very fun. I'm only in town for another week. Are you sure you want to pass this opportunity by?"

She pushed her chest up and out as she batted her long lashes at me. I'd always been the kind of guy who had things offered up to him on a silver platter. I'd never really had to work for much, and as a result, I'd never earned anything. Everything I ever had was given to me or had been taken without a thought as to whether I was worthy of it. I was sure it was Affton's influence, but I was wondering what it felt like to have something that I'd worked for, something that I'd earned.

"Yeah, babe. I'm gonna let it pass on by. I've learned not to answer the door to every opportunity that knocks."

She huffed and let her hand fall away. She put her hands on her hips and cocked her weight to one side, which was admittedly a very attractive look on her. She was spouting something about missing the chance of a lifetime and insisting that we would be mind-blowing together. I was only listening with half an ear to her tangent because Affton's blonde head was no longer bouncing on the surface of the water. The baby-blue board was upside down, the fins sticking up in the air. I yanked off my sunglasses and tossed them on the ground as I instinctively started moving toward the endless sprawl of water.

"Hey, Reed! You okay out there!" I cupped my hands around my mouth and called her name, the girl on the sand next to me forgotten. I started running. The rolling waves crashed into my knees knocked me back a step.

The board continued to bob up and down, but there was still no sign of Affton. She was a strong swimmer, but if she got caught in a current or hit her head on something under the water when she fell, there was a good chance she wouldn't be able to pull herself up to the surface.

I dove into the water, panic clawing at my throat and fear making my brain tumble with every worst-case scenario imaginable. If something happened to her, it would be all my fault. She was happy up at the house with her college reading list and puttering around talking to Miglena. I was the one who forced fun on her, and if she was hurt by it, that would fall squarely on me. I should've known better than to allow the lull of a good day to seduce me. I wasn't meant for good days. I wasn't allowed to get close to happy without getting burned by the brightness of it all.

I made short work of closing the distance between me and her board. It was only seconds . . . but it stretched into a lifetime. All those summers spent in the water to avoid my parents were suddenly worth something. I had my hands on the fiberglass and was getting ready to dive underneath it when the entire thing moved and Affton's pale head popped up on the other side. Her hair was streaming down her face, and she was coughing and sputtering as she swiped at the soaked tendrils hanging in her eyes.

She put her arms on the board so she didn't have to tread water and lifted her eyebrows at me as a lopsided grin turned her mouth up at the corners. "Got tangled up in the leash and lost which was way up. That was a pretty epic wipe-out. I'm glad you missed it." She reached behind her head to adjust the top of her bathing suit, and I stopped breathing again. "I think I almost lost my top. That would have been . . ."

I couldn't handle it anymore.

I thought my heart rate would slow back to normal once I knew she was okay. I thought my stomach would slide back into place. I thought my brain would quit somersaulting. I thought I would be able to breathe . . . but I couldn't. All I could do was reach for her. I needed to touch her, to feel her, to absorb her heat, to warm up everything inside of me that went icy when I thought the worst had happened. I needed her close so that I could prove to myself she was real and none of this was a dream.

I grabbed her by the upper arms and pulled her across the board. Her wet skin slipped easily over the surface, and she hit my chest with an oomph. Her arms automatically went around my neck and her legs brushed against mine as she scrambled to touch the sand under the water. I could touch, was standing solidly, but if I set her down, the water would be over her head, so she stopped struggling after a second and let me hold her even when one of my hands landed directly on her ass and the other one tangled in the ends of her messy hair. I used my hold to pull her head back, and before I could think about what I was doing, dropped my mouth over hers, swallowing her gasp of surprise and tasting her shock.

It was the best kiss I'd ever had.

It was wet and wild.

It was so hot I could hardly stand it.

She tasted sweet and made the sexiest little sound of amazement and wonder low in her throat.

Her fingers dug into my shoulders, and her legs shifted restlessly against mine under the water. Through the thin fabric of her bathing suit, I felt her nipples pull tight and harden against my chest.

I was capturing a fantasy, creating a memory I could hold onto later. Holding something that shouldn't be real, shouldn't exist in my hands. She pressed closer and followed my lead as I kissed her deeper and dragged her under.

It was the worst kiss I'd ever had.

It was too fast and slightly furious.

It scared her, I could feel it. I scared her. I didn't want to, but I couldn't stop myself.

I was used to taking, and she wasn't used to giving. So there was a moment when there was no question I was devouring her, swallowing her up in everything I felt, and I was leaving none of the amazing things she was untouched. She was meant to be savored and appreciated.

Our teeth clicked together. Our tongues clashed for control and both of us were holding on too tight.

It was obvious neither one of us excelled at kissing: her from lack of practice, me from lack of interest. After a moment, when my heart stopped hammering and her's started racing, we managed to figure it out.

It was still desperate. It was still frantic and a little bit unhinged. It was greedy and hungry because there would never be enough of my mouth on hers or hers on mine. I hadn't had a drink or a hit in almost a month, but I felt drunk on her taste. Loopy on the way everything about her went to my head and made my body feel too heavy and languid.

She always seemed to be the best and worst of everything.

The thin material of her suit was nice. The velvety softness of her skin was even nicer. I didn't think about pushing her, or if I was rushing things, I simply acted on instinct. She was okay. She was right in front of me, and she wasn't going anywhere, at least not anytime soon, and she was reacting to me. She always did. I couldn't get enough of it. Of her.

I slid my hand under the elastic waistband of her bottoms and grabbed a handful of softly rounded flesh. She made a noise that could have been complaint, but I decided to ignore it when she hooked one of her legs around my hips under the water and pressed her hips closer to mine. The water made her bob up and down, rubbing my cock along that secret, sensitive notch between her legs. The wet friction made me groan and had my teeth nipping down on the lush curve of her lower lip. I was sure the top of my head was going to come off. I hadn't had my dick inside a girl in a long time. Too long if I was ready to lose it just from rubbing up against her and from nothing more than a handful of ass. The truth was, I'd never had my dick anywhere near a girl who was like Affton and everything about her was so potent. She wasn't watered down or cut with any kind of filler. She was all honest response and heated reaction, and that was more of a turn on than being buried inside something easy and temporary had ever been.

I tugged on her hair again and groaned against her lips. I wanted to peel her top off and put my mouth on those stiff points poking into my chest. I wanted to strip her bottoms off and grind against her. I wanted to drag my throbbing cock through the heat I could feel burning between her legs. I wanted to watch her come and watch her crash. I wanted to plant myself so deeply inside of her that it would take a herculean effort for her to ever get me out. I wanted to be her first, and I refused to think about anyone who might be her last. That rule about sleeping with virgins was bullshit. Nothing more than useless words I used to wound and push her away.

I lied.

Thank God she already knew I was a liar.

I pulled my mouth off hers and watched as her foggy gaze struggled to clear. I lowered my head again to press my lips to the soft swell of her cheek. I pulled my hand off her backside and lifted it so I could smooth some of her hair out of her face. She was blinking rapidly and looking at me like she had never seen me before. Her lips were ruby red and swollen from the bite of mine. She could no longer pass as the innocent, untouched girl next door. Now she was the girl next door who had been felt up and fondled by the town fuck-up. She looked rumpled and ruffled. She looked wide-eyed and wild.

It was a good look on her.

"You scared the shit out of me, Reed." I moved my hands to either side of her face and dropped a quick kiss on her nose. "That was the opposite of fun."

She rested her hands on my shoulders, and I pulled us closer to the shore until she could touch the bottom. I felt her reluctance when she uncurled her body from mine, and we both sighed as she freed the tether around her ankle and found her own footing so she could move away from me.

"I didn't think you were even paying attention. You seemed pretty preoccupied." She didn't sound mad about the beach babe, just resigned.

"She was a distraction. They all are." I grabbed the board for her as we made our way to the shore. I stuck it in the sand next to mine as she wrapped herself up in a colorful towel and wrung out her hair.

"Well, I'm glad you weren't distracted for very long. That was kind of scary for a minute. It's good to know you were paying enough attention to me that you would have been able to save me if I needed it."

I shook my head at her. "I can't even save myself, Affton."

She pushed her hair back behind her ears and wiggled into her cutoffs making all my favorite parts of her body bounce and jiggle deliciously. "Well, you can try because as much as you want to deny it, you are trying, Cable. You didn't know if I was okay or not so you tried to help. Succeed or fail, you did try."

She nodded at my phone which was ringing from somewhere inside my own towel. "You should answer that. I'll be up at the house. I'll make us some lunch, and then we can tackle that studying."

She didn't say anything about that kiss, and I couldn't decide if I was grateful or irritated. One thing was for sure, nothing was going to be the same going forward. Everyone else had been a distraction, but Affton Reed, she was a destination. She was the place I wanted to go and maybe, just maybe, she was the place where I wanted to stay. She was the place I was going to have to work my ass off to reach.

I wanted to earn the right to have my hands and mouth on whatever part of her I wanted, because there was no way, now that I had had a taste, that I could ever walk away without savoring the entire thing.

eleven

AFFTON

I HUNG UP the phone after assuring Melanie McCaffrey, for what felt like the thousandth time this summer, that Cable was doing all right. I could tell in her voice that she was hoping his visits with Doc Howard and his time spent surfing and sobering up would bring him around so that he would finally accept one of her calls. She let him go, and now she wanted him back. She missed him, and I was the only link she had to her son. I didn't mind passing on updates, but when she started to pry, started to prod about anything beyond his progress and sobriety, I shut her down. Partly because I was still pissed that she twisted my arm to get me here, and I was petty enough to enjoy frustrating her, but mostly because it felt like I would be betraying the tenuous trust Cable had given me if I filled her in on how tangled his thoughts and actions were. She also didn't need to know he was doing a bang-up job of making me just as twisted up and confused as he always was.

"So, what's going on between the two of you?"

I gave Jordan a narrow-eyed look as she continued to lick her ice cream cone like she hadn't just shown up out of the blue, unannounced and unexpected. Instead of an explanation, she wanted to know why Cable and I were dancing around each other. She wanted to know why we each acted like the other was about to explode.

"You don't seem nearly as disgusted by him, or the situation, as you were when you left Loveless."

A group of teens around our age came pouring through the door of the hot pink building. It was hot out, and Jordan's inquiry was making me even warmer. I couldn't answer her question because I had no clue what was going on with me and Cable. We'd settled into an unsteady kind of truce. I went surfing with him in the morning, and he tried his best to study with me in the afternoon if he didn't have to meet with the doc or go in for a test. He had the attention span of a house fly so getting any kind of information to stick was work, but he was smarter than anyone ever gave him credit for. We didn't talk about that kiss. Not at all. Not ever.

But we thought about it.

It was there in his eyes. I felt it whenever he almost smiled. I dreamed about it at night, and I knew he thought about it whenever I leaned close to write something down and whenever I touched him . . . mostly on accident. Sometimes it was on purpose. However, neither one of us made a move to go back there. It was a place that was too precarious, too risky. There was too much at stake, and neither one of us was willing to take that kind of gamble on the other.

I sighed and stuck my spoon in my rapidly melting rocky road. Jordan ordered a cone, but I always ate my ice cream out of a bowl. I wasn't fast enough to avoid the mess that came from racing against the Texas heat. "We're making the best out of a bad situation. He's managed to stay straight since I've been there, not that he's happy about it." I lifted a shoulder and let it fall in a half-hearted shrug. "I think I've put a kink in his typical mojo with the ladies. That isn't tension you're feeling; it's his frustration." I pointed the end of my spoon at her as she smiled at a couple of the boys who walked by our tiny table, obviously trying to get her attention. "I'm happy to see you, Jo, but I still want to know why you showed up out of the blue. What happened?"

She swirled her tongue around the edge of her scoop, and one of the boys tripped over his own feet. It was a common reaction. Jordan was one of those girls who was inherently sexy. She didn't have to work at it at all. She just oozed confidence and sexuality. It didn't hurt anything that she was built along the lines of a Kardashian and had the prettiest, shiniest, thickest head of jet black hair I'd ever seen. Combined with her light blue eyes, she could pass as one of the girls who graced the cover of *Maxim,* but fortunately, she was smart enough to know her looks would only get her so far in life, so she actually had a spectacular personality. She was funny. She was sweet. She was savvy and smart. She was avoiding my gaze as I waited her out. I wasn't backing down until she told me why she was here.

She turned her attention back to me and lightly cleared her throat. "I missed you. You're going to be gone all summer, and then you're off to California where you'll probably forget all about me. Is it so unthinkable that I wanted to spend time with my bestie before she's gone?"

"Unthinkable, no . . . unlikely, yes." I cocked my head to the side and studied her closely. "You know you have an open invitation to visit, but it isn't like you to show up out of nowhere. Especially, when you know Cable can be so unpredictable. Lord knows how he's going to respond to having another woman invade his summer sanctuary."

"Yeah. What's up with the Russian hottie? Who is she?"

Miglena had been cleaning the kitchen when Jordan showed up: a task that was surprisingly easy since Cable had been making more of an effort to pick up after himself. There were fewer dirty dishes in the sink now, and I couldn't remember the last time I tripped over his shoes. He was still leaving his wet clothes wherever they landed, but neither Miglena or I said anything about it. Progress was progress no matter how small it might seem. She also agreed to stick around until I got back in case Cable needed a ride to the testing facility. The boy needed to clean his act up so he could get his license back. Luckily, Cable was still in bed, and I hustled my friend out of the house before he realized he was about to have another piece of his past occupying his present. I had a feeling he wouldn't do well with anyone from Loveless, and Jordan was impossible to forget.

"She's from Bulgaria, not Russia, and she's the housekeeper and Mr. McCaffrey's mistress, or she used to be." I couldn't stop thinking about the fact that Cable had sisters he'd never met. His life seemed so lonely. He really was disconnected, and it was clear it wasn't all his fault. "Apparently his dad cheated on his mom on a pretty regular basis. It's part of the reason neither one of them realized he was in trouble. They were too busy messing up their own lives to notice he was destroying his."

"Rich people are so complicated."

I let out a little snort. "You have no idea. And you can quit changing the subject. Talk to me, Jordan. Tell me what happened."

She licked the back of her thumb where some of her strawberry ice cream had dripped. "I was maybe, possibly, probably internet stalking Diego." She sighed and lowered her lashes. "I saw a bunch of pictures of him on Instagram kissing some girl. I mean *kissing*, Affton. This wasn't any peck on the cheek. I know we're not together anymore and that we're headed in different directions, but damn . . . it hurt."

"Oh, Jo. I'm so sorry." I reached out and put my hand on top of her free one. "That sucks."

"Mom asked me why I was crying, why I wasn't eating, and I lost it. I felt so stupid. I don't want to be hung up on some guy who doesn't want me anymore. I don't want to be the girl feeling sorry for herself . . . but I am. So, I packed a bag and left. I just needed some space." She got up to throw the rest of her cone away and was immediately set upon by the boys who had been checking her out earlier. She gave them a weak smile and shook her head at whatever they asked before making her way back to the table. She fell into the seat opposite me with a dramatic groan. "I figured you would be happy to see me. I know you were dreading spending day in and day out with your arch nemesis."

I grinned at that and pushed my mostly eaten ice cream away from me. "Obviously, I'm happy to see you, but Cable . . ." I trailed off, not sure there were words to describe all the things that boy made me feel. "He's not as bad as I thought he was going to be. He's not the same as he was when we were in school." We weren't enemies or friends. I wasn't sure what we were.

"You mean he's not broody, and moody, and smoking hot?" She lifted up her dark eyebrows and gave me a knowing grin. "He doesn't get under your skin and make you crazy anymore?"

I made a face and tapped my fingers on the top of the table. "Okay, he's still kind of the same, but he doesn't seem as desperate to destroy himself as he did back then. He's settled down some."

"Really? Are you sure he's not on his best behavior since you're here? What are the chances he'd go right back to the way he was if you weren't watching? Do you think he's changed for the better, or you're just hoping he has because of everything you went through with your mom?" That was the thing about best friends, they didn't have to have the entire story to know how it went. If they knew you well enough, if they cared, really, truly cared, they knew your story even if you didn't tell it.

It was my turn to avoid her knowing gaze. "I don't know. He seems like he wants something better. He won't talk about the accident, and when someone brings it up, he panics and breaks down. That's not how someone with no remorse acts. I think he wants to change but doesn't necessarily believe he can." I leaned closer to her and told her, "I don't think it's all addiction, Jo. I think he's depressed. Not sad but honestly, uncontrollably depressed. Sometimes he seems to have it all together, and he's a normal, cocky guy who is super annoying. Other days, he's beyond moody, and he acts like nothing in the entire world matters. Then there are the days he disappears inside himself. Those are the ones that are the worst." Those were the days he scared me, the ones where I could see him jonesing, itching for something to help lift the fog that surrounded him. "What if all of this is self-medicating gone horribly wrong? What if he got in too deep because the hole he was digging for himself never bottomed out . . . until he bottomed out?"

"I mean, do guys who have everything Cable McCaffrey has suffer from depression?" Jordan asked the question skeptically, and I couldn't blame her. On the outside, he didn't seem like he had any reason not to be the happiest guy in the world, but things like depression and addiction didn't work that way. They didn't care what you had. They didn't care what you lost.

I told her, "Anyone can struggle with depression. He isn't talking to his counselor the way he should be. He isn't being honest about how he feels about the accident or the time he spent locked up. He isn't looking for help, so whatever improvements he's made won't last very long." He wouldn't get better on his own. He couldn't recover without help.

She tilted her head to the side as she considered me thoughtfully for a long moment. "Are you sure you're not projecting what
happened in your past onto your current situation? Do you think
that maybe you're grasping at straws, looking for reasons Cable
did what he did since you couldn't find one for why your mom
did what she did?"

My fingers tucked into a fist so that my fingernails were digging into my palm. It was a fair question, one I'd asked myself
several times over the last few weeks. "My mom did drugs because
she wanted to be high more than she wanted to be a mom and a
wife. It stopped being about the pain management and started being
about the addiction pretty early on. From what I can tell, Cable
didn't enjoy any part of being an addict. He didn't use because he
loved it; he used because he felt like he had to." And sadly, I knew
deep down, if he didn't talk to someone, if he didn't let someone
connect with him, relate to him, then the chances were incredibly
high he would go right back to the only thing he knew made him
feel better.

Jordan dipped her chin down in agreement. "I don't want to see
you get all wrapped up in this guy, is all. You refused to let anyone
slow you down or get in your way all through high school. You
skipped every milestone you were supposed to have because you
always had your eyes on the prize, and now all of sudden, all you
can see is Cable. He's no prize, Affton. You need to remember that."

"He needs someone." I believed that with every fiber of my
being.

She frowned at me and leaned closer so we were both hovering
over the table, almost nose to nose. "That *someone* doesn't always
have to be you."

It didn't *have* to be, but I kind of *wanted* it to be. I could get seriously hung up on the idea of being someone Cable could confide

in. I wanted to be someone whom he trusted and relied on. I wanted to save him, just like he tried to save me when he thought I was drowning.

I grabbed my melted ice cream and pushed to my feet. "That person doesn't have to be me, but right now I'm the only option he's got." The only person he would let get close enough to touch those dark and dangerous places. "Let's head to the house and hope he's there and not out on the water so we can break the news to him that you're crashing with us for a little while."

She laughed and hooked her arm through mine. "You're not hurting for room in that place. You weren't kidding. It could totally be a hotel, complete with housekeeping."

It could be, but oddly there never seemed to be enough space. I could feel Cable everywhere. There was no escaping him no matter where I went in the house.

"I told Cable I wouldn't let Miglena clean up after me or cook for me while I was there. It's just too weird."

Jordan whipped her dark head around so that she was gaping at me, her mouth hanging open in disbelief. "You have the opportunity to be waited on hand and foot all summer, and you're wasting it? What is wrong with you, woman?"

I knew she was playing, so I elbowed her in the side. "Stop. You know I'm used to taking care of myself. Plus Miglena is the only person I've had to talk to all summer besides Cable. She's almost a friend now."

Jordan laughed and stopped next to my car. She drove a sweet Jeep Cherokee that her parents bought her for graduation, but she looked dead on her feet when she showed up at the beach house, so I offered to drive to the kitschy ice cream shop. "A friend who boned Cable's dad. That's so predictable, the rich dad banging the hot maid."

"She takes care of the house, and I think she took care of Cable when his mom didn't, so she's much more than a maid." I sounded defensive.

My bestie let go of her hold on my arm and held up her hands in a gesture of surrender. "I'm just kidding . . . about both. You never let anyone lift a finger to do anything for you, and from what I could tell in the few minutes I met her, she seemed nice enough."

I reached out and pulled Jordan into a hug. "This summer is making me crazy. I know you were teasing and even though the reason that brought you here sucks, I'm really happy to see you."

She hugged me back and whispered in my ear, "It's not the summer that's making you crazy, it's that boy. He's always been able to get to you, even when you didn't speak to or barely even knew one another. You thought you hid it, but I saw you watching him when no one else was around."

She wasn't wrong.

We got into the car, and she filled me in on the girl in the pictures with Diego. She was a redhead. She was in a bikini. She filled out said bikini spectacularly. What really sent her over the edge were the hashtags, #trueluv, #neverfeltlikethis, #myheart. She'd been serious about him, and it didn't appear he felt the same. I told her babes in bikinis were a common occurrence wherever Cable went, so I understood that burn of jealousy. The reason I fell off the surfboard that first time out was because I was distracted by the brunette kissing up on him on the shore. She was the same one he'd been groping in the water the day I snooped through his sketch pad. I didn't want to care about her and how she had her hands all over him, but I did, and it made me fall.

I considered telling Jordan about *the kiss*. Our kiss. Oh, that kiss. But since Cable and I weren't talking about it, it didn't seem right. If he didn't want to acknowledge that it happened, then neither did I. I didn't want it to mean more to me than it did to him. See . . . he was making me crazy.

When we got back to the house, Jordan was yawning every few minutes, clearly ready for a nap. It was obvious Cable was up and about as soon as we pushed open the front door. There was angry death metal blasting over the house sound system and the distinct smell of something burning coming from the kitchen.

Jordan and I both picked up the pace and found Cable at the stove, a spatula in hand as something in front of him sent plumes of smoke toward the ceiling.

"What are you doing? Where's Miglena?" I rushed into the kitchen and pulled the pan off the burner, wincing because it was so hot. He had the flame turned all the way up, and what appeared to be a grilled cheese was nothing more than a lump of charcoal now. He blinked at me, and he looked over at Jordan, leaning against the massive island, watching us with wide eyes.

"I told her to go home. Figured I could manage a grilled cheese on my own." He lifted a hand and rubbed it over the golden stubble that dotted his chin. "Guess not."

I dumped the pan in the sink and turned on the water. I waved a hand in front of my face and coughed through the smoke. "Since you told Miglena to go home, how were you planning on getting to your parole officer if you got called in?"

He squinted at me and settled his gaze on Jordan. "I know you, don't I?"

She nodded. "Yeah. We went to school together. I dated Parker Calhoun for a little bit when the two of you hung out. I've been to your house for a party or two."

I grabbed his elbow and pulled his attention back to me. "Seriously. What were you going to do if you had to go some-where? You know you can't miss those tests."

He swore at me and shook my hand off his arm. "I wasn't thinking about that."

I scowled at him and poked him in the center of his chest with my finger. "You weren't thinking at all."

He returned my look, both of us glaring and neither of us getting anywhere. After a minute of silence, he returned his attention to Jordan, that false, charming grin of his plastered on his face. "What are you doing here? Reed didn't mention we were having company."

She blew out a breath and leaned on the counter. "I came to visit my girl; she didn't even know I was coming. Wanted to make sure the two of you haven't killed each other yet."

His grin widened, and I saw Jordan react. It was impossible not to. He knew how to use that smile. He knew how to use all the weapons at his disposal in order to be disarming and enticing.

"No one's died yet. How long are you staying?" He didn't seem to mind that she was here, but I didn't trust that easy acceptance for a second.

"Just a couple of days. I have to get back to Loveless. I'm training for a new job this summer and can't afford to be gone very long."

That smile shifted to something cunning and calculating as he turned his head to look at me. Those dark eyes were planning, plotting, and I could practically see the wheels turning in his head. He was up to something, something I wasn't going to be on board with.

"Perfect. I've been looking for a reason to have a party. We should throw one while you're here. We can have a bonfire on the beach."

Jordan perked up at that. She was always down for a good time, and I was sure she was thinking about all the revenge pictures she could post on Instagram. She had no idea this was a test, some kind of game.

"That's a terrible idea. There is no way to monitor everyone who would be coming in and out of this house." There would be no way to keep an eye on him and make sure he didn't go back to his old ways.

"I've been so good. Don't you trust me, Reed?" He was taunting me, because that's what he always did. This was the Cable who wanted to prove a point. This was the dangerous Cable.

"I mean, sort of. But you can't expect me to trust a bunch of strangers. Who knows what they'd bring in or take out." If the house got looted and trashed, I would be the one held accountable.

He looked at Jordan who was switching her gaze between the two of us like she was watching a tennis match. He lifted his eyebrows at her and smirked. "Your girl is allergic to fun."

Jordan laughed and shrugged at me. "He's kind of right. You do get itchy and sneezy whenever someone tries to force fun on you." She was always saying I needed to live a little. She spent most of our friendship trying to pull me out of my secure shell of oblivion. She wanted me to experience things, both good and bad, so of course, she agreed to this nonsense. She didn't care how it would affect Cable, she wanted a wild beach blow out for me . . . and for her.

I glared at her and back at him. It was a bad idea. It was too much temptation and all too similar to the things that used to get him in trouble. "This is going to be awful."

Jordan clapped her hands together in excitement and Cable gave me a look I couldn't read. There was something going on behind those eyes, something challenging and hard. Every time I thought I had him figured out, he did something like this and threw me for a loop.

"Lighten up, Reed. A little fun and games won't hurt you."

No . . . but they might hurt him, and that was suddenly the focus of everything in my life: keeping things from hurting Cable James McCaffrey.

twelve

CABLE

"THERE ARE DIFFERENT kinds of broken, you know."

I cast a sideways look at Affton's girl to see if she'd gone too hard at the tequila that was floating around. "Excuse me?" She was a looker, for sure. I remembered her from Loveless. She was the kind of chick who wanted to see and be seen, but she was a good girl. She had to be for Affton to take her into her confidence. The sexy brunette narrowed her pale eyes at me, and I could tell there wasn't any kind of booze-fueled bravery behind her words.

"There's the kind of broken everyone can see. The kind that leaves a mess no one wants to get stuck cleaning up because it's obviously going to be a lot of work. And, even if you try to get it all, you're going to miss some of those sharp, jagged pieces. Then there's the kind of broken no one can see. The kind that's made up of hairline fractures and narrow little fissures that cover the entire surface. It's the kind of broken that's held together by some kind of miracle and pure strength of will. All it takes is one little bump, one wrong move, and that kind of broken shatters. There is no cleaning up that mess. There are too many pieces, and they scatter everywhere." She lifted her chin at me and narrowed her eyes across the room where Affton was talking to some guy who had wandered in off the beach a couple hours ago. "Do not be the guy who breaks her, McCaffrey. If you do, there is no coming back from that. There is no forgiveness and no second chance."

The house was packed. Music was blaring. Bodies were bumping and grinding as booze flowed freely while the fire on the beach burned big and bright. My dad would shit himself if he saw how many strangers were lounging around his perfectly decorated hideaway. My mom would blow a gasket if she knew how many bowls were being smoked and how many lines were being snorted. Some kid was handing out Molly, and there was a whole group of bikini-clad bodies rolling around on the sand as a result. It was everything I was supposed to stay away from. Everything that got me into trouble in the first place, but I'd been too distracted watching Affton, and too busy watching every guy who wasn't me watch her, to miss all my old vices.

She had on another one of those sundresses that made her legs look a thousand miles long, and I wondered again if she had a bra on or not since I couldn't see the straps. Her winter-tinted hair was messy, but not her normal, just-out-of-bed messy. It was messy in the way that took time and skill to craft. It was the kind of hair that made me think of tangled sheets and grabbing hands. It was sex hair. Rumpled and wavy, that hair should be spread across a pillow and clenched in fists. And that face. God, that face of hers. It didn't need any help to break hearts between blinks, but her girl had played with her makeup and her hair, so tonight, a typically stunning Affton Reed was something else. She was unreal. The gunk around her eyes made them look lavender and even more mysterious. The shiny stuff on her cheeks made her freckles glow.

And whatever was on her mouth made her lips resemble candy, and I was dying for a taste. Me and every other guy who caught sight of her.

"One of the few things I'm good at is breaking shit, babe. Thought you knew that." I picked up the can of 7UP I'd been nursing for the last hour and made a face as I took a sip. It needed a splash of vodka, but that's not what this party was about. Getting wasted wasn't the point. Staying sober was. I could do it, even though it surprised the hell out of me. I told myself it was to keep an eye on Affton, but somewhere in the back of my brain, there was a tiny voice screaming that I could do it for me as well.

Jordan cocked her hip and flipped her hair over her shoulder. Everything about her screamed high maintenance, which was one of the reasons I'd never made a move on her back in the day. I didn't do anything, or anyone, that took work back then, and Jordan Beckett was all kinds of work. Not to mention I knew even then that if I hooked up with her girl, there would never be a chance to hook up with Affton.

"I do know that. That's why I'm telling you to be careful with Affton. Handle her with care, Cable. I see the two of you getting ready to crash into one another, and I'm telling you, that is going to destroy her and no one is going to be able to put her back together. For once in your life, do the right thing." She poked me in the arm with her last words and then flounced away. Immediately, one of the guys I recognized from the waves was at her side. He offered her a beer, but she shook her head and told him she would get her own drink. He followed her as she disappeared deeper into the house. Smart girl.

But not as smart as her girl. I could see in those odd-colored eyes that Affton knew there was something more behind this party than my excuse to cut loose and an opportunity to piss off my old man. Her gears were grinding every time our eyes locked as she struggled to piece together my motivations.

It was easy. I was *trying* to do the right thing for once.

That's what the daily study sessions that were so boring I could cry were about.

That's what the grilled cheese had been about.

That's what sending Miglena home had been about.

And that was what this party, where I was staying sober and keeping my nose clean, was all about.

I wanted to show her I could make the right choices when I put my mind to it. That I did, in fact, know right from wrong and that I was capable of taking care of myself. I wanted to impress her. I wanted her to know she wasn't wasting her time, that I wasn't a lost cause. However, she'd been so busy fending off advances from other guys and so caught up in making sure the house didn't get trashed that she hadn't paid me any attention. Every now and then she would shoot a curious look my way, but that was it.

I'd like to imagine I'd miraculously earned a snippet of trust from her over the summer, but I knew it wasn't true. She was distracted, and I'd been on my best behavior for hours for nothing.

I finished the soda with a grimace and frowned when the big, blond guy, who had edged out all her other admirers, threw a beefy arm around her shoulders and pulled her to his side. He threw back his head and laughed obnoxiously, and even though I was across the room from her, I could see Affton recoil in horror. She was all about being unobtrusive and discreet. This guy obviously thought he hit the jackpot and wanted everyone to notice his good fortune.

The brute grabbed her by her shoulders and pulled her around so that she was in front of him. He said something to her and she frantically shook her head 'no.' The guy ignored her protest, wrapped his hands around her upper arms, and started to back her toward the open doors that led to the deck. He was trying to move her out of sight, trying to take her somewhere secluded. She clearly didn't want to go, and the only person who was allowed to lead her off her chosen path was me. I was the only one she was going to follow into the dark.

I braced my hands on the top of the island, hoisted myself up, and slid across the marble surface. I knocked over a handful of beer bottles on my way and almost knocked over a cute little redhead in a pair of overalls when I landed on the other side. I caught the girl before she went down and then bodily moved her out of the way as Affton's panicked gaze sought mine over the shoulder of the guy manhandling her. She didn't party. She didn't play. She didn't flirt and find stupid ways to kill her time. She had no idea how to handle this guy or the situation, and it terrified her.

They were on the deck when I caught up to them. He was telling her she was beautiful and trying to talk her into a walk along the darkened beach. She was adamantly telling him she wasn't interested. He pressed. She tried to pull away. I could see the way his fingers dug into her skin. He was holding her hard enough to leave marks.

I put a couple of fingers in my mouth and let out a shrill whistle that made everyone within a hundred yards go quiet and turn to look in our direction. She would hate a scene, but if this jackass started something I was forced to finish, I was going to need as many witnesses as possible to keep my ass from going back to jail.

"Where you going, Reed? You're not supposed to leave me to my own devices. Especially not when there's so much temptation around." I stepped around the two of them so that he would have to walk her through me if he wanted to get down the deck steps.

Her back stiffened and she looked over her shoulder at me, her eyes wide and pleading. "I'm not going anywhere." She turned back to the guy who was manhandling her and told him firmly. "I can't go on a walk with you, not that I want to anyway. Let me go."

She pulled back, and the guy let go of one of her arms but refused to loosen his hold on the other. She tugged until her back was pressed up against my front and I could feel her shaking. I put my hand on her waist and looked pointedly at the meaty fingers still digging into her muscle. "Every mark you leave on her, I'm going to make sure you get a matching one. Let her go and get out of my house." The words bit through my clenched teeth and were spoken low enough that the threat was clear.

He had an inch or so on me and was twice as wide, but he was slow. I could see him trying to put together who I was and how I played into his plans, and it was taking forever. He had brawn, but I had brains and my last name. I might be a screw-up but my parents weren't, and the kind of money and influence they had went way further than any right hook or kick to the ribs.

"We were just getting to know each other, weren't we, honey? I go to UCLA. I play football there. I told her if we went somewhere quieter, I could tell her all about going to college in California. She said she was curious." I looked at his fingers again, and he slowly started to peel them off. Her golden skin was an angry red as the blood rushed back in.

She practically collapsed against me as soon as she was free. I wrapped my other arm around her chest and brushed my lips against the back of her head. She slid her hand over the top of mine where it was resting on her middle and laced her shaking fingers through mine.

"I was not curious. I told you that was interesting to be polite. I asked you to let me go five times, and you didn't listen." Her voice got thready and thin. "Why wouldn't you listen?" She really had no idea how boys could be. Not all boys, or even most boys, but there were some who didn't listen, and they were the kind she needed to stay away from.

I kissed the back of her head again and looked at the guy who was taking in the way she was trying to burrow into me and the way she was glaring at him. I couldn't see it, but I could feel it. Her anger was hot, and her fear was practically vibrating along every line of her body. She was wound up, and she was going to snap.

Luckily, her girl popped up and diffused the situation in the way only a really pretty girl could. She was distracting and confident as she waded in. She caught sight of the way Affton was folded into me, the way the big guy and I were squared off, and she promptly put herself in the middle of it.

Hands on her hips, she pointed a finger at the blond brute and told him, "Go. I don't know what happened, but she does not shake. If you did that, you don't need to be here. You have a minute, and if you don't get gone, I'm calling the police." That would clear out the party and piss everyone off, and they would all blame him. Jordan was good, and she was ready to fight for her friend. I wondered what that was like. Having someone who cared enough to go toe to toe with the things that scared you so you could be afraid but know you weren't in the fear alone. My fear was lonely, hollow, and vast.

The footballer held up his hands and gave all three of us a dirty look. "High school girls are so fucking immature. This is exactly why I don't waste my time with them." He gave Affton a smirk as he turned to take his leave. "You're a stuck-up bitch, anyway. They're never very fun once you do all the work to get them naked and on their knees."

I made a sound that was closer to animal than human. I couldn't remember any other time in my life where I cared about anything enough to growl over it. I wanted to do more than that.

I wanted to put my fist in his face. I wanted to crack his jaw with my knee. I wanted to break his ribs and stomp on his fingers. In order to do any of that, I would have to let Affton go and turn around, and that wasn't happening. Right at this moment, she spun around in my arms and tucked her head under my chin as her arms wrapped tightly around my waist. Yeah, I wasn't going anywhere.

I looked at Jordan over the top of her head and told her, "Make sure he goes, and if he doesn't, shut the place down. It wasn't nearly as fun as I thought it was going to be anyway."

She looked at her girl locked in my arms and cocked her head to the side. She opened her mouth to say something, but I shook my head and cut her off. "I got her."

Jordan sighed and pulled out her cell phone as she headed for the steps off the deck. "That's what I was afraid of. Let me know if she needs me." She held up the phone and took off after the guy, following at a safe distance and corralling one of her admirers to have her back. Again, there was no doubt she was a smart girl.

I lowered my head so that my lips were next to Affton's ear and whispered, "Tell me what you need me to do right now, Reed. I'm used to being the villain, not the hero." I had no frame of reference for how to help her. I never cared enough to get involved before.

Her arms tightened around my waist, and when she lifted her head so she could look at me, her eyes were beyond the bruised blue that they turned when I used my words as weapons against her. "I need a minute. Someplace quiet, without all these people." Under her breath so softly that only I could hear she muttered, "I can't believe *this* is what Jordan thought I needed to experience all those nights I stayed home to study."

I took her hand in mine and started to pull her through the thriving party. People were starting to lose their inhibitions, and things were tinkering on the verge of crazy. She kept her eyes averted and her head down as I guided her through dancing bodies and entwined couples, heading past the theater room. She gasped and tried to pull me to a stop when she noticed there was a very graphic, very vulgar porno playing on the massive screen. I told her to ignore it and pointed out that whomever was watching that in a stranger's house wasn't someone she was going to want to walk in on unannounced. She'd had enough shock for one night. She didn't need to stumble across anymore.

I ushered her into my room, letting go of her hand so I could flip the lock on the door and hit the switch on the remote that made the floor-to-ceiling curtains slide shut. The fire on the beach caused interesting shadows to dance across the fabric and gave Affton's pale hair an ethereal glow. Of course, the girl *would* look like she was wearing a fucking halo when I got her alone and had her ironclad defenses down.

She wilted onto the edge of my bed. She picked up the notebook laying there, the one that I doodled in when my mind was being an asshole. Since I couldn't use narcotics to escape anymore, I drew. The strokes across the page, the scratch of the colors as I made a page come to life calmed me down and kept my hands busy.

She trailed her finger over the cover and looked up at me from under her lashes. "You're really talented, you know?" She cleared her throat. "I may have peeked one day when I was throwing your junk back in your room so Miglena didn't have to pick up after you. You're an artist, Cable."

I snorted and crossed my arms over my chest. "I mess around. It keeps me busy. Are you okay, Affton?"

She flinched when I used her first name. "I will be. That was scary. I'm not used to people ignoring me when I tell them something."

She was a fierce little thing but entirely unaware how the world worked. "Your girl is right. You don't shake, but you're quaking like a leaf. He shook you up."

She tilted her head back and squeezed her eyes closed. "This whole night shook me up. Too many people, too many opportunities for you to fall back on old habits. I hate feeling out of control."

I walked closer to her and reached out to push her messy hair away from her face. "You upset I didn't fail, Reed?"

She turned her cheek into the palm of my hand and whispered, "No. I'm proud of you, and that's almost as scary as having that guy shove me around and not take no for an answer. I really don't want you to let either of us down, Cable."

I bent down and put my lips on her forehead. "You need to have reasonable expectations."

She sighed and reached up so she could rest her hands on my waist. "What are we doing?"

I had no idea, but I was positive it was going to be the best and worst thing that had ever happened to me.

"Well . . . I'm going to ruin you, and you . . . you're going to do your best to save me." I slid my hand under the heavy fall of her hair and cupped the back of her skull. I knew where this was going and I was sure she did, too. I was going to get there faster, but that was okay because I might just wait on this girl forever.

"You've come to my rescue twice this summer already. You're the one doing the saving." Her voice drifted off as I stepped into her personal space. I was crowding her. I was pushing her. I was taking her somewhere she had never been before.

I was going to kiss her.

I was going to taste her.

I was going to fuck her.

I was going to be her first, which was scary, but not nearly as scary as the very real actuality that she was also going to be my first as well. I'd never done this with anyone I cared about before. Sure, there had been girls who cared about me, but I never felt the same. Affton was different. Some days, I couldn't stand to be around her. Some days, it hurt to be so close to her. Other days, all I wanted to do was get closer. One thing was absolutely clear to me, though, while I couldn't always tell how I felt about her, I did feel some kind of way. There wasn't a void in the center of my chest when I thought about Affton. There was something there, and something was so much more than nothing.

I was, without a doubt, going to break her, and there would be no cleaning up afterward. My pieces and her pieces were going to be scattered from here to hell and back. There would be no putting either of us back together.

thirteen

AFFTON

CABLE MOVED UP and over me. He put his knee on the edge of the bed next to my hip and pushed me backward. He put a hand next to my head as his face hovered over mine. Those midnight-colored eyes of his were unreadable, but the shadows were gone and in their place were all kinds of promises and plans. The outside light from the fire shining through the curtains cast his face in an orange-red glow that highlighted those demons in his soul he was always trying to outrun.

He was going to kiss me.

He was going to touch me.

He was going to taste me.

He was going to fuck me . . . and I was going to let him.

I wanted him to do all those things. This boy who couldn't get it together. This boy who hurt people without even trying. This boy who was so lost I wondered if he could ever be found. He was the one I was going to let in. He was the one I'd never been able to keep out.

His lips landed on the crest of one cheek and then moved to

brush across the other. His head tilted so his mouth was at my ear, his breath warm and damp against my skin. "You know where we're going, Reed? If you don't want to come along for the ride, now is the time to put on the brakes."

It was too fast. It was dangerous. It was illogical and definitely not smart. It was probably even somewhat unethical considering I was here through coercion and was getting paid to spend the summer with him. Those were all great reasons on top of the fact that I swore I would never care about an addict, to tell him this was as far as I could go, but common sense couldn't fight its way past all the other emotions that were churning and burning inside of me.

My usual focus was shot.

My typical calm and rationale was nowhere to be found.

Everything inside was buzzing and shaking. For someone who wasn't supposed to shake, I was doing an awful lot of it tonight. I'd never been so unsteady in my life.

"No brakes, but I might not be up to the speed you're used to when you go down this road." Once or twice things had gotten hot and heavy with Hayes when I was seeing him. I knew my way around the general landscape, knew when to turn right and when to turn left, but I had no clue how to park the car. I knew Cable traveled down this road on a regular basis, so nothing was new to him. I, however, didn't want to miss a single thing.

"I'll let you drive, but I'll navigate. I'll show you where to go, but you can set the pace." His voice was low, and his words were exactly what I needed to hear. He could be considerate. He could be kind. He could be understanding. He could be all the things he was so sure he would never be.

I turned my head so that my lips touched his. He tasted of his last smoke and something sweet. I'd kept him in the corner of my eye all night, falling back into the old habit of watching him when no one else was looking, even him. I was waiting for him to pick up a drink or disappear with something he wasn't supposed to be around. He never did. Other than stepping outside to smoke, he'd stayed within sight all evening long, eyes watching his old life happen around him. He didn't seem resentful or remorseful . . . he seemed sad. Maybe he finally realized everything that was supposed to make him happy never really did. It was all just noise. It was all distraction and diversion.

He kissed me back. His lips moved over mine as he lowered himself down so our chests pressed together. I never enjoyed feeling trapped, but in this moment, I never wanted to come out from under the weight of Cable James McCaffrey. His hands grasped either side of my face, and his breath mingled with mine as we both panted and groaned at the feeling of being pressed together. My nipples pulled tight. My legs shifted restlessly against his and my hips lifted and arched into his. Pretending they knew exactly what they were doing, my hands found their way to the hem of his t-shirt and started to push it up the hard plane of his back. Muscle flexed and tattooed skin moved under my fingertips as he reached up and grabbed the back of the collar so he could yank the cotton over his head in one swift move. It was practiced and effortless, but my breathing, after all that tanned and taut skin was pressed into mine, was not.

I felt breathless and overwhelmed, which wasn't helping at all when Cable's lips moved from my wet, kiss-stung mouth to the side of my neck. I felt the edge of his teeth and then the glide of his tongue as he licked along my pulse and nipped at the curve of my neck down past the curve of my jaw. One of his hands lifted from where it was braced on the mattress above my head and landed on my thigh where the edge of my dress had ridden up. I felt the burn from every finger as he used his thumb to draw circles on the sensitive skin on the inside of my leg.

It made the part of me that was pressed against the bulge in his jeans clench and quiver. It made me gasp and shift under him in anticipation. The tip of his nose skated across my clavicle, and I felt the rush of his lips dance across the crest of my breast. It made my nipples harden even more, and suddenly my entire body felt too heavy. I ached between my legs and both my breasts throbbed and lifted compulsorily toward that questing mouth. He was being gentle, but there was an edge to the way he touched me and the way he tasted my skin. I could feel the restraint he was using, the care he was taking not to scare me or move too fast for me to keep up. He was the boy who took what he wanted, did what he wanted, whenever he wanted, but he was reining himself in for me. It made me feel special and important. It made me appreciate that I was having this moment with him instead of someone else, but it also made me impatient.

I could hear people laughing and talking on the beach. The party still raged on outside. The real world, the one where this was a bad idea, the same one that was going to leave me upside down and sideways was so close. If he didn't throw a little more of the dangerous Cable into the mix, my typical caution was going to get loud enough that I couldn't ignore it anymore.

I wasn't scared of him or what was happening between us. If I was honest, the way he was making me feel right now was less frightening than all the other ways he had made me feel this summer. I understood that he was ridiculously good-looking and had broody down pat. Attraction was a no-brainer. I liked the way he looked, and my body liked the way he looked at me. It was the pull toward him—even though he was always pushing me away— that scared me. I was getting so wrapped up in how he was doing and what he was doing that I forgot to keep myself safe. I forgot that there was no room in my plans for Cable James McCaffrey. Berkeley was in my plans, McCaffrey and anything—other than my dad—that had to do with Loveless were not.

I curled the leg he was caressing around him, trailed the fingers of one hand up the line of his spine, and dragged my fingers through the longish hair at the back of his head. My fingers dug into his scalp as he started to move his hand up the inside of my leg. My dress went easily with his sliding hand, and I let out a little gasp when I felt the brush of his knuckles against the center of my underwear. The contact made my skin tingle, and I couldn't take the layers of clothing between us anymore.

I snaked my hands down to my hips and wiggled until I had my dress over my head. I was left lying underneath him in nothing more than a lacy pair of underwear and a strapless bra that was doing very little to keep my aroused body hidden from view. Cable bit out a dirty word and looked down the length of my body with heavy-lidded eyes. There were twin spots of pink on his cheeks, and his broad chest lifted and fell as he exhaled a deep breath.

"Didn't lie when I told you that you're a stunner, Reed. Also, not gonna lie about the fact that I was trying to imagine what you had on underneath that dress all night." The hand on the inside of my leg lifted and teased the edge of my bra. He slipped his thumb under the satin seam and traced the full curve that rested underneath. I held my breath, waiting, wanting his touch on the pointed peak that was practically begging for his attention. When his fingers did circle the stiff point, I squeezed my eyes closed and bit down on my bottom lip to keep from moaning. He rubbed leisurely circles around one nipple and then switched tactics. He ordered me to lift so he could pop the clasp and get rid of the barrier entirely. His lips landed on the other tip, the velvety point disappearing into the warm cavern of his mouth as I sank into pleasure and oblivion.

The drag of his teeth across the sensitive skin had me ready to fly apart. The press of his fingers, and the tug he gave the other side, made my body bow and quake uncontrollably. I felt wet and warm. I was restless and ready. I was wanting and waiting. Every sensation he sent shooting through my nerves felt bigger and better than the last.

My fingers curled into the hard blade of his shoulder as I arched myself upwards to grind against all the hardness that was pressed against my center. I didn't know what to do with all of that, but I did know I wanted to feel it without the rough fabric of his jeans between us. I had to let go of his hair to get a hand between us, and when I did, I made a beeline for the button on the top of his jeans. My fingers skipped over the rock-hard delineation of his abs, and I sighed as they flexed against my touch. "You aren't so bad yourself, McCaffrey." He really wasn't. He did bad things, made bad choices, tended to think bad thoughts about himself and everyone else, but he wasn't bad. And the outside, well, that was better than good. I wanted my hands and mouth all over every single inch of him.

He couldn't answer me because his mouth was busy marking up my breasts. His licking and sucking and swirling switched from one to the other until my hands were unsteady and made getting his pants open far more complicated than it should have been. While I was struggling, awkward and uncoordinated, one of his hands found its way to the material of my damp panties. This time there was no leisurely stroll around his intended target. This time there was no playing around. His fingers navigated under the silky surface as if it wasn't even there and I went completely still as he slid through damp folds and obvious pleasure. There was no hiding my reaction to him. There was no pretending that I wasn't as eager and ready for him as he was for me.

That was new.

The feeling of want. The feeling of being empty and incomplete without him. I enjoyed the things the boy who wasn't Cable had done to me, but I didn't feel desperate for more. Cable made me crazy. He made me irrational and wild. He was the only one who could distract me from all the other things that usually held my focus and kept me going. He obliterated what could be, because all that mattered was what was happening between the two of us right now.

I whimpered, half in distress and half in desire as I felt his fingers move. They shifted and slid. Searching and seeking until they found what they were looking for. His lips lifted from my chest and landed back by my ear. I shivered as he pressed in and whispered, "I can't believe you're going to give this to me. I really don't deserve it."

His touch was confident, firm as his fingers moved in and out of my slick center. His thumb found that spot, the one everyone insisted was magical. They were right. It only took a little tap, a soft stroke, and my eyes crossed, and my toes curled. I forgot all about getting his pants open and got lost in the pleasure that rolled over me from head to toe. His teeth nipped at my earlobe, and his tongue licked along the outer curve. I lifted my hips, frantically asking for something, something I didn't even know existed until this boy broke into my life.

I wrapped my fingers around the wrist that was caught between my legs. I could feel his pulse pounding and the flex of his fingers as they worked in and out of my body. My muscles clenched and everything inside fluttered. The sensation was foreign but not unwelcome as I rocked more firmly into his touch.

It took some effort to peel my eyes open, and once I did, my gaze was immediately caught by the heated, possessive look in his. He knew he was getting something I would never be able to give to anyone else, and the look he was giving me told me he planned on handling what I was handing over to him like it was more than something special . . . because it was. This was more than a hook-up at a party. To me, this was everything.

I moaned as heat and languid tension started to unfurl from my belly out toward all my limbs. "You might not deserve it, but I sure as hell do. I've always done everything exactly right, Cable. Having you here, with me tonight, giving something I've never wanted anyone else to have, is my reward for that."

The pad of his thumb pressed down on my clit and those long, strong fingers that were learning every hidden and secret place I had found a spot that made me see stars. I couldn't take it anymore. My fingers dug into his skin deep enough to leave marks. Both my legs lifted around his waist. I pressed my chest into his and writhed against him. The warmth that spread throughout my body started to scorch as everything on the edge of my vision went a little blurry, and every part of my body tightened and tensed with pleasure. I was getting shoved off a cliff and floating on clouds of pleasure. I was getting wound up and released. There was a shock similar to that of being dunked in freezing water that quickly faded to a spreading, spiraling warmth that rushed through my blood. It felt good. So good. Better than good. It felt amazing, and I was sure this was what being rewarded for a lifetime of making the right choices was supposed to be like.

Panting, breathless, I kissed his chin as he hovered over me, watching, waiting. I wanted to tell him it was so worth it. I wanted to explain to him that I was sure no one else could make me react and respond the way he did. He was the only one with a finger on my trigger.

All I could get out was a weak, "Oh, my." It made him chuckle, and his eyes never left mine as he untangled himself from my clinging limbs so he was standing at the side of the bed between my splayed legs.

He offered a hand and pulled my loose-limbed body into a sitting position. After he took the time to slide my underwear down my legs with efficient, sure movements. I found myself face to face with that impressive package hidden behind the fly of his jeans, and now that I didn't have his hands and mouth all over me, I could focus on getting to him.

There was a little tremor in my hands when I lifted them to the front of his jeans, but it was anticipation, not fear, making them quake. He watched me silently, waiting for my cue as to what he should or shouldn't do. He was being so patient I couldn't stop myself from leaning forward and dropping a kiss right above his belly button. Those tight stomach muscles tensed and one of his hands landed on the top of my head. I felt his fingers thread through my hair.

I popped the button and pulled the zipper down. He was wearing those black boxers he seemed so fond of and his arousal was ready to burst out of them. There was a lot of him, and I wanted all of it.

He stopped me from pushing his pants down so he could grab his wallet. He pulled out a little foil packet and handed it to me as he proceeded to get naked right in front of me. He wasn't shy. He didn't have a reason to be, but that was a lot for my sluggish and mostly sheltered brain to take in. Even in the dark with shadows playing hide and seek, I knew I was blushing scarlet and blinking rapidly.

He held out his palm and made a 'gimme' gesture with his fingers. I handed over the condom obediently and watched with wide eyes as he rolled the latex down the length of the shaft. He must have picked up on some of my worry and hesitation because a knowing grin tugged at the corners of his mouth.

"It'll be okay. We'll take our time and make sure it works. Don't be scared." He did that thing where he pressed me backward and crawled over me again, this time moving us both more fully onto the bed.

His mouth was soft when it touched mine. His hands were gentle as they skimmed over the surface of my skin, but his body was hard. His shoulders were stiff, his biceps bulged, and I could feel the tension in his thighs. The press of his cock between my legs was insistent and erotic. He was as hot as I had been and that thick flesh felt silky smooth against the inside of my thigh.

"At first, this isn't going to feel as good as what we just did. You know that, right?" His voice was raspy and rough. I had no clue how he expected me to answer when I could feel the tip of his erection gliding through the damp folds that were still hyper-sensitive from his earlier attention.

I'd heard mixed accounts about the first time. Jordan hated hers, but that could be because she ended up hating the guy she lost her virginity to. She said it was quick, all of it, including the discomfort. I had another friend who had no real issue when she and her long term boyfriend finally decided to do the deed. She said it was a little uncomfortable and awkward but that quickly faded.

The truth was, either way, I was happy to have the memory made with him. Good or bad, I wanted this moment with him.

"I think I'll live." Really, it was the first time in forever I was living instead of just going through the motions. I was experiencing something. Jordan would be so proud . . . after she killed me for giving it up to Cable.

He chuckled again and slowly tilted his hips into mine. One

of his hands skimmed between us and over my belly. I felt him wrap his fist around his straining shaft and a second later his body pressed slowly and steadily into mine. I caught my breath, and his eyes drifted closed.

"Good thing one of us is going to live through this, Reed. I'm pretty sure you're about to kill me."

There were a few seconds where everything inside of me resisted his invasion, but when I remembered to breathe and when he kissed me, I forgot about the odd sensation of being filled and taken. I forgot about the stretch and pull. I ignored the ache of discomfort and focused on the feeling of pleasure and passion that hid behind it.

True to his word, he took his time and made sure it worked for both of us.

We ignited.

We went up in flames.

We burned and singed each other over and over again.

It didn't take long to get swept up in the new sensation. I forgot all about what he'd already given me and demanded more. It was a heady feeling having that big, strong body moving in and over mine. The sounds he made low in his throat and deep in his chest were intoxicating, and I knew I would never forget the way his eyes blazed with black fire.

He fell apart first on a long groan and another slew of dirty words. I was content to float on the cloud of pleasure he left behind, but Cable wouldn't stand for that. His hand and questing fingers were back between my legs, and it only took a few well-placed strokes and a couple of skilled circles for me to break all around him.

He collapsed on top of me, breathing hard, body covered in a thin sheen of sweat. It took an obvious effort for him to lift his head and I could see a million questions in his eyes.

Was I okay?

Was he okay?

Was it good for me?

Did it hurt and did I already regret it?

How did we end up here and when could we get back to this exact moment again and again?

Did I still hate him or was it something closer to love now?

For once in my life, I didn't have an answer to a single one of them.

fourteen

CABLE

"I WASN'T DRIVING the night of the accident."

It was the first time I'd ever admitted that out loud and I wasn't even sure that the girl I was admitting it to was awake. It had been a long night for Affton. I didn't give her time to think or put her shields back up. I cleaned her up and kept at her until both of us were too sore and too tired to do much more than curl into one another and pass out. Being with her had been worth the wait. My mind and my body were finally on the same page. They both wanted her, wanted to take her and keep her. Both reveled in the fact that she was a good fit, soft and hard in all the right places and just the right amounts of both.

I sighed and watched as her hair sifted through my fingers. It really was sex hair now, messier than it had been before, since I dragged her back to bed after she took a shower and rolled her from one side of it to the other. It dried in a wild tangle that seemed to go in every direction, but the pale strands were soft and silky against my chest. Her head was tucked under my chin, one of her arms curled along my ribs, and her knee angled over my seriously satisfied cock. Never in a million years would I have ever pictured this scenario with this girl, but if I was being honest, it was a dream come true. As in everything she did, Affton was a quick learner and a diligent student. I would never take for granted that I was the one who taught her all about the kind of sex that left you exhausted and exhilarated at the same time. I'd finally found the kind of lessons I didn't mind working through thoroughly and methodically. After all, practice made perfect.

"I know everyone thought Jenna was in the car with me because we'd hooked up a few times and hung around with the same people, but that's not why she was there." I gulped, hoping Affton really was asleep so she didn't end up with the same nightmares I had. Once she knew the truth about that night, it would haunt her the same way it haunted me. She might sleep easy, but it was debatable if she would still want to sleep with me lying next to her.

I sighed and twisted a strand of nearly white hair around my finger. "Jenna and I had a lot in common. Same kind of upbringing. Same kind of affluence and status. Her parents were never around either, but at least she had a nanny who gave a shit about her and raised her."

Jenna Maley was similar to Jordan in that everyone knew who she was and wanted a piece of her. Unfortunately, she was similar to me in that she was forever searching for something that would cut through the fog of discontent that covered her every single day. She was lost like I was, and she was searching. We both learned quickly that we were empty and hollowed out. There was no point trying to use each other to fill those holes, but we understood one another, and Jenna was the closest thing to a real friend I had in Loveless. It just so happened that Jenna's nanny had a brother, and that brother had connections all over Texas when it came to getting any drug you could think of. Jenna started popping pills her shrink gave her and quickly moved on to harder stuff. She was the one who introduced me to all the stuff that was harder than a joint.

"She was my dealer."

No one in Loveless ever knew. She hid her habits better than I did and carried her sadness with more grace than I ever managed. People assumed I was the bad influence. They whispered that I was corrupting her and leading her down a path of destruction. Her friends told her to stay away from me, and when her parents were around, they pretended everything was just a phase.

She never walked away from me because we used each other as a crutch and we enabled each other to do awful things. Feeling alone and abandoned is bad; but what's worse is when another person tells you that those feelings are justified and that you are completely and totally isolated because no one cares. She made the asshole thoughts in my head sound reasonable and justifiable. She wanted me as low as I could get so she didn't have to live on rock-bottom all alone.

"I told Jenna my mom was sending me to rehab. That my mom tossed my room, found my stash, and lost her mind. She didn't want me to die. I mean, she didn't want me to cause a scandal for the family either, but really she was worried about me when she knew just how deep I had gotten." I blew out a breath. "Thanks to you." I hated her at the time, but the truth was Affton probably saved my life when she ratted me out.

Still no response from the sleeping beauty sprawled across my chest. I slid my hand under the hair that was curling softly against the back of her neck and cupped the back of her skull in my hand. I was holding on to her for dear life. I never wanted to let her go.

"Believe it or not, I wanted to go." I let out a breath and really wished my pants were closer so I could light up a smoke. I needed the nicotine to calm my nerves. I needed the familiar inhale and

exhale to lull my heart into thinking it was okay to open its doors
to this girl. "I was so relieved someone finally noticed. I was exhausted from the constant chase and crash. And, Jesus . . . the way
you looked at me that day you confronted me at school like I was
a lost cause, I could tell you really did hate me. I was sick and tired
of being that guy, but I'd been him for so long, I had no idea how
to shake him loose. I started to think he was who I was meant to
be, but then Mom offered a shot at help, and I was going to take
it. Jenna hated that."

She hadn't wanted to lose the guy who was her smokescreen.
Everyone was too busy watching me fall apart to pay any attention to her. She also didn't want to lose her best customer. If I did
blow or popped a handful of Oxy, then a bunch of other kids who
wanted to be like me, or at least thought they wanted to be like
me, would follow suit. Drugs for recreation were a big business
in middle America, and Jenna was making a mint off bored kids
who fell face first to peer pressure.

"She called and told me she wanted to meet. She was crying,
really upset. She said if I was going into treatment, maybe she
should go as well. I should've known it was bullshit. That girl didn't
want help, she just didn't want to be the only poor little rich kid
with an addiction in Loveless."

Affton mumbled something and shifted. Her hand curled
under her cheek on my chest so that her fingers were touching
every heartbeat. Her knee grazed my sheet-covered cock, and I
immediately went hard. She was going to be out of commission
for a day or two. I had no doubt about that. She was already sore
and moving stiffly. She took a lot and then asked for more. She
was pretty much the best thing ever, and when this all blew up
and blew away, I would always have this night with her to remind
me there was something in this world that was worth fighting for.

"I went to pick her up because she was a mess and in no condition to drive." I shook my head and wanted to kick myself for how obvious it all was now that I was thinking straight. "She set me up. When I got to her house, she was naked and wasted. She said she wanted to give me a going away party I would never forget."

And because I was an idiot and couldn't turn down a sure thing, I fell right into her trap. I figured if I was going straight and clean, I was allowed one last night of excess. It was the kind of reasoning that turned me into an addict in the first place. I wasn't immune to the consequences of my actions, even though I thought I was.

"I went on a bender. Drank until I threw up, fucked until I couldn't stand up, put so much shit up my nose that I can't believe my heart didn't stop. It was gluttonous and disgusting, but I knew everything I was accustomed to using to fake being fine was going away as soon as I got on the plane. So, I went all in. She knew I would." It was pretty telling that my dealer knew me better than anyone else in my life.

"I woke up sometime that night, hungover and totally wrung out. Jenna offered to drive me back to my parents' ranch, and since I was in no shape to get myself there, I agreed. I knew my mom was going to be pissed because there was no way to hide just how fucked up I was at that point, and I figured that maybe she would keep her cool if Jenna was there as a witness. My mom never wants a scene." I snorted, and Affton rubbed her cheek against my chest. Her other hand worked its way under my shoulder so that she practically had me in a full body hug. I knew she was no longer sleeping or pretending to be asleep. I slipped a hand under the covers and cupped the gentle roundness of her ass in my palm. Her knee brushed against my erection deliberately, and I closed my eyes.

"As soon as we got in the car, Jenna lost it. She wasn't looking at the road when she started driving. She started screaming that

I couldn't go, that I couldn't tell anyone what we'd been doing. She was worried I would spill who my hookup was. She came unglued." I remembered her face, blotchy with anger and streaked with makeup as she screamed and cried at me. I had no idea if she was high, or still high from the night before, but either was scary considering my car went from zero to sixty in half a second. "She didn't head toward the ranch at all. She took the road into town. She was going way too fast. She couldn't handle the car. I was begging with her, pleading for her to slow down or to pull over, but she wasn't there."

She acted like she couldn't hear me at all.

"I don't know if she was trying to leave town, or if she wanted to hurt herself and me. I don't know if she was so far gone that she was thinking about hurting someone else. All I do know is that none of it would have happened if I had been stronger. If I hadn't had to have one last hit of everything that fucked up my life in the first place. I was selfish, and because of that, Jenna died."

I knew she couldn't take the sports car through the heart of Loveless. She was being too erratic and too unpredictable. She was going to run someone over or run us off the road.

"Of the two of us, I was thinking the clearest, and I honestly had no idea what to do. I was just as messed up as she was. All that made sense was to grab the wheel and try and force her to get off the road." Only we'd been going way too fast, and I didn't look to see if there was anyone else on the road before I did. I was panicked, inebriated, and scared out of my mind.

"The car skidded on some loose gravel that was on the side of the road and fishtailed out of control. Jenna let go of the steering wheel and covered her eyes, and we careened from one lane to the other, clipping another innocent motorist in the process. My sports car hit the side of the road, front-end caught and flipped the shitty import end over end. Both Jenna and I were thrown from the car from the impact because neither one of us bothered with seat belts." I had to stop and clear my throat a few times before I could keep going. My fingers dug into the back of her head and into the side of her hip. I was going to leave marks on her with more than my words. "Uh . . . When Jenna was thrown, the car rolled over her, and she was killed instantly. For some reason, I was tossed far enough away that I only ended up with some minor bumps and bruises. I suffered a broken arm, several fractured ribs, and split my head open. I ended up with a concussion and rattled my brain enough that I didn't really remember anything that happened."

Affton moved. She put both her hands on the center of my chest and rested her chin on the back of them. When I opened my eyes to look at her, I could see that she was crying. Silent tears trailed over her cheeks as she watched me in the dark. I lifted a hand and smoothed my thumb over the wet streak. "The cops came to the hospital after I was awake and asked me what happened. At the time, I honestly couldn't remember. All I knew was that Jenna and I had gotten super fucked up the night before. They asked me if I was driving since we both had been thrown and landed in different places. They couldn't tell who was behind the wheel. It was my car, so I assumed I was the one driving. It was only after I admitted responsibility that they told me I was charged with vehicular homicide. That's when I found out about the other driver, as well. He almost died. For no other reason than he was in the wrong place at the wrong time."

"When did you get your memory back?" Her voice was quiet and thoughtful.

"Right around the time the trial started. Bits and pieces of it started coming back to me, but I was pretty messed up at the time. The judge wouldn't grant me a bond because he was tight with the Maleys and they wanted me to pay for what happened to Jenna. All of a sudden they were the parents of the year and Jenna had been some kind of angel. Everyone in town was whispering they knew I would eventually crash and burn, only no one knew it was going to be so literal. The family of the guy we put in the wheelchair sued my parents for pain and suffering, and that was the straw that finally broke the camel's back in their marriage. Mom ditched Dad and turned all her attention to trying to keep me out of jail." I rubbed my thumb along her bottom lip and lifted my left leg under hers so that she was pressed more firmly against my aching erection.

"Somehow, Jenna managed to avoid traffic cameras, and my reputation for reckless disregard of the rules preceded me. There was no proof that I wasn't the one driving, and the truth is, it didn't matter. I knew none of it would have happened if I had been able to say no, if I had been able to walk away from my vices . . . but I hadn't. That accident was as much my fault as it was hers. Sitting in a prison cell was nothing considering the price she had to pay. I deserved it . . . and probably more . . . but I wasn't driving."

I needed her to know that.

I wasn't sure why, but I just knew it was information she needed to know, especially now that we'd crossed a pretty major line in our relationship.

She blinked at me and exhaled long and hard. Her breath touched my lips in a phantom kiss and her words wrapped around me in an invisible embrace. "Are you looking for forgiveness, Cable? Because if you are, I forgive you, and I really think you should forgive yourself." She turned her head so that her cheek was once again resting on her hands. "Want to know a secret?" Her voice was soft and gentle. It was the first time she'd ever seemed hesitant and unsure with me.

I nodded in the dark and twirled the ends of her hair around my fingers. "Your secrets are safe with me, Reed." I couldn't promise that her heart would be.

"I wrote you a letter, more than one, when you went away. I apologized a hundred different ways for telling your mom what was going on with you. I knew nothing that happened that night would have been set in motion if I'd kept my nose out of your business. I tried to help you, and it all went so wrong. I felt as responsible as you for what happened that night." She let out a long breath. "I never sent them. I felt terrible about the accident and the fact you went to jail, but I was glad you got help. I was happy you couldn't use anymore. It was selfish and made me feel guilty, but it's the truth. You went to jail for something you didn't do, and you lost someone you cared about. I think you've been punished enough for making some poor choices along the way. Your penance is paid. You wanted to get help. You wanted to make changes; here's your shot. Don't blow it."

I rolled us so that she was underneath me and braced myself on my forearms above her head so I didn't crush her. "I wouldn't have opened them if you sent them. I wasn't in a place where I wanted to share the blame, and we both know I'm not exactly great at listening to what you have to say." She made it all seem so cut and dry. I'd screwed up, and it cost me everything. The only way to fix it was to fix myself, because that was the only part of the equation that could be corrected.

"Speaking of blowing things . . ." I wiggled my eyebrows at her and grunted as she smacked me on my unprotected ribs.

It was a lot, handing all my secrets and sorrows off to her. She didn't seem scared of my demons, but now she knew just how bloodthirsty and vicious they could be. I needed something that was familiar, something that was simple after all that soul stripping.

I felt raw and exposed . . . vulnerable. I was shaking in a different way than I had been at Doc Howard's office and my world had narrowed onto her instead of on that night.

She wiggled underneath me and rolled her eyes. "I can barely move. I hurt in places I didn't know I had, and honestly, my heart is very conflicted after hearing all that." I could see she was hurting for me, but also because of me. She said she didn't want me to disappoint her, but hearing about how bad my bad choices could be did just that.

I moved to push myself off her, to give her the space she obviously needed while she wrestled with my ugly truth. "You recuperate. I'm going to go make sure the house isn't trashed and pick up a little bit so Miglena doesn't walk into a garbage pile." I didn't get very far. Her arms locked around my neck and her legs circled my hips so there was no going anywhere. Her pale eyebrows lifted and a soft smile played around her mouth.

"We can wrangle Jordan to help us clean up in the morning. I'm not ready for you to go yet."

I watched her watch me and told her honestly, "If I stay, we're both going to end up moving a lot more than that, and I don't want you to do anything with me when you're confused or conflicted. I don't ever want you to think I'm taking advantage of you, Reed." I didn't mind manipulating her and motivating her with silly little games, but I refused to leverage her heart for my own pleasure.

She stared up at me for a long moment before tugging my mouth down to hers. It was a kiss that started slow and sweet but ended up wet and wild. I had my fingers between her legs and her fingers wrapped around my pulsing cock by the time we broke for a breath. Her gaze was glassy, and her breaths were choppy as she told me, "I've always known who you are Cable. I have never agreed with the choices you made . . . but about you, my heart has never been confused about you."

I chuckled and bent so I could brush my lips against hers again. "You hated me back then and hated me at the start of this ride. Remember?"

Her lips twitched. "Exactly. I hate you, Cable James McCaffrey. Now teach me how to suck your cock."

Nothing had ever been sexier than her sweet mouth saying those dirty things. They were words she wasn't used to saying, and I fucking loved them almost as much as I loved the knowledge that I was the only one who knew what it was like to be buried deep inside of her. For once, I didn't give a shit about being a bad influence. If corrupting her led to her tongue licking me and her lips sucking me, then I was happy to lead her down the road straight to hell.

If you think about it, love and hate really aren't that much different when you got right down to it. Both make you crazy. Both make you do things you never thought you would ever do, and both were so, so easy to get lost in.

I loved that she hated me . . . and I hated that I was pretty fucking sure I was falling in love with her. That realization ripped my heart into two pieces. There was the half that was elated I could feel something that huge and important and the other half that was losing its shit and trembling in fear. I didn't know how to do love or hate when it came to another person. I'd felt plenty of the latter for myself but never bothered to let myself have such a strong reaction to anyone else.

It would remain to be seen which side of my heart was stronger.

fifteen

AFFTON

I ENJOYED SEX . . . a lot.

At least, I enjoyed having sex with Cable James McCaffrey a whole hell of a lot. It was so much better than fighting with him. It was so much better than trying to manage him. It was infinitely better than being ignored by him, and it was so much easier than trying to hate him. Naked and tangled around one another, we finally found a level we connected on that didn't make either one of us want to pull our hair out. The words he used when he was inside of me didn't hurt. The way he looked at me when he had his hands on me healed us both. The way his mouth moved over mine helped me understand how he worked more than watching him and waiting for his next move ever did. Every kiss was flavored with desperation and dominance. He was as out of control around me as I was around him, and while those feelings terrified me, they thrilled him and made him hungry for more. He was swamped in feeling, overwhelmed by emotion, and loving every minute of it. He was no longer numb, which meant he was flying higher than any drug had ever taken him . . . which meant the potential crash back to Earth when it happened was going to be devastating.

There was no telling which version of Cable I was going to get on any given day; there was never any way to predict what kind of sex I was going to have with him, either. There were the nights that he crawled under the covers and took me slow and soft. There were days he backed me into the wall, hands frantic and motions rushed, getting in and getting off before I knew what hit me. There were moments when he was all short demands and bossy orders, but those times were often followed by lost minutes as he let me learn my way and take all the time I needed. It was always good, always breath-stealing and mind-melting. He was hard to keep up with, so I had to learn to let go and simply appreciate all the different ways he made me feel the same kind of pleasure. I never knew which way he was going to go, but I was happy to be along for the ride if the destination involved coming apart in his arms and under his hands.

Speaking of being under his hands . . .

At the moment, I was learning that I got off when his hands pulled my hair and his fingers dug into my hip as he powered into me from behind. I didn't love being face down with my ass in the air for a whole lot of reasons, but the main reason was that I couldn't see his face. I couldn't watch those eyes as they shifted from espresso to midnight as passion and pleasure chased his shadows away.

"You close, Reed?" His words were choppy, and I shivered all over when I felt the wet sweep of his tongue along the length of my spine. "This was supposed to be quick."

He had an appointment with the doc in town that he wasn't supposed to be late to, but when he came in from his morning surf session all sandy and wet, shaggy hair hanging in his eyes and that knowing smirk on his mouth, I went a little crazy. I sort of jumped him, which led to my current situation. I was close, but

the disconnect I was having because I couldn't see him was playing tricks on my overactive imagination. I didn't want to be some
faceless body to him. I didn't want to be a warm, willing place to
escape everything he couldn't deal with.

I wanted him to want *me* . . . and only me. The same way I
was bordering on obsession with him and only him.

His teeth bit into the curve where my neck met my shoulder
and I let out a groan. That was going to leave a mark; I had them
all over. Another thing I'd learned over the last week was that even
though I tanned easily, my normally pale skin was prone to bruises,
and I now resembled a road map. All my most sensitive places were
marred by Cable's mouth and hands.

"Reed?" He breathed my name into my ear, and I could tell by
the tremor in his tone that if I still had a while to get there, I was
going to be alone because he was right at the finish line. I could
feel his thick cock kick between my legs and the way his steady
rhythm sped up and became more demanding. The hand that was
tugging on my hair pulled harder, and I turned my head obligingly
so that his lips could brush across my cheek.

I peeled my eyes open and looked at him now that he was
so close. I should be alarmed that he could read me so well, that
he could see right through all that fog that covered up my usual
smarts and confidence. Before I could catch my breath, he had us
both up on our knees, my back to his front, his arm locked around
my chest as his other hand disappeared between my legs where
we were joined. He knew exactly where to touch, just how much
pressure to apply to get me where he needed me to be. However, it
was my name growled into my ear that was the thing that pushed
me over the edge.

"Come on, Affton, don't do that." He grunted, and his hips
bucked as my body squeezed him, tightening as I convulsed around

him, desire hot and wet rushing around his cock and triggering his own completion. "You gotta know that I don't need to be looking right at you to see you. You've always been there, every time I blink, I can see you on the back of my eyelids. I could draw you from memory." His lips landed on the side of my neck and his teeth dragged over the throbbing vein there as I struggled to catch my breath and calm my heart. One hand was still between my legs, but the other skated across my chest and lifted until he was cupping my jaw and tilting my head back so that he could nibble along the sharp line of my chin. He smelled like salt water and sex. It was intoxicating and so easy to get drunk on. "I used to jerk off to the memory of you when the lights went out and I got a minute to think when I was locked up. We'd never spoken, other than the time you chewed my ass. I hadn't seen you in years, but I knew the exact color of your eyes and the exact way your top lip bowed. I knew you had breasts that would be perfect and an ass that would make men weep. I saw you, Affton, I've always seen you."

He rubbed his thumb along my lower lip, and I had to follow the caress with a sweep of my tongue. "And even if I was blind and could never see you again, I would know the way you feel. No one else is custom made to take me and only me the way you do."

He was good at making our level of crazy make sense. He was also good at making me wonder if I really *was* custom made to take him and only him. And I wasn't just talking about his cock. I was talking about his intensity. His unpredictable personality. His quick-fire temper, changing personalities, and all his games. I'd been taking it all since before we were all up in each other's space, and now I was taking even more of it and sinking deeper in the mire that was Cable. At some point, I stopped struggling to get myself free because fighting only made me sink deeper. I wouldn't tolerate any of that from anyone but Cable; I took it because it came with having feelings for him.

I gasped as Cable gave my tender clit a little tug as he pulled out of me. He turned my head so he could plant a stinging kiss on my lips and climbed off the bed, naked body stretching, muscles slick from humidity and sweat. He ran a hand over his chest and shook his messy hair out of his face as he turned and headed to the bathroom, the view to die for as he told me, "Gotta clean up and get going. I'll be out in a minute."

I wiggled to the side of the bed and reached for my big Johnny Cash shirt on the floor. I needed to go rinse off before we went anywhere, too, but before I darted up the stairs to my own room, hoping that Miglena didn't see me along the way, I had to ask, "Did you really do . . . ugh . . . that while you were thinking about me when you were in jail?" It shouldn't be sexy. There was no way that should be a turn on, but it was. He was in a terrible place, suffering for a sin that wasn't entirely his, and unknowingly I may have been the single bright spot during his stay. I liked the idea of that far more than I should have.

He paused at the doorway and looked at me over his tattooed shoulder. His blond eyebrows lifted and that smirk that seemed able to undo me pulled at his lips. "In my old room at the ranch in Loveless. In lockup. In the halfway house. In that bed you're sitting on." He pointed at the interior of the bathroom. "In that shower, at least once a day regardless if I was hanging out with some other girl or not. You've logged a lot of hours in my fantasies, Reed. You've always had a starring role, and now that I know how good you feel and how you sound when you come, you're pretty much a solo act. I told you, you're pretty much all I see when I close my eyes, and I don't know very many guys who jerk it with their eyes open."

I blinked in surprise and licked my lips. "Oh, my." That was sweet, and hot . . . and sexy as all hell.

"You're cute when you can't find something smart to say. Get it together, Reed, we have somewhere we need to be."

Once he took his very fine, perfectly muscled ass into the bathroom, I got my wits back and made the trek to my own room so I could make myself presentable. There really were landmarks all over my skin from the places Cable had been, so there was no hiding what we'd been up to, but I did tame my hair and put on something that covered up most of the obvious red spots and tiny bruises.

We were in the car on the way to Doc Howard's office when he asked how Jordan was doing. She ended up staying a little longer than the weekend after hitting it off with the guy who helped her make my man-handler leave. She wasn't exactly a fan of the new developments in my relationship with Cable, but surprisingly, she was a fan of him. They had a similar way about them that drew people in, the charisma that was such a draw. While he'd been indifferent to her at first, after she jumped in to defend me with no fear, his demeanor had changed. He was never exactly warm and welcoming to anyone, but he acknowledged Jordan the whole time she was there and actively engaged with her until she left. For Cable, that was practically a seal of approval.

"She's good. Busy learning the ropes at her new job. Her ex called her after she posted all those pictures from the party, but she didn't answer." I shrugged. "The guy she hooked up with from here actually lives in Austin, so he's not too far away from Loveless. They've been in touch, but she says she wants to focus on work." She also lectured me on birth control and losing my head over some guy when my lifelong dream was within reach. She warned me to be careful, told me not to get sex-stupid, and then ordered me to make sure Cable was good to me and reminded me to always be good to myself. She really was the best friend ever and the closer it got to the end of the summer, the more I realized just how much I was leaving behind when Texas was in my rearview mirror.

"When she's ready, she won't have to wait long to find a guy to take her ex's place. She's a knockout." I pulled into the parking lot of the doc's office and turned to look at Cable. He pushed the door open and looked at me over the top of his sunglasses. "She's also a cool chick who seems loyal to the people she loves. A smart dude will see that and snatch her up." He inclined his head to the building. "You coming in to wait for me?"

Ever since his panic attack, I sat in the tiny, dingy waiting room during his sessions in case he needed me, but he stopped talking to the doc after that episode, so it was a wasted hour. I was starting to wonder if he needed to handle this without the safety net I provided. He was weird for weeks after I witnessed his breakdown. Maybe if he knew he could open up and let all that ugly out in a safe place that I wouldn't invade, he would talk.

"Not this time. I'm going to go to the store. Miglena made me a list. I told her it was silly that we both wasted time getting stuff for the same house, so we're trading weeks." She told me that she would do all the shopping and all the cooking. She reminded me that it was her job and that she was happy to do it, but I mentioned I needed something to keep busy with while Cable was at his appointment. The woman saw and understood more than his own mother. She immediately picked up on the subtext and told me we could alternate.

His forehead puckered in a little frown but he leaned over the console and gave me a kiss before swinging his long legs out of the car. "All right. I'll text you when I'm done." He climbed out of the car and bent down, so he was looking at me with a pensive look on his face. "I've been thinking a lot about Miglena and my sisters. You think she'd ever let me meet them?"

I hummed a little and lifted a hand and let it fall uselessly back onto the steering wheel. "I think you should talk to her if that's something you really want to do. I also think that's something you should talk to the doc about. If that's a step you take, it's going to affect not only your relationship with Miglena but also the one you have with your mother and father." I wanted to believe he was emotionally strong enough to navigate those choppy waters, but I wasn't sure. If he got caught in the rapids, he would go under and make no effort to find his way up and out of the churning water.

He tilted his chin down in a jerky nod and closed the door with a little more force than was necessary.

I was still thinking about his revelation and worrying about how this session was going while I made my way through the store. I was zoned out, lost in the land of Cable, absently adding things to the cart, including all the garbage he lived on since it was on Miglena's list, when I came to a sudden, jarring stop as my cart collided with another shopper. The impact was loud as the cans in both carts rattled. I put a hand to my mouth to stifle my startled scream of surprise and rushed to apologize to the other patron.

He was a young man, probably only a year or two older than Cable, cute in a clean cut and boring way. He looked as startled by the collision as I was, but his reaction was a laugh and a wave of his hand as I tried to tell him I was sorry for having my head in the clouds.

"Don't worry about it. I was looking at my phone, so I'm as much to blame as you are. Are you okay . . ." He trailed off, obviously waiting for me to fill in the blank with my name.

"Affton, and yes, I'm okay, just a little embarrassed. I'm not usually a daydreamer."

The guy cocked his head to the side and narrowed his eyes as he considered me intently. "Affton Reed?"

I made a face and nervously played with a strand of hair. "Umm, yeah. Do I know you?"

He shook his head and gave me a megawatt smile that was nearly blinding. "Naw, not really. I'm from Loveless. Well, not originally, but I graduated from high school there. I was a senior when you were a freshman. Trip Wilson." He came toward me with an outstretched hand I only shook in order not to appear rude.

I was right about him being a little bit older than Cable, but I didn't have any clue who he was. I didn't remember him at all from school, and it was a little creepy that he remembered me after all this time. Especially since I went out of my way to be so unmemorable. I never thought I stood out, but Cable told me I didn't have to try.

"What are you doing down here in Port Aransas? One last vacation before you head off to college?" He seemed friendly enough, but there was something off about the whole situation. It made the hair on the back of my arms stand on end.

"I'm down here staying with a friend for the summer. Who could say no to a summer on the beach?" I moved back to my cart with every intention of finishing my shopping so I could get back to Cable. This guy unsettled me, but it wasn't in the fun, challenging way my troubled lover did. "I've actually got to get back. Sorry again about that bump."

"The friend you're staying with wouldn't happen to be Cable McCaffrey, would it? I knew him in school a little bit, as well. We were friendly, and I heard he was living down here after he got released from prison. Guy's been through the ringer, hasn't he? I'd love to catch up with him and see how he's doing." He moved in front of my cart as I went to move around him. Maybe he knew Cable back then, or maybe he didn't. He obviously didn't know him now, or he would know that he didn't want any more ghosts from his past showing up on his doorstep.

"The friend I'm staying with is very private and isn't a big fan of company. Good luck reconnecting with your high school pal, but it seems he isn't in a big hurry to be found if he's hiding down here." I purposely pushed my cart around him but was brought up short when his hand landed on my arm.

I glared at his fingers where they clamped on my elbow and tried to jerk away as he told me, "Don't you think the rest of the people in Loveless deserve to know that their reigning prince wasn't responsible for the princess's death? Don't they deserve to know that money still has influence when it comes to the legal system, and the wrong person can go to jail for a crime they didn't commit if the price is right? Shouldn't Cable be given the chance to tell his side of the story? Don't you think people should know that Jenna Maley was the one at fault? She was driving, and she was the one who supplied your boy with the drugs that were found in his system after the crash." His fingers tightened their hold, and I had to really struggle to jerk free from his grasp. "Cable took the fall. His parents paid that multimillion-dollar civil suit and the Maleys paid to cover up their daughter's involvement. There is no justice in any of that."

I took a deep breath and let it out slowly, so I didn't lose my shit in the middle of the grocery store. I didn't know how he knew all that he knew, but I did know that Cable wouldn't appreciate any of it.

"That story doesn't belong to either of us and the only person around to tell it doesn't want to. He's been through enough. He doesn't need to get caught up in your quest for justice, or whatever this is."

"It's justice for him, Affton. You have to see that."

I bit the tip of my tongue to keep the truth in. I did see it, but I also saw Cable on his hands and knees that first time, struggling to breathe as tears rolled over his face when he tried to process everything that happened that night. He didn't need justice, he needed peace and forgiveness. He'd made his choices and suffered for them. He didn't need anyone else weighing in or sensationalizing them.

"If you ask Cable, justice has already been served. He did what he thought was right after doing something he knew was very wrong. He's trying to move on and do better. He doesn't need you dragging him back to the worst night of his life. Leave him alone. He's not going to give you what you want."

The man let me leave, and I felt his eyes follow me down the aisle.

I was sure I was being set up, that I was hovering on the edge of a trap.

I'd given him nothing specific, but he made me feel as if I'd given him exactly what he came for.

I needed to tell Cable trouble was coming and hoped that he was ready to ride the waves of it all the way to shore. After all, he'd been practicing staying on his feet when the storm swept through all summer long.

sixteen

CABLE

THE DOC HAD on another one of those loud, ugly Hawaiian shirts, and as soon as I hit the door of his office, he asked me if I'd rather spend my session with him today out on the beach instead of on his couch. He mentioned having early morning appointments and missing his chance to catch a few waves today. I knew he was more beach bum than certified medical professional, so I readily agreed. It was a short walk from his building to the shore, and once we were there, he immediately kicked off his flip-flops and sank his toes into the sand with a sigh. I took a seat next to him and let the warmth of the sand sink into my skin.

"I love the water. That's why I moved down here from Dallas after my divorce." He looked at me, but he had on a pair of dark Ray-Bans so I couldn't read his expression. "Why did you decide to come here when you got out of the program? Your relationship with your father is questionable, at best, and from the bits and pieces I've gathered, this place doesn't hold the best memories for you."

I pulled out a smoke and lit the tip as I contemplated his question. "I love the water, too. I've always been drawn to it, and I didn't think anyone would bother to look for me down here when I got out of jail. I wanted to be left alone."

He nudged me with his elbow and asked me if he could bum a cigarette. I'd never seen him light up and he never smelled like cigarettes, so I was surprised, but relinquished one without a fight. He made a noise of pleasure as he inhaled a toxic breath and turned his head back to the water. "How do you feel about this summer since you haven't had a chance to experience the solitude you were after?"

I grunted and flicked ash on the sand. "I dunno, I guess it made me realize I was never as alone as I thought. My mom is all over my ass, Affton doesn't let me get away with shit, and Miglena . . ." I trailed off and tried to put in order how I thought about the woman who had always been there in the background of my upbringing. "She's always done her best to let me know someone who cares is around. I only saw her in the summertime, and I always knew something was up with her and my dad, but when it ended between them, she still seemed to care. I guess I realized this summer it wasn't an act. She does care, and being alone with my asshole thoughts and dickhead brain isn't always what it's cracked up to be. It's good to hear what other people have to say because the shit I tell myself is what gets me into trouble."

He took a long drag on his cigarette and reached up to push his sunglasses onto the top of his head. "Did you ever stop and wonder why your brain has the tendency to be a dickhead, Cable?"

I shrugged and reached behind my head so I could pull my t-shirt off. I tucked it into the waistband of my jeans and tilted my head back, so the sun touched my face. "My dad is an asshole, and I look just like him, so I assume I inherited some of his assholishness as well. My mom is a control freak, and both have more money than God. I never wanted for anything, and I grew up knowing that the basic rules and regulations didn't apply to me. I was treated special, even though I never did anything to earn anyone's praise or approval. I've always been an entitled little shit, but I've never done anything with it to help anyone else or make the world a better place. I always figured my brain knew I didn't deserve anyone else's respect, and it took every opportunity to remind me just how worthless I really am." It was easy to give him all of that with the sun shining on my face and the sound of the waves blocking out the noise of my racing heart.

The doc made a considering noise in his throat as he continued to puff on the cigarette. "You're young. Maybe you haven't found your purpose and place yet. It's a lot to operate under the assumption that just because you were born privileged that you would automatically have a cause or passion to champion. You had to grow up, Cable, and that always comes with success and failure. Not even the wealthy are immune to the downs that often follow the ups. Typically, they're just better at hiding it than the rest of us. Money can't fix everything, kiddo."

He was right about that. It had never been able to fix me, and it hadn't done a damn thing to save Jenna.

"Money isn't the problem, Doc. Even without it, there are days when I can't get out of bed. There are moments when all I want to do is walk into that water until it covers me up and sweeps me away. I drift. I've always drifted. That's how I ended up an addict. Even when I felt shitty when I was coming down, I still felt something. I wasn't numb like I am when I'm sober." Affton was the closest thing I'd ever found to an anchor. She was the only thing that made me want to have my feet touching the ground more often than not.

The doc flicked his cigarette out in front of us and crossed his arms over his bent knees.

"That's why I asked if you ever wondered *why* you feel that way. You're smart despite your choices, Cable. You should recognize that feeling that disconnected from the people who care about you and not being able to process how your actions will ultimately affect others isn't how our minds typically operate. You've been living your life as if your only option is to be this way when that very well might not be the case. You may have some crossed wires or a chemical imbalance. That's not out of the ordinary and has nothing to do with how you were raised or the benefits you were born with. A little tune-up and commitment to using therapy to address your issues might make a world of difference. That drifting you feel would lessen, but you would learn how to deal with the weight of your choices. That kind of accountability would be good for you, my friend."

I made a face and finished my cigarette. "Seriously? You think giving the recovering addict drugs is a solution?"

He chuckled and shook his head. "I think there are options that might help you. Are you ready for any of that yet?" He shrugged. "Hard to tell, because you aren't honest with me and I don't think you're honest with yourself most of the time. I do know that you do not have to live the way you've been living. I do know that you don't have to risk your life and the hearts of the people who love you if you choose not to." He sighed and laid back on the sand. He folded his hands over his stomach and closed his eyes. "Where was your pretty little companion today? She usually hangs around waiting for you."

I bristled when he called her pretty again. "She had an errand to run. She's not my companion; she's my . . ." I paused for a second, not sure what Affton was, but I knew she was sure as hell more important to me than a companion. "Friend. She's probably the best friend I've ever had, actually."

It was true. She was my best friend, on top of being the best sex I'd ever had. She was up for whatever I brought to her. She had a dynamite body, one I now knew inside and out. It was more than the fact that I was the only one who had ever touched her, tasted her, filled her up, and made her scream. That made me dizzy with delight every time I thought about it, but what really got me was that both my body and my mind were invested every single time we were together. I wasn't fucking to forget. I was fucking to make memories. I wanted to remember every sigh, every gasp, every groan, and every single sound she made in between. I wanted the way her eyes turned amethyst when she came burned into my brain and the way she tightened and pulsed around me, only me, etched across my soul.

I leaned back on my elbows and squinted up at the sky. "I told her about the accident the other night." I'd pulled her into the darkest places I had inside of me, and she still fell asleep next to me that night. She still held onto me and encouraged me to do better, to be better. She didn't give up on me and even showed me that she had a little bit of the dark inside of her as well.

"That's good. How do you feel now that you found someone you trust enough to share all the details of what happened that night?" He sounded sleepy, but when I looked over at him, I could see that he was listening intently. The guy was good. He took me somewhere I was comfortable, somewhere that calmed me down, and got me to spill my guts. I hated his office and how out of place he looked in it. He fit in here on the beach, and it was so much easier to open up to a beach bum than it was to a shrink in an ugly shirt. He manipulated the master manipulator, and I had to respect him for that.

I chuckled a little. "Well, I didn't have a panic attack if that's what you're worried about." That was probably because I'd just come harder than I ever had in my entire life and she was still naked and draped over me. "We were both pretty vulnerable at the time. She made it easy to spill my guts." Because I did trust her even when everything inside of me rebelled at the idea.

He made another noise and peeled an eye open. "I can't say I'm surprised the dynamic between the two of you shifted into something intimate. There is obvious affection between you and you're both exceptionally attractive individuals."

I scowled at him and bit out, "Stop talking about how she looks. It weirds me out, and I still don't think it's ethical . . . or appropriate."

He laughed and flashed his teeth at me. "I was wondering when those protective instincts were going to show back up. You showed them before when I first brought up her appearance, and it made you obviously uncomfortable. I've been wondering if it was a fluke or not. I'm glad that you not only trust her enough to share with her, but care about her enough to defend her as well. Those are normal responses when you care deeply for someone, Cable. You are doing it exactly right. Have you two talked about what all of this means when the summer is over? You're well on your way to getting control of your finances back, and I'm sure Affton has plans for her future. She strikes me as a determined and bright young woman."

We didn't talk about it. It was an elephant in the room that gained weight every day. We also didn't talk about how she was still reporting back to my mom every couple of days on my progress or the way she felt about taking money for keeping an eye on me now that she spent pretty much every night in my bed. There was a lot we were avoiding, and it was much easier to have endless amounts of sex and slip deeper into whatever it was that we were building between us than it was to try and tackle all the obstacles that were standing in our way.

"She's going to Berkeley. She wants to be a shrink. Her mom died when she was little from an overdose, and she wants to stop that from happening to any other little kid who might have a parent in trouble. She's got a huge heart." So big there was no way she could hold onto the entire thing by herself. Eventually, she was going to have to let someone else help her carry the weight of it around.

"Ahhh . . . no wonder she's so understanding and sympathetic toward you. She has first-hand knowledge of how hard it can be to love someone struggling with an addiction. She seems to be a special kind of girl, Cable. I suggest you do your best not to mess things up." He closed his eyes again. "Put in the effort, kid. You won't regret it."

I pulled out another smoke and stuck it between my lips without lighting it. I narrowed my eyes against the glare off the water and watched as tourists jumped around in the gently rolling waves that hit the shore. "I don't want to mess it up, but I will. That's the way I work." I'd never wanted not to screw something up as badly as this thing with Affton, but I would, and even in knowing that, I still had no desire to leave her alone. I told her I was going to ruin her and she ignored the warning.

"Maybe you will, maybe you won't. Either way, you are human and are having a human experience. You are present for it. You are embracing it. What you aren't doing is drifting." He sighed again. "And as I mentioned, there are options out there. If you want to get serious about making positive changes for your long-term health and well-being, you let me know. I'd like to see you go from recovering to recovered, Cable. I'd like to see you succeed."

I lit my cigarette and puffed on it silently for a few minutes. My hands were covered in sand when I pushed myself back into a sitting position. I brushed them off and fished my cell phone out of my back pocket. I had a missed call from Affton and two from my mom. I really needed to get my head out of my ass and call my mom back; it'd been months since I had spoken to her . . . I'd been content to let Affton do my talking for me. The woman had to be losing her patience, and I didn't want her showing up unannounced. I really didn't want her to walk in on something she shouldn't because that would affect Affton.

"We have ten minutes left. You got any other words of wisdom for me or can I call my girl back and have her pick me up?"

The doc peeled his eyes open and gave me a grin. "You can take off if you want. I'm going to enjoy the sun until my next appointment. Afraid she's not a fan of fresh air and sunshine."

I barked out a dry laugh at that and rose to my feet. I had sand in my shoes that I needed to shake out, but I would take that over the beige walls any day. "Any time you want a chance to take a patient out of the office, I'm your guy." I stretched my arms up over my head. "And if you ever want to do a session on the water, I'm down for that, too. I'm a much better surfer than I am a patient."

He dipped his chin in acknowledgment. "We might have to try that. Surfing therapy. I could get on board with that, literally. I'll see you next week, Cable. Think about what we talked about today. Talk it over with your girl and maybe your mom. Get some other opinions and do some research, but remember that the choice is ultimately yours. You can keep going on the way you are, or you can see about making some changes. Either way, you have people in your life who will love and support you."

I muttered goodbye and made my way back to his office building. Affton's battered, old car was already parked out front, and she was pacing back and forth in a very agitated manner. She was tugging at her bottom lip so hard I was worried she might rip the damn thing off her face. She was also mumbling under her breath. She was so caught up in her fit that she didn't respond when I called her name and didn't stop moving until I was close enough to catch her shoulders in my hands. When I pulled her to a stop and asked 'what's wrong?' she immediately started shivering, and that lip she was yanking on trembled making me think she was about to cry.

"Do you know someone named Trip Wilson?" She leaned back on the trunk of her car and stared up at me with wide, imploring eyes.

"Yeah. We went to school with him. He was a few years older though. His parents bought the *Loveless Gazette* when they came to town. Trip considers himself a big shot reporter. He's been on my case about the night of the accident ever since I got locked up. He wants an exclusive or some garbage like that. I've refused to talk to him, but that hasn't kept him from calling and being a pain in the ass. Why?"

She leaned forward until her forehead was pressed against my throat. I wrapped an arm around her shoulders as both of hers went around my waist. Her hands locked at the small of my back as her entire body shivered. "I ran into him at the grocery store. Well, he ran into me. He bumped his cart into mine and then started talking about you. He knows you're here, Cable. He also knows more about that night than he should. He knows you weren't driving. He knows you took the blame to cover up Jenna's involvement."

I swore long and loud over the top of her head. My hands tightened convulsively on the back of her head and curled into fists in her hair. "How could he know any of that? You're the only one I told."

She shook her head against my neck, and her hands curled into the fabric of my t-shirt. "I don't know, Cable, but he knows. He was talking about justice and small-town politics. He mentioned not letting the Maleys manipulate the system to protect their daughter's image. He was intense, and he didn't seem to care when I told him you just want to move on with your life, that what's done is done."

"Fuck me." I didn't want to deal with Wilson, and I wanted to deal with the fallout of whatever he was planning on doing with that information even less. This was exactly why I didn't want to go back to Loveless.

She pulled her head back and lifted her lips in a wobbly grin. "Okay, but I don't think that will solve the problem."

Her sassy response startled a laugh out of me, and I couldn't resist dropping a kiss on her trembling lips. "No, it won't, but it's a surefire way to make me forget about the problem for a little bit. Let's get the groceries home and distract each other for as long as it takes to help me forget."

She blew out a breath and let me take her hand. "We can't avoid dealing with all the hard things forever."

She was right, we couldn't. But we couldn't fix them either, so we might as well focus on the *hard thing* that was currently between us. That one we could definitely deal with, and the solution was a no-brainer.

seventeen

AFFTON

I LET OUT a yelp of fright and curled into Cable's side. I'd spent most of the movie with my face buried in his shoulder, peeking through my fingers when I thought it was safe. I never really got the appeal of horror movies, way too much blood and guts for my taste, but I understood why he enjoyed them. I could feel his heart racing, and every once in awhile, he jumped just as high as I did. For a boy who spent so much time trying to chase down a real emotion, fear was as good as anything else that might come along. He got jacked up on the thrill of being scared because that was a normal reaction he didn't have to search for.

I heard him chuckle from above my head and his hand slid comfortingly up and down my arm as I burrowed deeper into him. "I told you we could watch something else."

I shook my head in the negative and opened my fingers wide enough to look at the massive screen just in time to see another amorous teen lose her life. If you were a pretty girl, you didn't last long in these movies. If you were a pretty girl who got down and dirty with one of the boys, you died even sooner. It didn't seem fair that as soon as the characters figured out the joys of sex, they took a machete to the neck.

"You sat through the entire *Fast and the Furious* franchise for me; I'll make it through this *Friday the 13th* binge." He insisted Jason was the coolest of all the horror movie killers. With his herky-jerky movements and the hockey mask, I was having a hard time figuring out how he chased all those teenagers through the woods without falling on his face. He didn't appear to get more coordinated or graceful as the movies progressed.

Cable's hand curled around the side of my neck underneath my hair and held me to his chest. I felt the brush of his lips against the top of my head and heard him laugh lightly. He was doing more of that lately . . . laughing. He'd started to take his sessions with Doc Howard more seriously. The two of them had even started spending the morning on the water together once a week. He talked to Miglena about his sisters. She was hesitant and unsure. She loved Cable as if he was her own, obviously, but she still had a complicated relationship with his father, and because she was an extraordinary woman, she worried about what meeting them would do to his mother. She didn't want to lose her job or put her girls in an awkward, possibly emotionally stressful situation. She told him she would think about introducing him to them, but she wasn't ready to pull the trigger just yet. He still hadn't talked to his mother, and her calls were coming more rapidly than before. He was making progress in the present, but the past and the future remained a convoluted mess.

My dad called and asked if he could come down and visit me. He sounded lonely and a little lost. It broke my heart to tell him no, but he still had no idea what I was really doing in Port Aransas, or that his job hinged on my success. Cable overheard the conversation, and when I told him I was going to have to go back to Loveless to see my dad and pack up my stuff before I left for California, he got quiet. Not a normal kind of quiet, but the kind that let me know he was gone. He slipped somewhere inside of his head far, far away where I couldn't reach him, and he stayed there for two days. I couldn't touch him, not physically or emotionally. He shut down, and he shut me out. It hurt. It hurt even worse when I realized what was going to happen when I actually left. If the idea of me going had that strong of an effect on him, actually leaving would cut him off from me completely. There would be no long distance love. No effort to make things work through the space that separated us.

It killed, but I had no choice other than to let death take me. I couldn't walk away from him, even if it would be better for both of us in the long run. I waited him out, and when he found his way back to me, I was there. We spent the next few days being lazy, reconnecting (having copious amounts of sex all over the house), and enjoying each other's company while we still could. Which led to the movie marathon that had been taking place all day. I told him I would commit to watching all the Jason movies if he would watch the *Fast and the Furious* movies first. I didn't tell him that he kind of reminded me of a much younger Paul Walker, and that's why the franchise was one of my favorites. He was a good sport about it until *Tokyo Drift*. That was almost a deal breaker. He powered through only because I put my hands in his pants and distracted him with a hand job that left us both messy in the best way. I was about to tell him it was his turn to distract me when my attention was caught by the twisting, intricate ink that was spread all over his shoulder. We were naked together on a very regular basis, but I was usually distracted by the other parts of him to pay attention to his ink. Up close, the lines were mesmerizing.

I touched a fingertip to the black ink and traced it where it wrapped around his bicep. "Did you have these when we were in school together or did you get them after?" After would mean he let someone drill into his skin while he was in jail. The idea made me shiver uncomfortably. We always used protection, but there was a time or two when we got carried away, and protection came as an afterthought. I wanted to keep the way he made me feel inside forever, but anything that he could pick up from a dirty needle, not so much.

He chuckled and gave me a squeeze. "Most of them I got before I got locked up. Went to a guy in Austin. He drew up some stuff that was okay. I took the drawings and made them better. He was impressed." He held the hand that wasn't holding me out and wiggled his fingers so that the spider web on the back of his hand moved and the black widow danced. "I did get this in the pen. There was this kid who got locked up a few months before my release who was a tattoo artist on the outside. His older brother was in a gang, and his shop got caught up in some nasty business because of those connections. The brother's gang had a whole crew on the inside that offered him protection and set him up with everything he would need to do ink while he was locked up. We shared a cell for a few months, shared some stories, so he hooked me up."

I cringed, and he must've seen where my mind was at because he dropped another kiss on the top of my head and told me softly, "I'm clean, Reed. Haven't been with anyone but you since I got out, and I got tested before I went into the sober living house. I would never put you at risk."

I traced the top of his shoulder. "So, you drew this?"

His chin lowered and touched the crown of my head. I was cuddling now instead of cowering. "I did. Figured if it was going to be on my body forever, I might as well be responsible for it."

I leaned back so I could look up at him. He took advantage

of my new pose and dropped a kiss on my lips. I immediately ran my tongue over the moisture left behind, tasting him and savoring that smoky, sunshine flavor that was his and his alone. "You're an amazing artist, Cable. Maybe you need to look at doing something with that for your future."

He blinked at me a few times and then cocked his head to the side. "Do you really believe I'm an artist?"

I brushed the end of my nose along the edge of his scruffy jaw and made my way up to his ear. Once I was there, I gently sank my teeth into the lobe and whispered. "Yes, you are. I told you I peeked at your sketchbook. You're ridiculously talented, and your tattoos are beautiful. I'm not surprised you designed them."

I skimmed my hand over his bare chest, pausing to rub lazy circles over the flat of his nipple with my thumb. I heard him suck in a breath and the hand that was still holding the back of my head slid in a smooth line all the way down my spine so that it was resting on my backside. All I had on was one of his t-shirts and a pair of boy-short panties that did little to keep him out as his hand went in search of warm skin.

"No one's ever really called me anything before."

I moved, so I kissed the side of his neck and nibbled along his collarbone. My fingers took a detour to those carved abs of his, tracking the defined lines between them and tickling the tensed muscle under the taut skin. "What do you mean?"

He grunted and shifted his weight as his cock started to stiffen and lengthen against the thin fabric of the long basketball shorts he was lounging around in. There was no missing that monster, but I had no desire to run and hide from this one.

"I was never a good student. I was never a good son. I've never been a boyfriend or even a friend to anyone. I've never had to work hard or be dedicated to anything. I'm not nice. I'm not successful or driven. The only thing I've ever been is an addict. I've been called that and now a felon and an ex-con. But never anything good or worthwhile. That's the first thing anyone's ever called me that doesn't make me cringe. That's something I wouldn't mind being."

He pulled in a sharp breath when I dipped a finger into the indentation of his belly button, and raked my nails through the thatch of golden hair that narrowed down to his obvious hardness. I let my lips follow the path my fingers had forged, slicking my tongue over his nipple and grinning when the motions made him growl.

I pushed my hand past the elastic at the top of his shorts and sighed when I encountered steel wrapped in velvet. I loved that he was so hard and so soft at the same time. I loved that his erection kicked in response to my touch and that he was already damp at the tip. I rolled my thumb across the silky head, spreading wetness and making his body clench as I went. I shifted my weight so that I was sprawled on my stomach, head above his lap, his cock throbbing and full in front of my face.

I rubbed my cheek against his lower stomach and sighed. The hot air from my breath made his thighs clench and his hand returned to the back of my head as the other smoothed over my ass, his fingers dipping into places and touching spots I hadn't been brave enough to let him explore before now.

"You don't have to try to be an artist, Cable, you just are. You're talented, and you're a whole lot of other things, as well." I swiped the flat of my tongue over his slick head and wrapped my hand around the rigid shaft. He grunted, and his hips lifted involuntarily, pushing his wide tip past my parted lips.

I sucked him in obediently, swirling my tongue around his width and twisting my hand around his base after sliding it up and down the part of him I couldn't take in. He groaned, hand fisting in my hair as he guided my bobbing motion up and down. I loved the way he felt in my mouth. I got off on having control of his big body. I was intrigued by the way his fingers felt as they tickled and tripped between the globes of my ass. It made me twitch and moan against the firm flesh I was licking and sucking for all I was worth.

I knew he enjoyed it when I traced the thick vein that ran along the underside of his cock. He liked it even more when I pressed my tongue against the sensitive spot right below the tip. I flicked my tongue over that tender skin and sucked as more liquid beaded up at his slit. He growled my name and pulled the handful of hair he was clutching. I was good at this because he taught me exactly what to do. Luckily for both of us, I didn't have too much of a gag reflex, and I actually got off on getting him off. I didn't mind going down on him, which was good considering how much time he spent with his face buried between my legs. Turnabout was fair play.

I gasped and jerked on him, my hand tightening and stilling as I felt the press of his fingers against that secret, sensitive place no one had ever touched before. At first, his touch was light, testing, and teasing. When I lowered my head another inch or so, until his tip was touching the back of my throat and making my eyes water, I felt him press in. I thought my body was going to levitate off the leather recliners. I was practically vibrating, caught between curiosity and terror. He always made me act out of control and pushed me to feel and experience things I never felt before. That unexpected finger pulled out and pushed back in, which had me dragging my teeth across his shaft in surprise.

He hissed in reaction and tugged on my hair. "Get up on your knees, Reed. Give me the hand that isn't working my dick."

It took a minute to move. When I lifted into that touch on my backside, he sank deeper and made me shudder. I didn't know if I was into it yet, but I was sure I didn't hate it. He stopped his persistent prodding when I lifted. I swallowed hard on the erection that was stretching my jaw as wide as it would go and put my shaking hand in his. He immediately dragged it between my legs and put my fingers between my dripping wet folds. He pressed my fingers to my swollen, aching center and told me, "Don't stop touching yourself until I tell you to, Reed."

He held onto my wrist as I started slow, steady circles and continued to suck him down as far as I could take him. I had to concentrate because I wasn't getting enough air. I tingled because all my nerve endings were alive and dancing with one another. It was a lot to take in, and I wasn't sure I could handle it.

Once I had a rhythm down and was moaning and grinding against my own fingers, Cable's talented touch was back at that place that had always been forbidden. He caressed the curve of my ass, rubbed his hand over each side, and then I felt that foreign pressure and his finger pressing in once again.

I was sure the top of my head was going to come off. Pleasure slithered through every muscle, passion pooled heavy in all my limbs. There wasn't a place I didn't feel. There wasn't a single part of my body that didn't feel owned by him. I didn't need to be in control because he was. He played me like I was an expensive instrument and my responses were music to his ears. I squeezed his cock and swallowed around the tip. He swore, and his hips lifted off the leather.

I was so wet that I could feel it covering my fingers and dripping down my legs. He must have felt it, too, because he stopped playing and really started working me over the same way I was working him. Pleasure tripped up my spine, and my thighs started shaking. My body fluttered, and my heart raced. I could barely keep moving as sensation overwhelmed me, but luckily, his body couldn't take it anymore either and spilled across my tongue as I collapsed in a heap across his lap.

I wiped my mouth on the material of his shorts where they were bunched up across his thighs and sighed in boneless satisfaction. His hand went from pulling my hair to stroking it softly, and his fingers went from fucking my ass to drawing random circles on the rounded skin.

I blew out a breath and told him quietly, "You are more than an artist, Cable. You are a good friend; at least, you can be, and you have been to me. You're a recovering addict, which means you are trying and making an effort. You are a survivor. That crash could have killed you. Losing someone you cared about so horribly could have been the end of you. Going to prison for a crime you weren't responsible for," I curled my hand around his knee. "That could have broken you, but you came out mostly whole." I rolled over on my back so I could look up at him and grinned because he was obviously taking in everything I said. "You're also dynamite in bed . . . and on the water. You're a lot of things, Cable, and always have been."

He traced the bridge of my nose and the line of my cheeks. His voice was low and serious when he told me, "You're a lot of things, too, Reed, and I'm pretty fond of all of them."

That was good to know because I was fond of all the things he was, too . . . even the bad things. The only difference was that I would still love all those things when I was halfway across the country and he . . . well, who knew how long he would remember all the things he liked about me once I was gone.

I was pretty sure I knew him well enough to know he wouldn't remember we were something worth fighting for.

eighteen

CABLE

"WHAT ARE YOU going to do when summer is over? Are you going to stay here or go back to Loveless?" Affton was leaning against the railing of the deck looking out over the water as the sun went down. The sea breeze was blowing her pale hair around her face and across her eyes. She had on another one of those dresses that made me think dirty thoughts and her feet were bare. Innocence and temptation all wrapped in the perfect package. I wanted her more than I'd ever wanted a hit or a bump.

I had my feet propped up on the railing next to her, and my sketchpad open on my lap. I told her I was drawing the sunset, but somewhere along the way she'd worked her way into the picture and I'd spent the last thirty minutes trying to make sure I got her freckles just right and the curve of her jaw perfect. I was drawing her because it was the only way I would remember her when we went our separate ways.

She'd been trying to hedge her way around what was next for me, and for us, over the last few days. I didn't want to think about it, so I didn't, but it seemed like Affton had finally reached her limit of tolerance for my evasion.

"If you decide to come back to Loveless, I'll be there for a little while. I should pack up the things from home I'm taking with me to Berkeley, and I want to spend some time with my dad." I'd noticed she'd been dodging his calls the same way I was dodging my mom's. When I'd asked about it, she shrugged and told me she wasn't sure what to tell him and that she hated lying to him. I wanted to feel guilty about it, but I didn't. It meant I got her all to myself. She was still talking about me going back to Loveless, and I had to force myself to concentrate on what she was saying. "If you're in town, we can hang out before I leave for school." She caught her flying hair in her fingers and turned her head to look at me. I took a deep drag from my smoke and shaded in the hollow at her throat. She wanted it when I kissed her there. She wanted it when I kissed her anywhere and everywhere. For someone who was so controlled and collected in most things, she was surprisingly open-minded and adventurous when it came to anything carnal. For a girl with boundaries a mile high and a heart encased in steel, she was wide open to any and all possibilities when she was naked and turned on. "I would like that, in case you were wondering. I want to see you before I go. I want to spend as much time with you as I can, Cable."

I've had people want to spend time around me before, but she was the first who actually wanted to spend time *with* me. That was why I didn't want to think about what was going to happen when she was gone and I was left to my own devices once again. I couldn't get my head around being accountable for myself. I couldn't imagine working to be better if it wasn't for her. She was the reason I learned to float. She was the one thing that made me keep my head above water the entire summer.

"I don't know where I'm going." I inhaled hard on the end of my cigarette and squinted at her through the smoke between us. "I don't think I'm ready to go back to the ranch. I'm not sure I can ever go back to Loveless. My dad's going to want his love nest back, eventually, so I can't stay here indefinitely, either. I'll have access to my trust fund again, so maybe I'll go somewhere I've never been, hit up some places where no one knows who I am or what I've done."

She sighed heavily and turned back to face the water. Her shoulders fell as she leaned over the railing. "So, instead of drifting away inside your own head, you're going to actually be a drifter." She sounded disappointed and sad. "You do know that you can't outrun your issues, right? All you're going to do is take them with you to a new place. Your view might change, but the luggage is going to be crammed full of the same garbage. All you're going to do is haul it from one destination to another. When are you going to settle somewhere and unpack?"

I tossed the sketchpad to the side and put my smoke out on the wood of the deck. I put my hands behind my head and watched as the sky glowed orange and red with celestial fire. She wanted answers I didn't have. I never wanted to hurt her, and I never wanted anyone close enough to hurt me, but that was where we were headed, and it didn't matter where she was going or where I ended up.

"Cracked that suitcase open with you this summer, Reed. It isn't nearly as heavy as it always has been. It'll be much easier to move around from place to place." She made a strangled sound low in her throat so I climbed to my feet and moved behind her. I braced my hands on either side of her body and pressed my front into the stiff line of her back. I rested my chin on her shoulder and felt her damp cheek press into mine. I hated that she was crying over me and because of me, but she wanted to face reality, and ours wasn't pretty or easy. "You've always known where you're going, Affton, and I've always been lost. Eventually, I'll find my way to wherever it is I'm supposed to be, but we both know that place isn't anywhere close to where you're headed."

She sniffed a little and lifted a hand to rub at her wet face. She put her hand next to mine on the railing and whispered, "It could be."

I sighed and turned my head so I could kiss her cheek. The beach behind the house was surprisingly empty, the only sounds were our whispered words and the beating of our hearts as they raced toward each other and away from the heavy truth that was hanging over us. "It could be if I were a different person, if I weren't bound to fuck everything up. The last thing you need is to spend all your time trying to fix me when you're working on building your future. You have always been made to do great things, Affton. Anyone who spends more than five minutes with you knows that." I wanted to keep her, but for once in my life could recognize how selfish and self-serving that was. For once, I wanted to do the right thing, not necessarily for myself, but for her. She would take me, making probably the first bad choice of her life, and I couldn't let her do that. "This summer with you is as close to great as I'm gonna get, and honestly, it's been more than I deserve. I didn't want anyone in my space, but I'm grateful that you are the person who showed up to share that space with me while I tried to figure shit out. This is the second time you saved me."

I moved my head so I could kiss her jawline and up behind her ear. She tilted her head to give me better access, and her sniffles turned into soft sighs. "I guess that makes us even then. You saved me twice this summer, as well."

I wrapped an arm around her middle and pulled her back more

firmly into the curve of my body. Her hips fit perfectly against mine. She sucked in her stomach when I shifted my hold so my hand covered the full roundness of her breast over the light fabric of her dress. I knew for sure she didn't have a bra on under the flowy fabric because I watched her get dressed this morning. We hadn't had to go anywhere, no call in for a drug test today, so she never bothered to put one on. Her nipple beaded up and poked into the palm of my hand as I moved my lips from her ear to the side of her neck. I licked a wet line down to where her neck met her shoulder and took a bite at that sensitive bend. She shivered against me and lifted one of her hands so that it covered mine on her chest. My thumb was rolling over her aroused flesh, making it rasp against the fabric of her dress.

"We can't control where we're headed, but we can make the most out of where we are right now." I couldn't see anything beyond her, and that was scary because there was a time in my life where I couldn't see anything beyond my next hit or my next line. She made me feel better than any of that stuff did, but when she was gone, I had no idea how I was supposed to find my way back to those kinds of feelings without my vices to get me there. I was going to be cold again, empty and alone. I'd spent most of my life that way, but now that I knew there was a different way to be, it was going to suck going backward.

I put my other hand on her thigh where the hem of her dress rested. I felt her skin pebble up in reaction, and she shifted slightly against me. My zipper started to dig into my dick, and all the blood rushed from my brain to other places in my body. I got hard when she breathed, but when she wiggled against me and subtly pushed her breast harder into my touch, I turned rigid. There was no give where my cock was concerned, and I made that known by pressing the stiff length into the fullness of her backside. She sucked in a breath and curled her hand into a fist on the wooden beam where she was leaning.

"We should go inside." Her voice was strained and thin. A mixture of desire and resignation threaded throughout her voice indicating she understood this was all we had . She rubbed her cheek into mine and pressed back into my seeking cock. I wanted my jeans and her dress gone so I could rock into that sweet valley in front of me. I wanted to bend her over a little bit more, so I could drag my tip through her wetness and sink into her pulsing heat. I wanted to get on my knees and put my mouth on her as the setting sun reflected the colors of fire off the water, making the sound of the waves hitting the shoreline battle for supremacy over her screams of pleasure and moans of delight. I wanted to take her without a thought as to who might be watching or who might come along while I was buried deep inside of her. I wanted to claim her, make her mine, and have the rest of the world know it.

I let my hand move up her leg, chasing goosebumps and feeling her stiffen as I took more of her dress up with me. When I got to the top of her thigh, I let the material go so that it covered my hand as I traced the seam of her pretty, lacy panties.

I put my lips to her ear and told her, "I dig it right here." I really did. Here with her, with the water, the thrill of being outside and doing something that was usually done behind closed doors. I'd had sex in public places before, but it was always rushed, and I was usually too high to appreciate the natural rush of anticipation and excitement that made my blood heat and my skin tingle. I was too fucked up to care. All I was after was the release, it didn't matter where I was or whom I was with. Neither of those things were true now. I cared about Affton, and I cared about this moment in a place that helped soothe all my jagged edges.

"Cable . . ." She was hesitant and nervous, but she didn't protest when I hooked a finger along the side of her underwear and started to pull them down. I had to let go of her breast so I could lower myself to my knees behind her. I smoothed my hands along the firm line of the back of her legs, taking her undergarment with them, and getting an eyeful of her perfectly shaped ass while I was down there.

"No one can see you. The deck is up too high, and the slats in the railing keep you covered. Anyone who happens by will simply think we're two people cuddling during the sunset. It's romantic."

She snorted and looked down at me as I nudged her knees slightly apart so I could get my hand between her legs.

"I don't think romantic is the right word for it." She shifted her feet and bit down on her lip to stifle a gasp as my fingers found her damp center. She was already slick and hot, her body welcoming and ready, even if the rest of her wasn't.

I grinned up at her and put my free hand on her hip so that her dress folded in the back but was still down and covering her in the front. I was the only one who could see her sweet, slippery folds. I was the only one who could feel her body quiver and quake as I slipped my fingers inside of her and flicked them back and forth. I was the only one who could taste her, and I wanted to eat her up.

"Tilt your hips back toward me a little bit." She muttered something under her breath but obeyed my command. She was always so responsive when we were together this way. She was chasing after the same sensation as I was, always eager to feel the things only I made her feel.

I sank my teeth into the plump flesh of her backside, which made her yelp and look back at me through narrowed eyes. I grinned up at her, pulled my wet fingers out of her dripping center, and stuck them in my mouth. Her eyes widened in surprise, but they quickly got heavy-lidded and dropped with desire.

"You gotta keep quiet, Reed, or the jig is up." I reached in front of her and circled her clit with quick strokes. "Or you can be loud. Doesn't matter to me. I'll know how I make you feel, either way." Because I would have her pleasure all over my tongue.

I put my mouth over her and started to lick and fuck her with my tongue. I couldn't help but grin against her opening as she gave a startled little shriek. She pushed her hips back against my face and grabbed my wrist so she could grind against my fingers as I toyed with her clit. I could feel her body quickening and pulsing around me. Her thighs were shaking, and she lifted on her toes to give me more access. I growled in approval and sank my tongue more deeply into her. She moaned in response, and I heard her say my name. Nothing ever sounded better, my name on her lips as the waves broke.

I tugged on her tight little clit harder than I normally would and felt how much she was into it as her pleasure rushed across my tongue. She tasted so good and responded so sweetly. All I wanted to do was make her react this way all the time. She was amazing when she was rigid and uptight, but when she let loose and let go, she was spectacular.

"Cable . . ." There was a warning in her tone, and I heard voices drifting up from somewhere out on the sand. They were laughing and chattering away, but all I could focus on was how close she was to coming and how hard my cock was. I didn't care about them; I cared about her and making the most of every minute we had left together.

I gave her one last, long lick and lifted to my feet. I opened my pants and pulled my cock out. It was pulsing in my fist, wet at the tip and dying to be inside of her. It took a minute to pull a condom out of my wallet and roll it down the shaft. I kept waiting for her to change her mind as the voices got louder and closer, but she waited silently in front of me, eyes locked on the water. I squeezed a handful of her ass as I braced one hand on the railing and pressed my hips into hers. She whimpered a little bit and leaned back against me, tilting her head as my lips landed on her neck.

"They think we're cuddling, remember?" This was as far from cuddling as we could get, and if anyone looked close enough, they would know that.

I used my hold on my cock to guide myself through her folds and pushed inside of her in one long, smooth stroke. Her body clamped down on mine, her heat surrounding me, greedy walls fluttering around my shaft. I breathed into her neck, buried my nose in the curve of her shoulder and lifted a hand to cover her breast. I wanted her dress gone so I could feel the velvet softness of her nipple against my palm, but I didn't want to push my luck. She was still mostly covered from the front, and I was so close to her in the back that you couldn't fit a piece of paper between us. My pants were hanging off my ass, but I didn't care. I would fuck her buck naked in front of the entire town, but I knew she wasn't that kind of girl. She had far more discretion than I did, and I didn't want her to regret any of the things we did together.

I palmed her breast and rolled my thumb over her nipple. I rocked my hips into her and grunted in satisfaction as she pushed back into me. It was a slow grind. We barely moved against one another. I thrust steadily, making sure not to jolt her or press her into the wood too hard. It was softer and far more unhurried than the first time we did this. It wasn't fucking. I knew because that was all I had ever done before Affton, and this was different, down to the core.

My heart was thudding heavy in my ears. I could feel every flutter of her pulse. Pleasure coiled low at the base of my spine and I felt her spine stiffen. She raised her arm and curled it behind my head, her fingers threading through my hair.

I sank my teeth into the tender skin my lips were drifting across and sucked hard enough that she was going to have a mark long after this moment was nothing more than a memory. She whispered my name and came apart. Her body pulled on mine, sucking me into a swirling vortex of heat and satisfaction. When I followed her over the edge, it was a languid fall that was both sensual and carnal. It was something better than sex and gratification.

It was a connection.

It was the thing I'd always been looking for and had never been able to find. Never even realized it was what I'd been searching for in the bottom of bottles and the aftermath of snow-dusted lines and dime bags.

I huffed out a breath and leaned back so I could drop a kiss on the top of her head. She fit so perfectly against me; too bad I didn't fit anywhere in her life.

"That's what I call making the most of our time together." We both sighed as I pulled out of her lax and loose body and hitched up my pants so my dick wasn't hanging in the breeze.

She slid her dress down around her hips and looked at me through unreadable eyes over her shoulder. "I'm going to miss you, Cable James McCaffrey."

I believed her. She really would miss me, after everything I'd done, and all the things I was bound to do. That's why saying goodbye was going to gut me. The only thing I'd ever missed was oblivion. She was so much more than that. She was everything.

nineteen

AFFTON

ONE MINUTE I was sound asleep, snuggled into Cable's side, his arm heavy around my waist, and the next I was in the middle of a whirlwind of McCaffrey fury.

I blinked as the heavy curtains that covered the big glass door were yanked open and lifted a hand to cover my eyes against the light. I gasped when Cable bolted upright, sending me sliding to the side as the covers were pulled off of us and a newspaper came flying directly at the center of his chest.

Standing at the end of the bed was a clearly furious Melanie McCaffrey. Some of her polish and poise had rubbed off, and she looked ready to breathe fire and rain brimstone down around me and her sleepy son. Cable rubbed a hand over his face and blinked lazily at his mom as he reached for the newspaper she threw at him. I tugged the sheet closer to my chest and did my best to make myself as small as possible. It didn't work. The woman's furious, dark gaze pinned me in place as it skipped between me and her son.

"You weren't driving the night of the accident." It wasn't a question. It was a flat statement of fact that came out sounding brittle and broken. "You went to jail for no reason. You cost your family a fortune in a civil suit when you weren't at fault. You let me fight for you. You let me defend you to everyone when it wasn't necessary." She paused, sucked in a breath, and crossed her arms over her chest in a combative stance. "You divided your father and me. I left him because of you, and not once did you think to tell me the truth, Cable. I've always been on your side, but now I'm not sure that *you're* even on your side."

Cable swore as he scanned the headline and article below. Wordlessly, he handed me the paper and slid his long legs to the side of the bed. His mom locked her gaze on me as Cable climbed from the bed, naked and unashamed, even though it painted a pretty clear picture as to why we were in bed together. He pulled on the shorts he'd discarded last night and pushed his hands through his messy hair in aggravation.

The newspaper trembled in my hand as I read the bold print at the top of the page.

NEW EVIDENCE SHOWS LOCAL HEIR TO
THE MCCAFFREY FORTUNE NOT AT FAULT IN FATAL COLLISION

The byline read Trip Wilson, and the article went on to state that under orders from the sheriff, an investigation had been launched into the accident at the urging of the resident press. The Loveless Sheriff's Department brought in an accident recreation specialist that used digital technology to map the scene and recreate different scenarios until they found one that matched where the vehicles ended up and the victims had been found. Apparently, the recreation showed that it was impossible for Cable to be driving. It went on to quote an anonymous source (me) as saying he had been through enough and didn't want to address anything about that night. It also outlined the cost of the trial and the taxpayers' cost of keeping Cable locked up for a crime he didn't commit. It came across as inflammatory, just one more way the rich took advantage of the less well-to-do, rather than sympathetic. So much for justice. The article speculated that Cable wasn't the one responsible for the drugs found in both his and Jenna's systems that night. The Maleys were up in arms over the revelations and were quoted as saying they would not let their daughter's memory be tainted by the new evidence. Loveless's two wealthiest families were about to go to war, and from the looks of things, Melanie was willing to drag Cable right into the middle of it.

He tossed me his t-shirt from the floor, and I slithered into it, keeping one eye on his mom, because she looked like she wanted to throw something a lot heavier than a newspaper at me.

"Mom . . ."

She held up a hand and cut him off. "I don't want to hear it, Cable. I've been worried sick about you. I did my best to do right by you and for you. All I wanted to do was help you, and you couldn't even be bothered to pick up the phone. I sent someone down here to keep an eye on you, and you took her to bed. Has he really been clean all summer? Or have you been covering for him so you could continue to play house with him? You get my son and my money; it seems I underestimated you, Affton. I'm sure your father wouldn't be as proud of you now if he could see how you've been taking advantage of my son."

I narrowed my eyes at her and followed Cable's lead by climbing out of the rumpled bed. "You blackmailed me into giving up my summer. You threatened my dad's job. How dare you stand there and try and lecture me about taking advantage of someone. I'm here because you forced me to be." I saw Cable wince out of the corner of my eye, but I couldn't take it back because it was true. I wanted to be here with him now, but I wouldn't have been here in the first place if she hadn't forced my hand. "And no, I didn't cover for him so that I could spend the summer sleeping with him. He's stayed clean, gone to his meetings with his therapist, and generally done everything he was supposed to do to stay out of prison. He's tried to do and be better. Maybe you should stop and take an inventory before throwing all those ugly accusations around."

She opened her mouth to argue, but Cable moved faster than I'd ever seen him move before. He was in front of her with his hands on her shoulders before she made a single sound. He gave her a little shake and her attention snapped to him as her hands went up to circle his wrists. It wasn't a pretty confrontation by any means, but then again, nothing with this family ever seemed to be easy.

"Don't. Whatever it is you think you're going to do or say to Affton . . . just don't. This has nothing to do with her." His voice was rough, and I couldn't help but be a little pleased that he was defending me. He never got worked up over much, tending to slide toward cold and icy rather than hot and heated. Now, he was all kinds of fire and flames. It clearly took his mother by surprise. I couldn't tell if she was thrilled or terrified by his explosive show of emotion. She seemed to settle somewhere between the two.

"She was supposed to keep you safe, not sleep with you. I promised her a small fortune. Having sex with you was not part of the deal. You don't need any more complications in your life. You do not need some girl working her way under your defenses when you are at your lowest and most vulnerable." She closed her eyes briefly, and I watched her pull her composure back together in a way that only really rich and really practiced people could. This was a woman used to keeping what happened behind closed doors firmly locked in a box so that no one else could see her suffering and sorrow. "You need to be focused on you, not on someone else, Cable."

I couldn't argue with her there. I also couldn't tell her that everything had been focused on him from the start. I wanted the same things she did . . . to help him. To save him from himself. The difference was that he let me in . . . all the way in. I got to the places no one else had ever seen. The places where his shadows kept everything dark.

He swore again, and I started to slowly edge my way toward the door. They needed to work this out between the two of them. I no longer cared if she paid me or not, and if she was going to fire my dad, there was nothing I could do to stop her. There were still a few weeks of the ninety days left, and I had done my part. Cable was clean, he wasn't going back to prison, and he could actually do his own laundry now. I honestly believed he would pass his GED test, and he was taking his sessions with the doc more seriously. He seemed to be thinking about his future more and more, so any way you looked at it, I had more than held up my part of the bargain. If she wanted to punish me for sleeping with Cable, then so be it. I didn't regret a minute I spent with him. He was worth every tick of the clock.

"Mom, all I've ever focused on is myself. That's why I didn't tell you I wasn't driving that night. I wanted to pay the price for my bad choices, so I did, regardless of it being right or wrong. That's why I didn't tell you I was doing drugs. I wanted to escape and disappear into something that wasn't real, so I did. That's why I haven't answered your calls all summer. I didn't want to face your guilt and pity. I feel bad enough as it is . . . I couldn't handle you feeling bad on top of it. I knew you were holding something major over Affton's head to get her to stay with me, and I fucked her anyway because she makes me feel good." It was my turn to flinch, but he was right. He did sleep with me even though it had way more consequences for me than for him. "It's always been about how I feel or don't feel, but these last couple of months, she made me see that it's also about how I make other people feel." He laughed, but it was nasty and sharp. "I usually make them feel shitty, and that's something I need to change. It's something I want to change because of Affton."

He had definitely made me feel like garbage at certain points this summer, but he also made me think, challenged some of the things I thought I knew about myself and him. There was no denying he made me feel really, really good, more than he made me feel bad. It twisted my heart in knots to know I was the one to open his eyes to the effect he had on others. He was his own kind of drug. Addictive and problematic. Once you had a little bit of him, you wanted more, but once you had all of him, it seemed impossible to live without him flowing through your veins.

His mom softened a little, just a little, but it was enough that he let go of her shoulders and took a step back from her. He shook his head and took one of her hands in his. "Leave Affton's dad alone, Mom. If you mess with his job or his future employment, you won't hear from me again. When I turn twenty-one, you can't hold the trust over my head anymore. I'll be free to do what I want with that money, and if you toy with an innocent man, I promise you I will use it to disappear." His tone was soft, but the threat in it was very real. He meant it. She could tell and so could I.

I felt tears burn at the back of my eyes. I thought hating Cable James McCaffrey was overwhelming. Hating him had nothing on loving him. I felt the heat and weight of the shift in my emotions completely consume me. I felt it overtake me. I felt it spiral, uncontrollable and wild throughout me. It was the only thing I could feel, and that was scary because I could see the end of us staring at me directly in the face. He was wandering, and I was settled.

I darted out the door as he called my name.

I was running.

Running from what I was feeling. Running from his defense of me and my father. Running from his reunion. Running from his self-realization and redemption. Running from an empty goodbye and tearful parting. I needed to get away from everything that was Cable James McCaffrey before he really did ruin me.

He told me he would. I should've listened.

Blindly, I pulled on a pair of shorts so I was covered up. Then I threw open the closet in the guest room and started throwing dresses and t-shirts into the open duffel bag I tossed on the bed. I was cramming stuff into the bag by the fistful when Cable came into the room, still looking pissed and slightly shaken up.

"She's not going to mess with your old man, Reed. She promised me she wouldn't."

I kept on shoving clothing and miscellaneous things into bags. I could only glance at him for a minute, or I would fall apart. "Thanks for that."

"What are you doing, Affton?" His voice was gruff.

I tucked a piece of hair behind my ear and cut him a look out of the corner of my eye. "Packing. I think it's time I go back to Loveless. You made it almost the entire summer without a single slip up. You did a good job, Cable. You don't need me anymore, and I don't think I can do this with you any longer knowing it's going to end anyway. I miss my dad, and I miss Jordan."

"What is 'this' exactly, Reed? You can't fuck me anymore knowing it's going to end, or you can't care anymore? Which is it?" Mean Cable was back. I'd still take him over chilly, vacant Cable any day. Mean Cable wanted a fight; ghost Cable didn't care about anything.

"Either. I'm all kinds of tangled up in you. Right now, if I struggle to free myself at the end of summer, I'm just going to get even more stuck. If I cut myself free right now, you can go do whatever it is you need to do to find your way, and I can get myself back on track." I couldn't remember how to travel that road anymore. I had my path all mapped out, and Cable had tossed the directions out the window. I heaved a sigh and closed my eyes briefly. "You need to be okay for you, not for me or for anyone else. You need to want that for yourself, Cable."

I heard him grunt, and when I opened my eyes, he had both my bulging bags in his hands and was headed out the door without a word. It shattered my heart, but I told myself it was for the best. It was better to pull the Band-Aid off quick. Not that a Band-Aid would help heal the wounds that leaving him sliced across my heart.

I grabbed my last little bag filled with my toiletries and makeup and followed him to my car. He already had my bags stashed in the tiny trunk and was leaning against the side, arms crossed over his chest, and a thunderous scowl etched across his handsome face. There was a lock of blond hair hanging over his forehead I wanted to brush away, but if I touched him now, I wouldn't be able to let go. I would be the one clinging frantically and desperately as he tried to cut himself loose. I'd tried to hold on to my mother, and having her slip through my fingers nearly ended me. Losing my grip on Cable would crush me, so letting go was the only option.

"Would you stay if I asked my mom to leave?" His voice gave me goosebumps. He sounded as if he was in pain and I hated it.

I shook my head in the negative. "No. It isn't about her. It's about me and you. Our time's up. You told me it was bound to happen. Let's not let our crappy start and our bittersweet ending ruin all the good stuff that happened in the middle. I loved getting to spend the summer with you, Cable. I'm so proud of everything you've accomplished. I'm proud of you."

Throwing caution and my heart to the wind, I pushed up on my toes so I could wrap my arms around his neck in a hug that had to strangle him. His arms wrapped around my waist and his face buried itself in the curve of my neck. Neither one of us wanted to let go, but we had to.

"I'm gonna miss you, Reed."

"I'm gonna miss you, too. But you know where I'll be if you ever find yourself on the West Coast . . ." I let the sentiment trail off and pulled back even as he tried to pull me closer. I wanted to tell him to keep in touch, but that would hurt too much. Instead, I told him, "If you ever need me, Cable, I'll be there. I will talk you through your bad choices, and I will support you through your good ones. You are not alone, *ever*. Remember that."

It was clear he wanted to say something, but his eyes shifted to almost black, and he let me go. He pushed off the car and started back up the stairs to the front of the house without a goodbye. Again, I told myself it was all for the best, but that didn't stop the tears from breaking free or my hands from shaking so badly I could barely turn the key in the ignition. I was turning to give him one last look and maybe, hopefully, get a wave or a smile to remember him by, but what happened next was anything but a memory I wanted to have forever.

Instead of looking at me or watching me drive off, Cable had stomped up the stairs and paused at the front door. I could see his back tremble from the effort he was exerting to keep it together. It wasn't enough. In a split second, his fist landed against the heavy wood of the door. I thought I could hear the timber shudder from inside my car. I was going to pull away and leave him to vent when the sound of breaking glass made me jump out of the car. His next strike missed the wood and had gone through one of the decorative glass panels that sat in the door. It was heavy glass, hurricane rated, so there was no way his hand was okay after smashing through it.

"Cable?" I called his name to make sure he was all right, and when he turned, I screamed because he was covered in blood. It was spurting out of his hand and running down his forearm in a scarlet river.

The door flew open, and both Miglena and his mom appeared. They both had a similar reaction to mine. Lots of wailing and hands flapping uselessly about as I ran up the stairs, pulling his t-shirt I was still wearing over my head so I could wrap his hand. Up close and personal, it looked even worse than I imagined. There was blood everywhere, and several of his knuckles were swollen and buckled at a weird angle.

I wrapped his hand up and realized he hadn't uttered a sound or flinched at all. Zombie Cable had taken over, and that wasn't good. "Call an ambulance."

Miglena jumped to follow the order while Melanie looked at her son as if she had never seen him before. "What did you do?"

I wasn't sure if that question was for me or for him, so I didn't bother to respond. I was too worried that Cable seemed completely shut down. He was in that place where nothing could reach him, not even pain. It was ten times worse than his breakdown in Doc Howard's office and twice as frightening.

He was gone, and I wasn't sure anyone was going to be able to get him back.

twenty

CABLE

KNEW I should be screaming in pain or freaking out at the amount of blood that was soaking through the bandages the paramedics had wrapped around my hand, but I was numb.

Affton was leaving.

She was going back to a life that had no place for me in it.

I knew it was coming; hell, I had been bracing myself for that goodbye for weeks, but I wasn't prepared for the hole it left in my chest. It was a double whammy, her taking off and my mom showing up and shoving all my selfish decisions in my face. I'd already decided when I got back access to my trust that I would repay her and my dad for the money they fronted in the civil suit. I would also cover all the legal fees. That was going to put a dent in the total sum, meaning I wouldn't be able to live off the amount indefinitely. I was going to need to figure out my life, find something I was good at, and make money from it. I was going to have to do what Affton had been urging me to do all summer long . . . find something I gave a shit about besides her.

I could hear the sirens overhead wailing and the squawk of the radio on the EMTs' shoulder as they raced me to the hospital. The guy told me my hand was for sure broken, but it was the out of control bleeding that had him concerned. He was worried I nicked an artery, and if that was the case, I was going to need surgery to stop the bleeding.

I wasn't sure what happened to Affton. She disappeared when the ambulance showed up saying she needed to go find a shirt. I was loaded on a stretcher and racing toward the hospital before she reappeared. If I was in her shoes, I would take the opportunity to make a stealthy exit. I clearly didn't handle our goodbye well, and if I was her, I would be worried about what might happen next. It wasn't her fault I lost it.

It was mine.

All those years longing to feel something, aching for genuine emotions, but when I finally felt them, I couldn't handle it. My chest was caving in. My skin felt too tight all over my body. My brain was two sizes too big inside my skull. Everything was swirling, chaos, and confusion. I knew I needed to tell her I would miss her, too. I needed to tell her that I believed her when she said she would be there no matter what, that I would never be alone. I needed to hear that from someone I trusted and cared about. But all I could do was feel fire and fury burning under my skin. I didn't intend to hit the door; it wasn't planned. The first thud pulled my churning thoughts from despair to something solid and tangible, something familiar . . . pain. I knew what to do with that, so I put my fist through the window and destroyed my hand.

It took my attention off my destroyed heart.

The stretcher was pulled out of the back of the ambulance, and I was immediately rushed through the halls of the emergency room. There was a flurry of activity as I was wheeled into one of the trauma bays. Rapid fire questions were thrown at me by several nurses, and I saw a young female cringe slightly when she unwrapped the bloody mitt securing my wounds.

"Looks like the window won, Champ?" She flashed me a smile, but it had no impact. I felt like I was watching it all happen to someone else. I was gone. Floating somewhere where nothing hurt and nothing mattered. I couldn't even get excited or concerned about how twisted and mangled my knuckles looked. There was no way I was getting out of here without a cast, and that sucked because all the damage was done to my dominant hand, but even that couldn't pull me out of my zombie haze.

"Your blood pressure is a little elevated, but that's to be expected. Are you on any medications? Do you have a history with any medications we need to be aware of?" One of the nurses tapped the bend in my arm and inserted an IV. If I wasn't drifting, separated from myself and everything happening around me, I would have told them that I was a recovering addict . . . or maybe I wouldn't have. Either way, I said nothing as clear bags of fluid were hung above my head and pumped into my newly clean veins.

"We're going to have to put you under to set those bones in your hand, and it seems you nicked an artery. That little bugger won't stop bleeding unless we get a little stitch in it. You sure did a number on yourself, handsome." I was feeling a little woozy. Possibly from whatever she put in the bags hanging over my head, or maybe it was from blood loss. I remembered a doctor coming in, followed by my mother, who was crying and shaking. Words were exchanged, paperwork was signed, but I was sleepwalking through all of it. Between each blink I found myself looking for a familiar face with almost purple eyes and freckles. I wanted her to kiss me and tell me it was all going to be fine. I wanted her to hug me and tell me this was all no big deal.

She wasn't there, and I couldn't blame her because neither

was I. I vaguely felt my eyes getting too heavy to hold open. I felt my mom squeeze my good hand. The lights above me started to move, and then everything was gone. Everything went black, and I really was drifting, lost in an abyss I wasn't sure I would ever find my way back from.

When I woke up, I was in a hospital room, and there was no longer a way to shut out how much I hurt all over, inside and out. My busted hand felt like it weighed a thousand pounds and sure as shit there was plaster wrapped all around it. My head was fuzzy, and my mouth was dry. It was like coming down off a particularly potent high. I lifted my good hand to rub my eyes and blinked when a guy in a lab coat came through the door. He had a tablet in his hands and was squinting at the screen. His tie was crooked, and his shoes squeaked on the floor as he made his way over to the side of my bed.

"How you feeling, Mr. McCaffrey?" He sounded bored, and somehow that was reassuring.

I lifted my injured hand and let it fall. "Been better."

"I bet. You shattered two of your knuckles, dislocated two fingers, and gave yourself a hairline fracture along your wrist. You've got an army of stitches holding your hand together, and that arterial bleed was a bitch to close." He looked up from the tablet and lifted an eyebrow at me. "On a scale of one to ten, what's your pain level?"

I wiggled the tips of my fingers that were sticking out of the cast and sucked in a breath as sharp, searing discomfort shot up my forearm. "About a nine." It wasn't anything I hadn't felt before. I'd been more banged up after the accident that night, but it definitely didn't feel good.

"I'll have one of the nurses bring you something for the pain. Your chart says you're not allergic to anything, is that correct?"

I swallowed hard and licked my lips. Now was when I was supposed to come clean. Now was when I was supposed to make the right choice and tell him I didn't want narcotics.

"No, I'm not allergic to anything." I felt the hole in the center of my chest widen and the space between me and Affton grow bigger than it already was.

"Great. I'll have the nurse bring in something that goes in the IV, and I'll write you a prescription for something when you are discharged later today. Your mother has been in and out of your room waiting for you to wake up. I'm sure she'll be happy to see you're functioning properly. You gave her quite a scare."

He didn't know the half of it.

I didn't care that my mom was worried about me. What I cared about was that I was going to have something in my system soon that made me forget I didn't care.

The doctor went over a few things with me, mentioned I should consider anger management classes, and told me my stitches were going to itch like a son of a bitch when they started to heal. I closed my eyes when he left the room and didn't open them again until I heard the door open. I was expecting the nurse with my painkiller or my mom with her tear-stained face. What I got was the pale blonde hair and purple-blue eyes the color of a bruise. Her pretty face was pinched in concern, and her eyes were wounded.

I blinked at her as she made her way over to the side of the bed. When she took my good hand in hers, I couldn't stop myself from flinching at the contact, and she immediately let me go. She sighed and reached up to tuck her hair behind her ears. "That was stupid, Cable. You were the one who told me we weren't going in the same direction. Did you want to be the one who veered off first? Would that have been easier for you? Because if it would, then do it. You pull the plug, so I'm the one who's left watching you leave."

I closed my eyes again and turned my head away from her. "That's not it. I knew we had to end, but I wasn't ready for how that was going to feel. I'm not used to . . . emotion." I wasn't used to feeling anything, and she made me feel everything. "It needed somewhere to go." I snorted. "I was kind of hoping all those feelings were going to go with you when you left."

She moved to the other side of the bed and touched her fingers to my cast. She sighed again and bent down so that her lips touched the plaster. "Those feelings aren't mine to take. They're yours to keep. You need to learn how to deal with them without hurting yourself."

If that's what feeling normal meant, I much preferred being shut off and locked away. At least when I was numb, my heart didn't hurt.

"Cable McCaffrey?" We both turned and looked at the door as a male nurse said my name. He was wheeling a machine into the room and reading information off a little vial of something in his hand. "Is that you?"

I nodded. "It's me."

He rattled off my date of birth and asked me a couple more questions while Affton watched him through narrowed eyes.

"We'll get you fixed right up. As soon as this hits your system, you'll be feeling right as rain."

Affton stiffened next to the bed and shifted her gaze back and forth between the two of us. "What is that you're giving him?"

The nurse gave her a look and then looked back at me. I didn't say anything, so the moment dragged on until it became oppressive and uncomfortable. Finally, the nurse cleared his throat and told her, "It's Dilaudid. It's for the pain."

Affton hissed out a wounded, painful sound and stepped away from the bed. "He didn't tell you that he's a recovering addict?

There is no way in hell you should be injecting him with an opiate of any kind."

The nurse looked at me and then back at her. "Umm . . . that's not in his paperwork anywhere. This was prescribed by the floor doctor."

"He's also on parole. If he gets called in for a drug test with any kind of opiate in his system, he's going back to jail unless someone clears that he needs it with his parole officer." She stared at me so hard I could feel the press of it against my skin. "Don't take that, Cable. Do not start back down this road. If you don't watch where you're going, you'll end up exactly where you've always been headed."

The nurse waited, obviously uneasy and unsure. My hand was throbbing, and so was my head. "Give us a minute, will ya?"

He looked at the vial in his hand and then up to Affton. "She's right. If you're in recovery, you shouldn't mess with this stuff. The doctor wouldn't have approved it if he'd known."

I sighed and pushed my good hand through my hair in aggravation. "Just bring me some Tylenol or Advil for now."

Once we were alone, I waited for her to unleash on me. I could see every line of her body tensed in anger and her face was flushed with barely contained fury. She looked an awful lot like she did that day she confronted me in the parking lot. She called me an addict then and told me I needed help. I had no idea what she was going to call me now.

"My mom started off using pain pills." Her voice shook, and her knuckles turned white as her hands clenched into fists at her sides. "We were in a car accident. She got severely injured. She ended up needing a whole bunch of back surgeries and she never really got her range of motion back. The doctors gave her OxyContin for the pain, and at first, she used it only when she really needed it."

"Come on, Reed . . ."

She held up a hand and cut me off. "You said you would listen when I was ready to talk about my mom, so listen. I remember her starting to act different. She'd always been active in my life. She came and helped in my classroom; she took me to Girl Scouts and dance class. We did something together every Sunday, as a family, and then all of a sudden she was too tired for all of that. She never wanted to leave the house. She never wanted to do anything with me and dad. She said it was because she hurt all the time, and I don't doubt that was part of it, but the painkillers," she shook her head. "They helped at first, then they hurt. Soon, she needed more than she was prescribed. She started doing crazy stuff and jumping from doctor to doctor to get more." She laughed, but it was jagged and sharp. The edges of it cut against me and sliced across my soul. "When the doctors wouldn't prescribe them to her anymore, she started begging my dad to go for her. She wanted him to lie for her. That's when I really started to realize things in my family were falling apart." She lifted a shaking hand to her mouth and blinked away tears. "When my dad wouldn't do it, she burned my arm with an iron so that she could rush me to the ER."

"Jesus." I'd noticed she had a patch of pale skin on her upper arm that never tanned and was slippery smooth to the touch, but I never asked about it . . . because I was an asshole and she deserved so much better than me.

"When my dad found out what she did, he took me and moved out. He told my mom if she didn't get help immediately, he was going to file for divorce and get full custody of me. She went."

Affton crossed her arms over herself so that she was giving herself a hug. "She stayed in a program for thirty days and came out with all kinds of lies about appreciating what she had and wanting to save her family. What she didn't tell us was that she met a woman in rehab who educated her on how much easier and cheaper it was to get high on heroin than Oxy. She moved from pills to street drugs in the blink of an eye."

"Things went downhill fast from there. She left me alone. She forgot to feed me. She didn't care if I made it to school on time or not. She stopped being a mom, and she stopped being a wife. All she wanted to be was an addict. My dad tried to help her, but she made it clear she didn't want anything to do with getting better. She wanted to be high more than she wanted to be a family."

She sniffed and rubbed her arms with her hands. I wanted to hug her, but I had a feeling that if I got too close, she might break . . . exactly how her girl, Jordan, warned me she would. I didn't just bump into her, I crashed, and she shattered.

"She got arrested. The judge offered her a plea deal if she agreed to go back to rehab. She went, but unwillingly. Dad filed for divorce and was in the process of taking full custody of me when she got out. I was just a kid, but I knew she didn't have much time left living the way she did. She was a walking, talking corpse the deeper into her addiction she fell. She scared me."

She rubbed her fingers over her cheeks as the tears she was keeping in check broke free. "I was the one who found her. She hadn't returned any of my calls, and she missed a big dance recital, nothing new, but by that time I was pissed. I wanted to tell her I was done, that she wasn't my mom anymore. I wanted to tell her Dad and I deserved better, and she was gross and sad. I wanted to hurt her the way she hurt me. I skipped out of school early and walked to her apartment. When I opened the door, I found her lying on the floor. She was blue." She stopped breathing for a second, and when she started speaking again, her words held barely any sound. "I didn't know what was wrong, so I touched her, and she was so cold. I sat on the floor and cried, calling her name over and over until a neighbor came to see what was going on. My dad was so mad. He was mad at her. Mad at himself for letting me still see her. Mad at me for being so upset over a woman who hadn't bothered to be my mother in a long time. It was the only time I've ever seen him cry."

She was shaking so hard I was sure she was going to fall over. Groaning with effort and pain, I swung my legs over the edge of the bed and reached out my good arm so I could snag her around the waist. She didn't struggle because of the tubes and wires attached to all the different places on my body, but she didn't make pulling her between my legs and into my chest easy, either.

"I can't love another addict, Cable. I won't." She sobbed against my neck, and I brushed my lips against her forehead. "I hate Cable the addict, but I love Cable the recovering addict, even if he's not always who you choose to be. You need to learn to love him, too."

"I can make good choices for you, Reed. Can't seem to get a handle on making them for myself."

She put her arms around me loosely and gave me a squeeze. She sniffed loudly and pulled out of my embrace. My neck was wet from her tears, and my pulse was erratic from having her so close and hearing her history.

"Try."

I chuckled and gave her a nod. "I'll try."

She gave me a weak smile and pushed her hair out of her face. She loved me and hated me. I loved and hated her for that. "I'm pretty sure when I get the hang of all these feelings, when I learn what to do with them, I could learn to love you, Affton Reed."

Her eyes widened, and she put her hands over her heart. She flushed again, but this time it was a pretty pink. She stuck her tongue out and licked her lower lip, eyes glowing with promise and challenge. "Prove it, Cable James McCaffrey."

With those final words, she disappeared out the door and out of my life, leaving me alone to make the right choice for myself . . . to at least try and be worthy of loving her and being loved by her.

All I could do was try. Even if I failed, at least I was trying . . . her words haunted me long after the door closed behind her.

twenty-one

AFFTON

Berkeley ~ Close to Thanksgiving break

"I WAS WONDERING if you wanted to get some pizza or a cup of coffee sometime before break starts?"

I was looking down at my phone, barely listening to the guy walking next to me. I wasn't even sure what his name was, but he'd been persistent in his efforts to get me to go out with him over the course of the semester. We were in the same intro to psychology class, and he'd been moving steadily across the giant auditorium the last few months until he worked up the courage to sit next to me. At first, he asked me if I wanted to study together, and when I turned him down, he switched to subtly asking me if I wanted to hang out during a bunch of group events. I always said no.

It wasn't that he wasn't cute; he was. He was tall, lean, and looked very academic. He wore glasses that were trendy with their thick, black frames, and sweaters over button-up shirts. He also wore tightly fitted jeans and ankle boots. He was pretty much a walking advertisement for hot college guy who took himself and his education seriously. There were plenty of other girls who gave him the eye day in and day out, but he didn't seem to notice. He had his sights set firmly on me, even though I barely spared him a glance. I could hear Jordan telling me it was time to move on. I could hear her telling me to live a little, to embrace everything college had to offer, including very cute boys who were the opposite of Cable in every way imaginable. There were no scruffy, surfer boys in my psychology program. There were no boys who were lost and desperately trying to find their way. These guys had all worked just as hard as I had for their place in that classroom, and they weren't about to blow it by living recklessly. It should have appealed to me, they should have appealed to me . . . but they didn't.

I looked up from my phone and blinked at the guy trying to piece together what he'd just asked me. Since he was staring at me expectantly, I figured he had asked me out again. I had to say no, hated that I couldn't even imagine saying yes to someone who wasn't Cable, but there was no other choice. I wasn't about to lead anyone on. Even though I was single, technically unattached, and free to do whatever and whomever I wanted . . . I couldn't. As always, my stupid heart was still tangled around and caught up in all things Cable James McCaffrey.

I hadn't heard from him since I walked out of the hospital.

I had no clue if he turned down the painkillers and pulled himself back on the right path.

I didn't know if he had gone back to his old ways or if he thought about me every minute of every day, the way I thought about him. I wondered if he missed me so much that it was all-consuming. In the dark, I wondered if he imagined me when he woke up alone and lonely . . . the way I imagined him.

I didn't know anything, but my heart didn't care. It refused to let me let go completely. It refused to let me consider this cute boy's invitation or any of the others that came my way. It wouldn't let me move on.

"I . . . uhhh . . . well, I can't really get away before break. I have a project due, and my dad is coming to town so we can spend Thanksgiving together. I don't really have any free time." I tucked a piece of hair behind my ear and noticed we had almost made it all the way to the building where my apartment was located. Thank God Melanie McCaffrey came through with the money she promised me. Otherwise, I would have been stuck in one of the open dorm rooms, sharing my space with a stranger, and living with no walls. The idea of using a communal bathroom made me gag. As it was, I still had to share the apartment, but at least there was a living room and several closed doors separating us. It was totally worth the extra money.

And my dad really was coming to visit. When I left Port Aransas, I went back home and immediately spilled my guts about everything. I think it was seeing Cable in the hospital, all those tubes attached to him, that pushed me over the edge. It reminded me too much of all the times my mom had faked an injury or illness to get herself committed so she could score. I told him about Melanie and her threat. I told him about the money, and my summer spent trying to help Cable stay clean. I told him about the accident, the truth, not the garbage that was in the papers, and I told him all about falling for the absolute wrong person and how hard it was to walk away. I apologized for lying and waited for him to fix it all like he always had.

My dad shocked me by calling his boss at the brewery and quitting on the spot. He had some choice words for Melanie McCaffrey, but I begged him to let it go. She loved her son and refused to let him ruin his life. I reminded him we'd both been there with my mom. He said he refused to work for a woman who would manipulate his daughter that way. He agreed that Cable wasn't someone he would ever pick out for me, considering his history and his issues, but he didn't judge me for falling so far, so fast. He held me while I cried and told me to believe in the good parts Cable showed me, but to stay aware of the bad ones. He was the best dad ever, and he handled my first broken heart like a pro. But he couldn't fix what was broken. He couldn't console me when I fell apart after calling the hospital to check on Cable, only to be told he'd checked out against doctor's orders. The only person who could help the heartache had disappeared like a puff of smoke, drifting away in the darkness just like he always warned me he would.

My dad also told me that he had been considering for a long time what he was going to do once the house was empty. His whole life had been working to keep a roof over our heads and to take care of me, but now that I was venturing out on my own, it was time for him to live a little. Within a month of me getting to school and getting settled, he sold our house and used the money to buy an RV. He told me he wanted to see the country. He wanted to travel and experience all that life had to offer. I had been worried all along about Melanie uprooting my father, but as it turned out, the man was a rolling stone. He was never in one place for very long, and I got a postcard once a week from places I'd only ever seen in magazines and on TV. He was making his way to California from Seattle to spend Thanksgiving with me, and I couldn't wait to see him. He had no regrets about leaving Loveless behind, and I actually envied his carefree attitude. People only had power over us if we allowed them to.

"Are you seeing someone, Affton? Do you have a boyfriend back home or something?" He looked confused rather than confrontational. He really didn't understand why I wouldn't give him a shot. "I admire your drive and I think how smart you are really is sexy, but this is college. There is more to life than what's in our books. I really want the chance to get to know you better. I think we would be a good fit." He sounded so sincere, and he was right; he was a much better fit than the boy I left behind and couldn't forget.

I shifted and tucked a piece of hair behind my ear. "I . . . uh . . . I'm not . . ." I stumbled to a stop, almost tripping over my own feet as we reached the front of my building. The guy next to me grabbed my arm to keep me from tumbling over as I went still, mouth hanging open, breath wheezing in and out, heart pounding so hard it hurt, because there was no mistaking the familiar figure sitting on the steps of my building.

There was a cigarette dangling out of his mouth, and his eyes were locked on my elbow where the boy was still holding on. I blinked rapidly to make sure he was real, and when he didn't disappear, I remembered to breathe.

He climbed to his feet, and I automatically took a step toward him. Pulled, as if he was magnetic and I was a piece of metal. Tugged, because he was the sun and I was nothing more than a planet caught in his orbit. He moved me without even trying.

He looked different, better. His dark blond hair was shorter than it had been over the summer, cut close to his head on the sides and in the back, but longer on top and slicked back. The pale white pieces from the summer sun were gone and so were the shadows in his eyes. Those chocolate-colored orbs were clear and sharp, never wavering from the point where the boy who wasn't him touched me. The scowl on his face was familiar, and so was the swagger as he stepped closer to me and my unwanted companion. Neither one of us spoke, but there was an entire conversation that took place as we stared unblinking at each other.

I pulled myself together enough to shake loose of the hold on my arm and looked at my classmate with genuine regret. I wish I had been able to see him, that he had been able to break through, but the only one who had ever been able to climb over all my walls was Cable. Now, he didn't even have to scale them. There was a door to my heart, and he was the only person who had the key. We were right out of a terrible movie. I was the otherwise smart and intrepid heroine making the dumbest choices when it came to men. This man. Standing next to me was the perfect example of who and what I should want, but everyone knew I was going to go for the guy who was obviously all wrong for me.

"I'm sorry." I looked at the guy from my class out of the corner of my eyes. The apology would sound more sincere if I bothered to learn his name. "I don't have a boyfriend, exactly . . . it's complicated." Cable had never been something as simple as a boyfriend, and he never would be. "I'm not interested in seeing anyone else."

Cable stopped a couple feet away, and I could feel him. I could feel his tension and his intensity. I could smell his cigarette and the sun and sand that always clung to him. I could hear him inhale and exhale, slow and steady as if he was trying to keep himself in check. I could see his eyes shift from brown to that darker color that was almost black. He was feeling things, so many things, and he was working through all those emotions, not running or hiding from a single one of them.

My would-be suitor let out a dry laugh and turned on his heel. "You can't see anyone else, even if you were interested. You've been looking through anyone who approached you all semester, and now I know why. You only have eyes for whoever that guy is. You have no trouble looking right at him. I'll catch you after Thanksgiving break. My offer to study still stands. I meant it when I told you that I dig the fact that you're as smart as you are pretty. See you later, Affton."

He walked away, and Cable came closer. He put one of his

hands in the pocket of his jean jacket and used the other to pull the cigarette out of his mouth. His sandy brows lifted and the corner of his mouth turned down as he asked, "Did I interrupt something?"

Typical Cable. No hello. No greeting of any kind.

I cocked my head to the side and answered his question with one of my own. "What are you doing here?"

He dropped the cigarette to the ground and put it out under the toe of his sneaker. He lifted a hand to the back of his neck and looked down at the ground as he answered. "It was time." Could it be that easy and that simple?

"I haven't heard from you in months." There was no hiding the accusation in my tone. I'd been worried about him. I'd missed him and grieved for him. It rankled that he was acting like we'd barely been apart.

He swore and lifted his head so that he was looking at me. Everything was in those dark eyes. Every minute we spent separated, every second spent divided and drowning in loneliness.

"Can we go somewhere and talk?" He shifted with uncertainty and blew out a breath. "It can be somewhere public if you don't want to be alone with me."

There was a time when the last thing I wanted was to be trapped one on one with him. For the last several months, being alone with him was what I dreamed about at night. It was a fantasy I let play in my head when I was having a particularly bad day. It was what kept me right where I was when I knew it would be so much better to emotionally walk away from him.

"We can go up to my room. It's nothing special, and I have a roommate, but it's quiet and close." He owed me an explanation. Hell, he owed me a whole lot more than that, but to start, I would be happy with him telling me where he had been and why he hadn't reached out.

He nodded and followed me into the building. We didn't talk in the elevator on the way up to my floor. I waved absently to a couple of girls who lived down the hall from me. I was surprised they knew my name since I didn't go out of my way to hang out or engage with anyone. I was less surprised they were curious about Cable and wanted an introduction. I didn't give them one. Luckily, the apartment appeared to be empty when we got inside. I wasn't sure where any of this was going between the two of us, but I didn't want an audience for any of it.

"How do you like your roommate?" I threw my bag on the floor by the bed and watched as Cable meandered around the tiny room checking out the small touches I added to make the place feel more homey.

There was a chair at the desk, but that's where he was standing, so I took a seat on the edge of the bed. My skin prickled as his eyes followed the movement. Me and him in a small space that was mostly taken up by a bed was probably not the best idea I'd ever had.

"She's fine. She's a fellow psych major so we have a couple classes together and a lot of the same assignments. She's quiet. She has a boyfriend who lives in the Mission district across the Bay, so she's gone a lot. She isn't Jordan, but I like her." I liked her more than I thought I would. She was serious and driven, and she never asked why I always seemed to be sad and lost.

Cable slid his hands into the front pockets of his faded jeans and leaned back against my desk. His voice was quiet and intense when he told me, "I missed you, Reed."

It made my heart squeeze. It hurt. It hurt so bad that I put a hand to the center of my chest and pushed against the pain. "Why didn't you call me then? Or text, or email? There were lots of ways for you to reach out to me, Cable. You've always known exactly where I was." All I wanted to know was that he was okay. I wanted to know he was making good choices and trying to be better. Not for me, for himself.

"I didn't take the painkillers or the prescription for Oxy." He pulled his hand out of his pocket and held it out in front of him so I could see all the fine white lines that now cut across his fingers and the back of his palm. His spider web tattoo had voids in the ink where he was scarred, but it didn't make the tattoo look any less badass. "That sucked. I really, really wanted something to take the edge off, but you were right. If I started slipping down that hill, I would snowball, and there would be no controlling the avalanche of destruction that followed. I told them no for you, but after talking with Doc Howard, I realized I told them no for me, as well. Besides, my mom lost her shit when she heard what they were trying to give me. I think that doctor is still trying to grow some new skin after she ripped him a new ass."

I wanted to cry in relief. "That's amazing, Cable." I was so proud he worked through what he was feeling and came to the right conclusion. It gave me hope . . . for him . . . and for us.

He chuckled and pushed his marked hand through the front of his hair. "When you told me you were going, I lost it. I didn't want the painkillers for my hand; I wanted them for my heart. I wasn't used to caring about anyone the way I care about you."

At least he said *care* and not *cared* because the past tense would have shattered the paper-thin composure I was holding onto. "You were the one who said we had to end. You were the one who told me there was no place for you in my life." I would have made room for him if he asked, but instead, I ran before he could chase me away.

A grin tugged at his mouth, and I wanted to feel it against my lips. Along with his eyes being clear, it appeared that some of the weight that held down his soul had lifted, as well. That smile was real. It was genuine, and there was nothing but self-deprecating humor behind it. No malice or manipulation.

"You gave up so much of your life for one addict. I couldn't let you give up any more for another. There isn't room in your life for someone who isn't willing to try and recover."

That was sweet but also heartbreaking. "You were trying."

He shook his head and moved off the desk. He made his way over to where I was sitting and lowered himself next to me on the edge of the bed. Instantly, everything in my body tensed. When we touched, there was always an electric current passing from him into me. I was intently aware of how close we were and how easy it would be to close that distance.

"I wasn't really trying, Affton. I was going through the motions. If I were really trying, I would have been honest with the doctor when he asked me about my history. I would have let Doc Howard help me the way he wanted to all summer. I would have left you alone until I got my shit together and could offer you something other than sex."

I flinched a little at that, but he reached out and put a hand over mine where they were locked together on my lap in front of me. His voice was low and intimate, soothing, even when he told me, "Don't get me wrong, I don't regret a minute we spent together this summer, and I would still take my shot if it meant I got you naked, but you deserved better, and I don't blame you for taking off. You didn't have a choice. I did need to get better for myself first, and only after that would I be good enough for you. You asked me to prove I could love you and that's exactly what I've been doing."

Since he'd been a ghost and I had no clue what he'd been up to, I had a hard time believing he was proving anything to anyone. "How have you been proving that?"

He rubbed his thumb in a circle along the outside of my wrist. I had to bite my tongue so I wouldn't moan. I missed the feel of him. I missed the way I felt because of him.

"After you left, I told my mom I was ready for her help. I was ready to really try and make some significant changes. I didn't want to be an addict anymore, I wanted to be a recovering addict. We talked to Doc Howard, and he helped me see a specialist. Between therapy and medication, I got a lot of my shit straight. I mean, I'm still a mess. I'm clinically depressed and have all kinds of anxiety because of the accident and all the stuff that happened after, so I doubt I'll ever been one hundred percent even-keeled. But for the most part, I don't feel as alone or as untethered as I did. Most of the fog has lifted, but there are still days I struggle to see through the haze of it all."

My pulse jumped, and I was sure he felt it because that grin turned into a full-fledged smile. He was still the only one who could make me react. The guy from my class was right. I looked through everyone else because I only had eyes for Cable.

"I spent a month on the shore getting used to the prescriptions and finding what worked. There were a few that made me feel like a zombie and some that made me feel like I was crawling out of my skin. But ultimately, we found a good balance of meds and therapy. I also told my mom I wanted to meet my sisters, and after some initial resistance, she agreed that it would be good for me. Miglena took a little longer to convince, but eventually, she relented after being assured she wasn't going to lose her job. My mom also promised to make sure my dad follows through with child support for both of them. She's done paying to keep them away. We both know how ruthless she can be when she sets her mind to something. Money won't be as tight for her, and my dad can't keep pretending like none of his children exist. The oldest one looks just like me, and the younger one obviously takes after Miglena. They are the sweetest little girls. Eight and six years old. We went for ice cream. They asked me if I could teach them to surf." His eyes were still on mine and his lips quirked into a slight grin. Some of the tension in his broad shoulders seemed to dissipate when I stayed right where I was. I doubted I would ever be able to pull away from him again.

He sounded so proud and so pleased that I got a little choked up. "That's amazing. I'm so happy for you." He needed all the love he could get and the kind of love that came from two innocent little girls who had no idea where he had been or who he had been was the best kind. It was pure and unwavering.

"I also went and talked to the guy Jenna hit in the accident, the one who ended up in a wheelchair. I wanted to apologize and tell him that if he ever needed anything to make his new normal easier, to let me know. He told me he read the article in the paper and knew I wasn't the one responsible for the crash. He asked me if I was still using and when I told him I wasn't and that I'd been clean since that night, he told me he could forgive me and that he would pray for me. He was happy we both lived. He called it a miracle, and I realized I'd been living my life the wrong way. I was pissed I survived instead of being grateful I got more time to make things right. He's a better man than I'll ever be, but I realized I could learn a lot from him. If he could forgive me if I was trying, then I sort of felt like I finally had permission to forgive myself."

He trailed off a little bit, possibly thinking about the girl who had made such a huge impact on his past, or maybe, I hoped, thinking about the one who was going to have everything to do with his future.

"When I was feeling steadier, I told my mom I wanted to go to that program she set up for me before the accident. I stayed clean all summer but just barely. If you hadn't been there, I wouldn't have made it. I needed to learn how to cope with the cravings and how to live without a crutch. Getting the clearance to go away within the confines of my existing parole stipulations took a lot longer than I expected, but it was worth it. I learned that my rock-bottom isn't as low as some others and that my struggle isn't unique. I won't ever be recovered but I am in recovery, and it feels damn good. That's where I needed to go . . . where I needed to be . . . in order to end up here with you. I thought there were endless roads to travel, but there was only one that was going to take me where I really wanted to be. I left the program a couple weeks ago. I would have reached out sooner, but I needed to know I was making the effort for the right reasons and not just because it was what you needed from me. I had something to prove."

I blinked hard so I wouldn't cry. I pulled my hand out from underneath his hold and laced my fingers through his. "I'm impressed." I really was. "I was proud of you before; I'm in awe of you now."

He reached up and caught a rebellious teardrop with the end of his finger. "Don't cry for me. Not anymore. I'm not the guy who makes girls cry anymore. I'm not the guy who doesn't care when those tears are for me anymore."

I sniffed and blinked against the rest of the moisture that gathered. "I can't help it. I wasn't sure I was ever going to see you again, and if I did, I had no idea what version of Cable I was going to get. Nothing prepared me for this version."

He lifted an eyebrow and leaned into me so that he could bump his shoulder into mine. "What version is this?"

"The wide awake one. The reasonable and rational one." I had no idea what to do with this Cable, but I knew if I couldn't resist any of the other versions of him, there was no way I stood a chance against this one; this one made all kinds of sense and had my heart fluttering like a million butterfly wings in the middle of a whirlwind.

"Since I'm putting it all on the table, I need to tell you I'm the one who paid you for giving up your summer. It was the least I could do after everything you gave up, and the truth is, I wanted to have a part in you living out your dreams. I wasn't sure there was going to be a spot for me in them anymore. I had no clue how long it was going to take to get myself straightened out, and I wouldn't blame you for not waiting around." His smile fell, and his eyes narrowed. "You definitely didn't seem to hate having Mr. Four-Eyes walk you back from class."

He wouldn't blame me for not waiting around? Did he not know me at all? I'd been waiting on him since I first saw him all those years ago. The hate I knew for him was actually compassion, love, a need to protect something that wasn't mine to protect. He made me feel for him when I was scared. My mom had hurt me in ways I would never heal from. I didn't want him to do the same thing. Even though I was halfway across the country from where we started and stopped, my heart wouldn't move away from him.

I left because I loved him and he told me it wasn't possible. I ran because I wanted him more than I wanted out of Loveless. I bolted because even when I was convinced I hated him, he was still the only one I could see and the only one who really saw me.

"I don't even know his name," I whispered the words as he tilted his head so that it rested against the side of mine. "I don't even know what he looks like."

Cable snorted and tightened his hold on my hand. "He was standing right next to you, Reed. He was touching you."

There was jealousy there, and I had to admit I didn't mind it. "He could have been standing right in front of me, and it wouldn't matter. You're the only person I see. You're the only one I feel in here." I touched my fingers to my chest and felt my heart kick in agreement. "No one else can withstand the cold."

He turned his head so his lips could touch my cheek. That small touch made me shiver from head to toe. "Ice is nothing more than frozen water, and you know how I feel about the water." I felt him smile right before his lips touched the corner of my mouth. "It's pretty much my favorite thing. I adore you, Affton. I want to learn how to love you. Show me how."

I did everything right.

I never misstepped.

I was careful, controlled, and had all the plans.

I was focused, attentive, and driven. I'd worked my ass off to get exactly where I was.

I told myself nothing and no one was going to hold me back or slow me down. I rolled over everyone who got in my way and never looked back.

I'd never had anything handed to me or had anything come easy.

Including love. Nothing was more challenging than loving Cable James McCaffrey. I guess it was a good thing that I knew nothing would be more rewarding than learning to be loved by him.

twenty-two

CABLE

I WAS FEELING a lot of things. It took a minute to isolate and work my way through all the different emotions, but I was doing the work, and I was grateful to have the problem of being overwhelmed. It was how I knew she was the right choice for me, even if I wasn't the best choice for her.

I was jealous. Blindingly and obsessively so. It made me a little crazy, and I wanted to find the guy who had been walking by her side, the one who had touched her like he had the right and break all his fingers. It burned seeing her with someone who wasn't me. It tied my guts in knots when I realized how good he looked standing next to her, how right someone else would be for her. I would have walked away, disappeared before she could catch sight of me if she had looked happy. I would have let her be if she said she cared about the guy in skinny jeans and glasses. Instead, she was back to being the way she was all those years in high school. She was flying high above him, and he was trying his best to reach her. She was still untouchable. I was the only one who weighed her down enough to touch her. When I got my hands on her, I was never letting go.

I was happy. My heart swelled and lifted as soon as her blonde head came into view. Her hair was longer and the beachy waves from the summer were gone. She had done something to tame it; the pale strands were severely straight as they hung around her face. Her golden tan was also gone, making her freckles pop on the bridge of her nose. She'd lost some weight, defying the freshman fifteen, and her face had that blank, controlled look on it she used to wear when she was dreaming of leaving Loveless. I knew some of the changes in her appearance were because of me, but I was so excited to see her, to be near her, that I let the guilt slide.

I was relieved that when our eyes met, the world still stopped. The jackass at her side didn't matter. The months apart didn't matter. The questions and concern radiating off her in waves didn't matter. The only thing that mattered is how she saw me, really saw me, the same way she always had. She didn't look through me or around me. She looked right at me and moved toward me because she couldn't help herself. I was so thankful that our connection hadn't been broken, that time and distance did nothing to dilute the chemistry that pulsated and pounded between us. I was elated, honestly, thrilled she agreed to talk to me and was still comfortable with me enough that she didn't demand we do it with witnesses.

I was sad. Unhappy because she looked so sad. I hated I did that to her. Hated that I was the one who made her eyes turn that bruised color and put her back up on the pedestal where no one could reach her. I was worried she was going to tell me she'd moved on. Not necessarily from me, but from having to deal with me. I knew she cared; it was clear in her eyes and the way she fought to hold herself together. She deserved someone easier, and I wouldn't have blamed her if she went out and found him. I was worried she'd had her fill of loving an addict, that she didn't have any faith left.

I was nervous I hadn't done enough to prove to her that I really did want to love her and that I was worthy of being loved by her.

But then she invited me inside, gave me the time to tell her what I needed to and now I was feeling things that were much more familiar where she was concerned. I was lost in the kind of emotion and sensation I'd associated with her and the way she got under my skin from the start.

And now, here we were in this tiny apartment, and I was turned the fuck on. She looked so prim and proper on that narrow little bed. She was still stunning without even trying, and my hands were dying to slide over the ice she'd encased herself in when she had walked away from me all those months ago. She looked like the ice princess she'd always been accused of being, but I knew it wouldn't take much to thaw her out. I'd been without her long enough. I needed to reacquaint my hands with her soft skin and my mouth with her sunny, spicy taste. I wanted to rumple her up and make her hair wild again. I wanted to break that cheap bed and remind her that she might be frosty to everyone else, but for me, she burned.

I told her we had to end, that I didn't fit in her life, but I was wrong. What we needed to do was begin. We needed a real chance to start something without my demons and her ambitions hanging over us. We needed to see what was between us when there wasn't a clock ticking down our time together, reminding us we were bound to go our separate ways in a matter of moments. We needed to see if we had what it took to make it work between us because it was never going to be easy. I was never going to be easy to love.

I wanted to ask if I proved myself. I wanted to know if she felt I was finally worthy of all that she was. I wanted her to tell me that she could see I was really trying for once, and I understood *all* my actions had consequences that affected more than just me . . . finally. But I kept quiet. She told me I had to figure out the right choice for myself and that's what I did. I couldn't push her because I was asking her to make the wrong choice by picking me for the foreseeable future.

Finally, after what felt like an eternity and a half, she turned her head so that our foreheads were touching. Her lips were nothing more than a breath away from mine, and when she spoke, I swore I tasted her words and felt the brush of her eyelashes as she let her eyes drift closed.

"You don't need to learn how to love me, Cable." She lifted her hand and put it on the side of my face. I sighed as her thumb swept wide circles over my skin. It made me shudder, and all the other emotions that were scrambling for recognition faded behind the overwhelming amount of passion and hunger I had for this girl. "I think you have all along, in your own way. I just needed to recognize that's what it was."

I made a noise in my throat and clenched my fists so I didn't grab her and throw her on the bed when the tip of her tongue darted out to touch the very center of my bottom lip. I felt that tiny touch all the way through me. It made my body tight and deflated the balloon of pressure that was in the center of my chest so I could finally breathe normally for the first time in months.

"I spent close to ninety days with you and more than ninety days without you. Gotta say I preferred the days with you, Affton. Even when I thought you were the enemy." Little did I know she was always going to be my biggest ally. She realized I was my own worst enemy before she even knew who I really was, and she'd never been scared to fight for me and against me when I so desperately needed it.

I wrapped my fingers around her wrist and felt her pulse flutter excitedly against my fingertips. Her lips lifted into a tiny grin that I wanted to kiss permanently onto her face. "That's okay. I preferred the days I spent with you even when I thought I hated you. I never really did. I wanted to, I believed I did, but my heart never let me. It didn't listen and loved you anyway."

I moved my other hand so I could grab the back of her head. I threaded my fingers through her hair and touched my lips to hers. "Thank God your heart isn't as smart as the rest of you, Reed."

Her grin grew into a smile, and I couldn't stop myself from kissing her. She was the light I needed to see through the dark. She was the goodness that took up all the room inside of me where the bad got to play. I would always have my demons, but this girl did her best to tame them. I did love her in my own broken way and always had. I just had to make sure that was enough to keep her.

Her lips tasted sugary and sweet. She always tasted good, but whatever this was, it wasn't her. When I pulled my head back and smacked my lips together, she giggled a little. I lifted an eyebrow and ran my tongue over the sticky coating on my mouth. "Strawberry?"

She reached out a finger and traced the wet trail I left on my lower lip. Her eyes got heavy, and her cheeks turned that pretty pink I loved. She bit down on her lower lip and nodded. "Lip gloss. Jordan convinced me I need to make more of an effort now that I'm in college. She told me I'd been planning for this my entire life and I wasted high school refusing to fit in. She took me shopping before I left Loveless and loaded me down with stuff she insisted was necessary." She rolled her eyes and shifted her touch to my top lip, tracing the dip and stopping at the corner of my mouth. "I almost poked my eye out trying to figure out how to draw a perfect cat eye, and my freckles look weird under all that stuff she picked out for my face. Lip gloss is as good as it gets."

I stuck my tongue out again and this time licked the side

of her thumb. "It's enough. You don't need any help." I lowered the hand that was tangled in her hair to the back of her neck and pulled her down until we were facing each other on our sides on the narrow little bed. "You don't have a lot of room to work with in here, Reed." I tried to keep it casual, but she had to know what I was getting at. This bed was way too small for two people to sleep in and I was hoping against hope that she'd been in it alone while I was in rehab.

"I don't need much room. It's only me. It's been only me all semester. I study and sleep; that's about it."

I covered her cheek with my palm and leaned forward so I could kiss her again. This time the sweetness didn't surprise me, and I licked along her lips until she let me into the natural sweetness I was craving. Her familiar taste popped on my tongue and made memories explode in my head. She was everything that was right in my world, and I doubted I'd ever be able to get enough of her. I swirled my tongue against hers and let my teeth nip at her lower lip. Her hand curled around my bicep and one of her legs lifted and hooked over my hip.

I pulled away to catch my breath and told her, "The beds in rehab were narrow, too. There was only room for one, and I can't say I minded that at all."

She stared at me for a long moment and then asked in a small voice, "What about before you left for the program? Your bed in Port Aransas is definitely big enough for two."

She spent enough nights tangled around me naked and sweaty to know that was true.

Of course, she wanted to know about the time I could have done my best to fuck away her importance and her memory. I'd used girls to get away from my problems for years, so I wasn't surprised she thought she would be so easily replaced. "When I first got out of the hospital, my hand was pretty messed up. I was mad at myself. I was mad at my mom. I was mad at you. Maybe the idea of fucking around crossed my mind once or twice, but it was simply reactionary. It was the same thing as all those girls at the start of the summer, a habit I used to avoid the real issues that were tearing me apart. I got on a bunch of different meds to try and regulate the depression and anxiety. Some of them really messed me up. I could hardly function, and the last thing I wanted to think about was sex. When I finally found a combo that worked for me, it was easy to understand that if I wasted my time on sex with someone who wasn't you, then I would never have a shot at ever having sex with the only person I really wanted to again. Those consequences to my actions were crystal clear, and the thought of never having you under me or over me again just because I was blindly doing what I have always done was enough to make me rethink some of those bad choices I'm so well known for."

She studied me for a second while she tried to figure out how much truth was in my statement. She must have decided to believe me because when our lips met again, she was kissing me. It was her tongue teasing mine and her teeth doing the biting and tugging. She put her hands under my jacket on my shoulders and started to push the fabric down my arms. I couldn't help her get the heavy fabric out of the way fast enough. I also managed to get my hands under the bottom of the bulky sweater she was wearing and tugged it up over her head. Her hair floated around her face in a silky slide as she shook the static out of it. We faced each other, breathing heavy, back in this place we both knew so well, but now we weren't visiting. We were staying here permanently . . . together.

She got her hands under my t-shirt and started to work the cotton up my torso. She sighed when she uncovered my abs and let out a little groan when she reached my tattooed shoulders. I grabbed the back of the collar and yanked the thing over my head. I grabbed her hips and rolled so I was on my back and she was straddling my waist. Her leggings did nothing to keep the heat and hardness of my erection from pressing right against her center. Her eyes widened, and her breath hitched. She put her hands on the center of my chest and leaned forward so her hair surrounded our faces. Her lapis eyes were intense with a vast array of emotion, some I couldn't identify because they were too big and too bold to name. I was surprised she had enough composure left to ask, "What happens next, Cable?"

I laughed and lifted my hips up so that she bounced a little. "I know it's been awhile, but I doubt you forgot how to do this in that short amount of time. You had an amazing teacher. Those lessons had to stick."

She made a face at me and moved one of her hands, so she was gently cupping my jaw. Her eyes bored into mine, not giving an inch, demanding I give her every ounce of my newly acquired sincerity and honesty. "You know what I mean. I wasn't even planning on going back to Texas for break. My dad is coming here to see me. How are we supposed to do this when we aren't in the same state?"

I knew by *this,* she didn't mean sex. She was always better about thinking further into the future than I was. With a little grunt of exertion, I rolled her underneath me and started working on getting her out of the lacy tank top she still had on. One thing I would miss about Texas was the weather. She never had this many clothes on back home. "We aren't going to be in separate states. You need to be here, and I need to be where you are, so I'll be close by."

I had her top off and was reaching behind her to pop the latch on her bra when she suddenly pushed up so that she was sitting in front of me. She tossed her bra onto the floor, and it was a real struggle to continue the conversation with her pretty tits in my face. I reached out my scarred knuckle and rubbed it over the velvety surface, pleased to see she still reacted to the smallest touch and the lightest caress.

"What do you mean you'll be close by? What did you do, Cable?" She sounded equal parts pleased and panicked.

I decided she needed a distraction, so I stood, pulled my belt off, and went to work on getting my jeans open. The wild-eyed stare she had pointed at my face immediately dropped below my waist when I set my trapped cock free. It was pressing insistently against the thin material of my boxers, the rigid outline and plump head clearly visible. She licked her lips and started to lift a hand out to touch, but she always was too focused for her own good.

"I want you in my life, but I have to finish school. I owe it to my dad, I owe it to all those little kids who might lose their moms, and I owe it to myself. This is everything I've worked my whole life for and as much as I want you and this," she pointed a finger between the two of us. "My future is not something I can give up in order to have it."

I tossed my wallet on the bed next to her, then I took a step back so I could kick off my shoes and peel my pants the rest of the way down my legs. I heard her bite back a moan and hid my grin. While I was on my knees in front of her, I got her shoes off and pulled those stretchy, ass-hugging leggings off her deliciously long legs.

"I don't want you to give up a damn thing." I kissed the inside of her knee and used my hands to pull her legs apart. She said my name, but I ignored her because it had been way too long since I'd been this close to her shiny, sweet center. She was already glossy and wet. She shivered under my touch and tensed as I leaned closer so that I could breathe her in as I slid a finger through her pouty, pink folds. "All I want is to be part of the future you're creating. I only need a slice of it, and I'll give you a slice of mine." She couldn't be the only thing that mattered to me, because my entire world would crumble if things didn't work out between us. I'd come too far to fall back down that slippery slope. "Remember the guy I told you I was locked up with? The one who used to own a tattoo shop?" She mumbled an affirmative but it was barely a sound because my fingers were stroking her, sliding inside of her and slipping over her clit, twisting and pressing down with each pass. Her hips lifted on the edge of the bed and she didn't argue in the slightest when I lifted one of her legs and braced it on my shoulder. I sank my teeth into the inside of her thigh and grinned against the sting as she yelped in response. Good thing her roommate wasn't around. There was going to be no mistaking this for quiet cuddling.

"I talked to him before I left Texas. He gets out of jail in another month or so, and I asked him if he would be interested in getting out of the gang life. I thought maybe he could move out here and we could go into business together. You were right about art. I love it, but I can't imagine sitting in a classroom having someone else critique what I do. I thought Emilio could teach me not only how to run a tattoo shop but also how to tattoo. I think it's something I might enjoy doing, and if it turns out not to be my thing, I can just run the business end of it. I don't think I'd be a bad silent investor, and I dig the idea of giving someone in a shitty situation a way out."

I curled my finger against her silken passage and honed in on the spot that made her eyes cross and her toes curl. The way she moved against me and wrapped her hand around my wrist was the same as all of my most favorite memories. I dragged my nose along the crease where her leg met her hip and sighed when her hips lifted toward my open mouth. I let out a little hum of approval and told her, "I'll be around, but I won't be in your way. We'll make this work."

I didn't give her a chance to respond. My mouth was watering, and I had to have a taste before I lost my mind. I covered her clit with my lips and tugged. She came all the way up off the bed and clutched her hands in my hair. There was a lot less of it to hold onto now, but she made do. She lifted the leg that wasn't over my shoulder onto the edge of the bed, dug her heel into the mattress as she rode my face, and writhed against my flicking tongue. She fucked herself on my fingers until illicit, sexy sounds filled both the room and my head. I dragged the edge of my teeth over the trembling flesh I had between my teeth and felt her entire body bow. She gasped my name and pulled on my hair hard enough that it hurt.

I never wanted to be without this again.

I never wanted to go without her again.

She made making the right choices easy, and she made trying to be the right choice for her a challenge I was ready to face head-on.

She whimpered and twisted wildly under my mouth and hands. There wasn't a single place on her that I would consider cold. She melted against me and rushed liquid and warm everywhere I touched. She was close to the edge, pent-up emotions pulling her closer and lifting her higher and higher up the harder I worked at her, but I didn't want her to go over without me.

This wasn't the end either of us were facing alone, it was the beginning we got to face together.

I sucked hard on that tiny bundle of pleasure and gave it one last swirl with my tongue. I let her ride my fingers a little bit longer, tapping her g-spot and winding her up to the point I could see she was ready to snap. Her chest was flushed. Her eyes were wide and dark. Her nipples were pulled into points so tight they looked painful, and her teeth were embedded in her lower lip so deeply I was surprised she didn't draw blood.

She was beautiful.

She was broken.

She was mine, and I was going to do whatever it took to keep it that way.

I asked her to hand me my wallet. While I scrambled with shaking hands to pull a condom out, she finally got her hand on my cock, and I almost fell on top of her as my legs turned to Jell-O. She circled the shaft with her hand and used her thumb to trace the throbbing vein that ran along the bottom. She circled the tip, slowly and deliberately. Her lips landed on the taut muscles right above my belly button, and I had to reach out and put my hand under her chin before she blew my mind by blowing me. I wouldn't last. The second her mouth touched the tip, I would be done for, and this was a moment I wanted to last.

"We'll have to save that for the encore, Reed. I want to make it through the first act before you get your mouth on me."

Her eyebrows lifted but she shifted back on the bed to make room for me as I crawled between her spread legs and made my-self comfortable at the notch between them. I sighed in heavy satisfaction as her warmth surrounded me and sucked me in as I glided my erection through her slippery folds. The head of my cock bumped into her swollen clit, and we both jolted in response. I placed a sucking, searing kiss on the tip of one of her breasts and closed my hand over the other as I braced myself on my forearm over her head. This tiny bed really didn't have a lot of space for either of us to move, so she curled her legs over my hips and sank her heels into the curve above my ass as I situated myself at her entrance.

I groaned against the side of her throat, and her sigh shifted my hair as I let myself sink into her slow and steady. Anywhere she was happened to be my favorite place to be, but being inside of her, making myself at home against her sensitive walls and in her wet heat was my second favorite. I belonged there; it was a place she kept secret and special just for me.

She was still achingly tight and outrageously responsive. She squeezed and clutched my cock in the best way possible, and her chest rose and fell to brush against mine like she was trying to catch her breath after a race. It was clear she missed this as much as I did. It was obvious she belonged to me as well as with me, the way I belonged to her.

I rolled the velvet bud of her nipple back and forth and started to move as I kissed along her neck. She shivered against me and rocked her hips up in a greedy manner. I laughed into her ear and put my mouth over hers so I could catch and savor every cry and every plea. Her legs tightened around me as I started to move faster, push deeper, asking for more, taking what was mine.

She pulsed around me, body quickening and fluttering along each stroke. She made me harder than I thought I'd ever be. Her softness was intoxicating and sensual as she writhed and begged for release beneath me. I let her work herself up until she was practically bucking against each thrust and demanding I go deeper, thrust harder, fuck faster. When she was as out of control as she always seemed to make me, I let go of the nipple I was torturing and moved my fingers back between her legs. She swore in relief and immediately let sensation take her over the edge. Her pleasure rushed furious and frantic across my pounding erection, and her body tightened to the point I almost couldn't move. I was being strangled in desire and choked in passion, and nothing had ever felt better.

My orgasm unfurled from the base of my spine and raced

through the rest of my body. She wrung every single scintilla of pleasure out of me, leaving my limbs heavy and hard to move as I collapsed on top of her, sweaty and spent. I kissed the side of her head as I struggled to roll off her so that I wouldn't crush her. I was surprised when she refused to let go of me so that when I finished rolling over, she ended up sprawled across my heaving chest, her hair everywhere as we stuck together with sex and perspiration.

She was tracing the shape of a heart on my chest when she asked, "You have it all planned out, don't you, McCaffrey?"

I threaded my fingers in the hair at her temples and kissed the crown of her head. I needed to pull out of her and ditch the condom before all those plans I'd meticulously been working on were blown to hell. While the idea of tying her to me forever through a baby didn't freak me out nearly as much as I thought it would, we were both too young, too new, and too unsteady for that kind of complication. Besides, I promised her I wouldn't derail her future, and I meant it.

I lifted her up and set her down next to me so I could climb to my feet. "First time in my entire life I've ever looked past the day I was currently struggling to make it through. It was easy though . . . when I looked ahead all I saw was you, Affton."

She smiled, and it made me smile. I was so glad I wasn't numb anymore. It would suck not to experience all the great and exciting things this girl made me feel. She was right . . . I was wide awake. She forced me to open my eyes.

"You're all I see, too, Cable. And I love the way you look standing there in my future."

I would never stop proving to her that I had earned my spot there or make her ever question her place in my forever.

This was our beginning. . . .

epilogue

AFFTON

Ink Addict Tattoo Shop ~ Four years later

I SWEPT THROUGH the doors of Cable's shop and was immediately greeted by not only the pretty, heavily tattooed girl behind the counter but also the ever-present buzz of busy tattoo machines. I spent a lot of time in the eclectically decorated, brightly painted building, so the sound was nothing new. Cable's art was splashed across the walls, and there was no longer any question in his mind, or anyone else's, that he was indeed an artist. I hardly noticed it over the tingling excitement that was whipping through my entire body. I had a smile on my face that stretched as wide as the East Bay, and I was practically bouncing up and down on my toes as I reached the counter.

The girl seated behind it lifted her purple-tinted eyebrow and gave me a grin. "Good news, I take it?"

I liked all of Cable's staff, but Van was my favorite. She was the same age as me and was just finishing up school for a graphic design degree. She wanted to design book covers and websites for authors, which I assumed would be a pretty cool gig. Cable hired her after his third receptionist asked if she could switch to apprenticing under Emilio. Cable's old cellmate had only been in town for a couple of years and had already made a name for himself as one of the best on the West Coast. Tired of hiring help and shuffling people around, he made sure he found a replacement who loved the industry, appreciated the art, but had no interest in becoming an artist. He was not only a good boss but a savvy businessman on top of it. Van was a godsend, and she was the closest thing I had to a best friend, next to Jordan.

"Great news. Is he busy?"

It was a dumb question. Cable was always busy. His brain and his hands didn't stop. He was Emilio's first apprentice and best student. For someone who had hardly any experience under his belt when it came to the art and talent of tattooing, Cable picked it up like he was made to do it. I think he thrived in the creative environment. He found his outlet. And while Ink Addict was his baby and his pride and joy, it was just the tip of the iceberg in all the different pots he had his spoons stuck in. He invested in a surf shop down in San Diego. He was the financial backer for a bar. He offered up the initial investment in a clothing start-up, and he helped develop an app that aided addicts who wanted to find help and find it quickly. So, even though he depleted a huge chunk of his trust fund paying back all the debt he accrued through the accident, building up this place, transforming the empty barbershop next to it into a livable space he could call home, and paying me the amount his mom owed me, he was doing just fine making a living on his own. Who would have ever thought that once he got sober and started really living his life clean, he would be such a force to be reckoned with?

"He's got a client, but they've been at it forever. I would say he's only got twenty minutes or so left on her." Van looked at the clock shaped like a T-rex as she answered.

I nodded and slipped around the desk so I could wind my way through the shop to the back where Cable had his station set up. His was the only station that was enclosed and private. It used to bother me considering the amount of naked woman he had in there day in and day out, but when he explained he needed to shut everyone else out in order to concentrate on what he was doing, I couldn't fault him for wanting the barrier between himself and the activity of the rest of the shop.

I stopped when Van reached out a tattooed hand and grabbed my arm. "Hey. I'm super proud of you. We all are."

I nodded and wrinkled my nose so I wouldn't cry all over her. "Thank you." They all knew how important this next step was to me. They all knew how hard I worked and how much I sacrificed to reach the next level. It was touching to have my accomplishments recognized instead of ridiculed.

She squeezed my arm and winked at me as the chime over the door dinged. "Drinks later to celebrate." It wasn't a question.

"Absolutely."

I waved to a couple of the other guys who lifted their chins in greeting. Emilio was bent over his drawing board and not with a client, so I swung by his chair really quick to get a congratulatory hug. Milo was as distractingly good looking as Cable. Van was the one who started calling him by the shortened version of his name, and since he never told her to knock it off, it kind of stuck. He didn't really look like a Milo; he was too dangerous for that. He was all dark hair and golden eyes that saw way too much and gave away too little. His edges were even rougher and more jagged than my boy's, and at first, I was terrified of him. He wasn't unpredictable and wild like Cable. He was too quiet, too contemplative. I got the feeling that he was always up to something and none of it was good. Eventually, I got over any reservations I had about the ex-con. He was a good mentor for Cable and an outstanding business partner. He seemed to have left most of his demons behind when he moved out to California, but every so often I could see they caught up with him. He was not only Cable's confidant, he was also his closest friend. My boy still struggled to connect, to attach and let others become attached to him, but Milo was in. He was family. He was loved.

After another congrats on my good news and another promise to throw back celebratory drinks later, I made my way over to Cable's station. A sliding silk screen painted with cherry blossoms that looked like something from a high-end sushi restaurant served as the door. It was mostly see-through but offered enough privacy that he could work in peace and his client wouldn't feel confined or exposed in the small space. I rapped my knuckles on the surrounding wood to alert them to the fact I was there and slid open the screen.

He was working on a girl who was probably around my age. She had dyed black hair, blunt cut bangs, and a ring through her bottom lip. She was lying on her side facing me, her shirt pulled up and tucked into the bottom of her bra as he worked on something that covered the entirety of her ribs. It appeared to be a steampunk-inspired butterfly, intricate and detailed. It was very cool, and I told her so. She grimaced up at me, obviously in pain, but got out a short, "Thanks."

Cable had expensive wireless headphones covering his ears. I knew he was listening to something loud and aggressive as he worked. He wasn't one to chat with his clients. If they wanted friendly and engaging, they went with one of the other artists in the shop. If they wanted art, and if they wanted expensive skin, they came to him. He didn't do flash. He didn't do cobbled together ideas. All he did was custom, one-of-a-kind pieces that were brilliant and beautiful. He was picky about who he worked on and who he gave his art to, so it was a good thing he made money other ways. No one liked a temperamental tattoo artist.

He finished the line he was working on and lifted his buzzing machine off the girl's skin. Sensing someone behind him, he looked up at me, those dark eyes still able to undo me with little effort. He had on latex gloves that were slick with blood and ink, so I reached out and lowered the headphones off his head so they circled his neck. I kissed the corner of his mouth as he lifted a questioning brow in my direction.

"You get in?" He'd been almost as anxious as I had been waiting on the acceptance letter. No one knew how important it was to me as well as he did.

I clapped my hands together in front of me and grinned like a lunatic. "I got in." I wanted to scream it from the top of my lungs, but it came out as a whisper.

His grin was as big as mine, and my heart swelled at the pride that lit up in his eyes. "Of course, you did, Reed. Was there ever any doubt?"

I rolled my eyes at him. Of course, there had been doubt.

My sophomore year was much tougher than I anticipated. Keeping my GPA up had been a struggle. Not only was the school work tougher than I imagined but my dad had suffered a mild heart attack while climbing a fourteener in Colorado. It all threw me off my stride, and so had the pressure of juggling school and my relationship with Cable. He lived in an artsy, industrial area of San Francisco called the Dogpatch. He converted an empty storefront into a sprawling apartment right next to the tattoo shop. It wasn't the world's longest commute by any means, but between his working hours and my endless studying, we both found ourselves letting our relationship slide. He was too tired to come to me; I was too stressed to make time for him. Before either of us had realized it, we'd gone weeks with barely a phone call between us or any kind of contact. We were drifting away from one another, and it didn't seem like either one of us had the strength to pull the other back in. The current was carrying us farther and farther away from each other.

But then my dad almost died, and before I could get the whole tearful panicked explanation of what happened out to Cable, he had us both on a plane and on our way to Colorado. He didn't leave my side once while dad had surgery. He didn't bend. He didn't break. He held me together when I fell apart, and I wanted to kick myself for not trying harder to hold onto him. I remembered how it felt when I let him go before and I never wanted to be there again. Neither did he. When we got back home after my dad was declared hearty and whole, we had a heart to heart about making our relationship more of a priority, about putting one another first. I decided I would rather commute back and forth from his place to school than risk that chasm opening again. I moved in and relished every second of sharing my life with him.

Once I was away from the school instead of being there twenty-four-seven, I could shut my brain down. I could study in the shop while he worked. The buzzing in the background was surprisingly soothing. I could be in bed waiting for him when he had a late night, and he could stay up and watch movies with me when I had a cram session. Plus, I adored his home, *our* home. It was unique and so very him. Edgy, but with lots of soft nooks and crannies to hide away in. His art decorated the walls. His outlet to quiet his restless mind was still the most beautiful thing I'd ever seen. It was also nice I didn't have to worry about running into my roommate's naked boyfriend coming out of the bathroom anymore. The only naked boyfriend I ran into was my own, but that was just fine with me. I couldn't get enough of him and never turned down an opportunity to get my hands on his nakedness. It was so much better to be anchored to him than floating away from him.

He rubbed his forehead with his forearm and looked at the twisted metal and glass clock that hung on the wall. "Give me a half hour, and I'll be over to congratulate you properly. I'm so fucking proud of you, Reed." He smirked at me as his client shifted uncomfortably in front of him. She was caught in the middle of an intimate moment and she knew it. Luckily, she had enough tact to let us speak without words for a minute. Finally, he cleared his throat and told me, "Can't wait to call you Doctor Reed. That's gonna be hot as fuck."

I tossed back my head and laughed. I was still a long way away from earning that title in front of my name, but my acceptance into the graduate program was one step closer. I was almost there. I was going to have a Ph.D., eventually, and he could call me Doctor Reed along with everyone else I planned on helping.

I dropped a kiss on his mouth as he lifted his head toward me. He asked his client if she was ready to finish and when she gave a stiff nod, he asked me to put his headphones back on his head so he could finish up. I complied and wished the girl good luck before practically skipping back through the shop. Van stopped me for a hug before I hit the front doors and I happily returned it. I texted my dad and Jordan the good news as I bounced next door to the converted space I called home.

Dad was still traveling. He'd convinced Cable and me to spend a week with him at the Grand Canyon. I thought Cable was going to hate being cooped up in the tin can my dad called home, but he loved it. We were supposed to meet up with him again at the end of summer when he planned on driving down through Baja. Cable wanted to go surfing, and I wasn't going to pass up time with my dad or his new girlfriend. He met a fellow wanderer in the Badlands of Utah. She was a lady biker named Bianca, and I liked her a whole lot. She put her bike on a trailer behind my dad's RV and never looked back. She was good for him and came from a well-off place. She didn't have the kind of money Cable's family did, but she married well and divorced even better, so I no longer worried about my dad running out of funds and getting stranded somewhere.

Jordan was six months pregnant. The guy from Austin, the one who wouldn't let her chase my attacker alone that night on the beach, had been serious about getting to know her and starting something up. He pestered her until she gave him a chance. Turned out he was a firefighter, a true hero type. He proved to be impossible for her to resist. She got engaged before she was twenty-one and now had a baby on the way. She couldn't be any happier. We still talked at least once a week, and Cable and I had gone back to Loveless for the wedding. I was her maid of honor.

I also texted Melanie McCaffrey. She still wasn't my favorite person on the planet, but we both loved her son, so we forced ourselves to find common ground. She checked in frequently to see how he was doing and, surprisingly, to see how I was doing. She wanted what was best for him, and since he decided that was me, she did her best to play nice. She still worried about him. We'd both gotten used to her showing up unannounced, but neither of us ever asked her to leave. She had started dating one of the lawyers she'd hired to represent Cable all those years ago, so she seemed less miserable than she had when we first got together. It didn't hurt that Cable's father was in the middle of an ugly paternity suit with two different women. He was making headlines in Loveless that were far more inflammatory than the ones Cable had been a part of.

Melanie frequently asked me probing questions about his sobriety and the handle he had on it. I always told her he was working on it because that was the truth. He slipped up now and again. He still smoked like a chimney and enjoyed whiskey on the weekends. He never overindulged and kept himself to a firm two-drink limit. It wasn't something I encouraged because I knew how easy it was for those two drinks to turn into four or five, but I didn't fight with him about it either. I trusted him, and as long as he was honest with me about how he was doing, I believed in the limits he set for himself. I trusted him not to cross them. Milo was a bit of a stoner, and there were days Cable came home smelling like weed. I knew it wasn't simply from being in the same shop as his friend. He was always truthful when I asked him if he'd been using and he always agreed to talk to Doc Howard about it if I asked him to. Cable had a therapist here in San Francisco he saw a couple times a month, but he still checked in with the man who originally gave him a safe place to address his feelings. Doc Howard had even come to California for a visit. He and Cable met up in San Diego for a weekend of surfing. The line between patient and friend had blurred at this point, but it didn't matter. Cable was comfortable with the older man, and it was apparent Doc Howard had a soft spot for my boy, as well.

Occasional indulgence wasn't healthy for an addict, we both knew that, but as long as he addressed it, as long as he kept trying, I supported him. He knew my story, and he knew I refused to have another ending like the one I had with my mom. I trusted him to never put me in that position again. He knew I wouldn't love an addict again, but I had no trouble giving my heart to a recovering one for as long as the recovery lasted.

I flew through the front door and stopped to pet the white and gray fluff ball of a kitten Cable had gotten me for our last anniversary. He called the little cat Razor because of his claws and the way he tended to sink them into any unsuspecting toes that happened by. I called him Sweetheart because he was so fluffy and adorable. I loved the little guy almost as much as the man who got him for me. Cable told me it was good practice for when we had kids. I laughed it off, but it was something we'd talked about.

Our future was together. However that looked. He wasn't a huge fan of marriage considering how his parents had ended up, but he did want to start a family somewhere down the road. He had grown increasingly close with his half-sisters over the last few years and was amazingly good with them. It didn't surprise me that he wanted kids, but I was a little shocked at how open and honest he was about his concerns that when we reached that point, he would end up passing along some of his less desirable traits to his child. I couldn't tell him not to worry. Depression was partly influenced by genetics, but I assured him any kid of ours would have two parents who understood what they were struggling with. We would recognize and address it before it overtook their entire life the way Cable's had. It was a war we knew how to prepare for and one we knew how to win.

For now, we had a ridiculously cute kitten and stupid amounts of sex as we enjoyed being together and building a life together. I couldn't find much to complain about on any given day, even when it was a day Cable slipped up or disappeared inside his own head. As long as he was screwing up or struggling somewhere close by, I was happy and always willing to help in whatever way I could.

Distracted by the kitten, I tripped into the kitchen in search of that celebratory drink a little early. We never kept any hard liquor in the house, but Cable always had a six-pack in the fridge for when

Milo dropped by to watch football or shoot the shit, and I usually had a bottle of white wine somewhere for really rough days after class. Sometimes learning was hard.

I jolted to a stop when I saw the cool, pressed concrete counter of the kitchen island covered with an array of flower bouquets. There were at least twenty of them in all shapes, sizes, and colors. They were vivid and breathtaking. I had no idea how I missed the glorious, floral scent filling up the space when I walked in. There was a teddy bear dressed like Sigmund Freud with a giant balloon that had CONGRATULATIONS written across it in bright script. There was also a silver bucket amidst the flowers that had a very expensive bottle of champagne sticking out of it. I put a shaking hand over my mouth and took it all in.

I heard the kitten meow and Cable's low voice mutter something to him as his sneakers squeaked across the floor. I looked over my shoulder at him as he approached. His brown eyes were deep and dark with emotion, and all I wanted to do was drown in the way he was looking at me.

"How did you know I got in?" My voice shook, and I practically collapsed against him when he finally untangled himself from the cat so that he could get his arms around my waist.

I felt his lips touch the back of my head as he muttered, "I've been checking the mail for a few weeks and putting it back for you before you get back across the Bay. I knew the letter was coming and I wanted to surprise you."

I let out something that might have been a whimper and rested my head on his shoulder. "You saw the letter, but you didn't know it was an acceptance letter. What if I didn't make it in the program?"

He chuckled and hugged me harder to his strong body. "I didn't need to look to know it was an acceptance letter. I know you, Reed. I know hard you work. It wasn't going to be anything other than a yes. That's what you deserve."

I turned in his embrace and threw my arms around his neck. He smelled of cigarettes and the disinfectant they used in the shop. I planted a wet, smacking kiss on his mouth and giggled when he hefted me up so that I could wrap my legs around his lean waist. He walked me backward until my ass hit the countertop and he wasted no time settling himself between my legs.

I ran my nose along the shell of his ear and whispered, "You're going to make me cry."

He pushed me back a little to work on pulling my shoes and jeans off and one of the vases of flowers went careening to the floor. He looked up at me from under his lashes, eyebrow cocked as that smirk I loved more than anything played around his mouth.

"I'm not the guy who makes you cry anymore, remember?"

That was a lie.

He did make me cry . . . all the time. Sometimes they were happy tears like the ones threatening now. Sometimes they were furious tears that burned and scalded when they ran down my face. Sometimes they were sad tears I couldn't control when he still seemed lost and adrift. And sometimes they were a combination of all three because he overwhelmed me with all that he was and all that he brought into my life . . . both good and bad.

Once I was naked from the waist down, he yanked my t-shirt over my head and stripped my bra down my arms. When I was totally naked in front of him. he smiled and slid his talented hands over my collarbone. "I am the guy who makes you come repeatedly though. Only me."

Well, that was true.

I pulled at his t-shirt and sighed when he dropped his jeans and seated himself between my legs once again. The head of his cock tapped my clit like it had a homing beacon, and my eyes rolled back in my head as I wound my arms around his neck and played with the soft, shaggy hair on the back of his head.

"You're the guy who does both."

He chuckled and lowered his head so he could touch his mouth to mine. "Can't argue with that. I love you, Affton."

I sniffed and then groaned as his teeth nipped at my lower lip. "I love you, too, Cable James McCaffrey."

He kissed me to shut me up. I kissed him back to say thank you. He then proceeded to make me both come and cry as the flowers skidded across the counter.

Thank goodness I had made the right choice by picking the absolute wrong guy to love and perfect guy to hate.

thank you

IF I'M A new author to you, thank you for picking up Recovered.

If you loved Cable and Affton I strongly suggest you check out the rest of my New Adult titles, starting with the internationally bestselling Marked Men series.

Everything began with Rule:

www.jaycrownover.com/markedmenseries

Opposites in every way . . . except the one that matters

Shaw Landon loved Rule Archer from the moment she laid eyes on him. Rule is everything a straight-A pre-med student like Shaw shouldn't want—and the only person she's never tried to please. She isn't afraid of his scary piercings and tattoos or his wild attitude. Though she knows that Rule is wrong for her, her heart just won't listen.

To a rebel like Rule Archer, Shaw Landon is a stuck-up, perfect princess-and his dead twin brother's girl. She lives by other people's rules; he makes his own. He doesn't have time for a good girl like Shaw-even if she's the only one who can see the person he truly is.

But a short skirt, too many birthday cocktails, and spilled secrets lead to a night neither can forget. Now, Shaw and Rule have to figure out how a girl like her and a guy like him are supposed to be together without destroying their love . . . or each other.

If you know someone struggling with addiction and or depression, please don't let them navigate that road on their own regardless of how bumpy it may get.

National Suicide Prevention Lifeline

Call 1–800–273–8255

Available 24 hours everyday

www.suicidepreventionlifeline.org

National Addiction Hotline

Call Now *1–888–352–6072*
www.nationaladdictionhotline.com

IF YOU MADE it this far thank you so much for reading Recovered! I would be so very grateful if you would leave a review on whatever platform you read, or listened to, this book on. A review, good or bad, is the best gift a reader can pass along to an author. It's also a great way to see more of the books and characters you love!

acknowledgments

OBVIOUSLY, I HAVE to thank the first guy who ever broke my heart. Without him, there would be no Cable. If he ever stumbles across this book, I'm sure I'll get an earful . . . lol.

If you have purchased, read, reviewed, promoted, pimped, blogged about, sold, talked about, preached about, or whined about any of my books . . . thank you.

If you are part of my very special reader group The Crowd . . . thank you.

If you have helped me make this dream of mine a reality . . . thank you.

If you have helped make my words better and helped me share them with the world . . . thank you.

If you have held my hand and helped me through the tough times when it feels like everyone's against me . . . thank you.

I'm throwing out a random thanks to my mom in this one. She's been reading *Recovered* in my newsletter along with all of you. I never let her meet the boy who inspired Cable because we were a mess and I didn't know how to handle him and us when I was younger. She told me that she feels like she finally got to know him through this book, which was the ultimate compliment in my mind. If I made Cable real enough for her to recognize everything I felt back then, well, then I did my job right.

I also have a pretty special girl gang of professionals who help me turn my words into an actual book. First off is my amazing agent Stacey. Then there's my PR guru KP Simmon, who makes sure I behave. And as always, my wonderful assistant Melissa Shank deserves a medal for putting up with me. I wouldn't make it through a release or a regular ol' day without this team of impressive women.

If you are looking for an editor, I can't recommend Elaine York enough. I love getting to work with her. I adore her insights and her commitment to each project I send her way. She doesn't pull any punches, and she's not scared to tell me when I'm not quite there yet. She makes me work for it, and as a result, my readers get the best book possible. She immediately recognized Cable and Affton as people who I intimately knew and could tell this story came from somewhere real. I think that's special. She's smart as hell and has a way of seeing nuances in a story I'll admit to never even thinking about. She's also really good at pointing out when my characters magically lose clothes during the sexy scenes . . . lol. Unlike when I publish traditionally, I got to pick who I wanted to work with when it came to self-publishing. For me, Elaine was the only choice.

The same thing goes for Hang Le and Donya Claxton. Hang was my one and only choice to work with when it came to my covers. She's brilliant. I love her style and her flare. She takes what I want and makes it better than I could imagine. Pretty sure her beautiful covers do more to sell my books than anything I do. Donya found and captured the perfect Cable. I sent her an idea and she took her special skills and sent me the magic of the perfect picture.

If you want the pages and the guts of your book to be pretty, then you need to hit up my friend, Christine Borgford. She's one of the kindest, most supportive humans I've ever met, and not just because she's Canadian! She really loves books, romance, and the reading community. She wants our words to be as pretty as possible. Formatting is important. End of story. It makes your book look pulled together and professional. Let Christine play with your pages; you won't regret it.

My friend, Beth Salminen, handled all my copy edits and proofreading this go around. Beth is wicked smart and super funny. The only thing better than writing books is getting to work on them with people who care about making your words the best they can be. It's a bonus when that person also wants the writer to be the best she can be. If you are looking for a pretty blonde to cross your t's and dot all your i's, you need to give Beth all your money.

I want to thank Pam Lilley, Karla Tamayo, Meghan Burr-Martin, Sarah Arndt, and Traci Pike for giving up their valuable time and precious moments to go over the rough draft of this story. If you read it in my newsletter, you know my rough drafts are R-O-U-G-H. It takes an intrepid soul to take all my run-on sentences on. They don't get anything out of the deal other than my undying gratitude and unwavering thanks. There are some very special readers out there in Booklandia, and I feel like I've been so lucky to have most of them in my court since the very beginning. If you notice fewer errors and fewer typos in this book, it's all thanks to these lovely ladies.

Feel free to appease your inner stalker in all of these places. I love to connect with my readers.

about the author

JAY CROWNOVER IS the International and multiple *New York Times* and *USA Today* bestselling author of the Marked Men Series, The Saints of Denver Series, and The Point and Breaking Point Series. Her books can be found translated in many different languages all around the world. She is a tattooed, crazy haired Colorado native who lives at the base of the Rockies with her awesome dogs. This is where she can frequently be found enjoying a cold beer and Taco Tuesdays. Jay is a self-declared music snob and outspoken book lover who is always looking for her next adventure, between the pages and on the road.

GUYS!!! I finally have a newsletter, so if you want to sign up for exclusive content and monthly giveaways you can do that right here: www.jaycrownover.com/#!subscribe

You can email me at: JayCrownover@gmail.com
My website: www.jaycrownover.com
www.facebook.com/jay.crownover
www.facebook.com/AuthorJayCrownover
Follow me @jaycrownover on Twitter
Follow me @jay.crownover on Instagram
www.goodreads.com/Crownover
www.donaghyliterary.com/jay-crownover.html
www.avonromance.com/author/jay-crownover

CPSIA information can be obtained
at www.ICGtesting.com
Printed in the USA
LVOW13s1018010418

571865LV00049B/733/P